The Palm-Wine Drinkard

and

My Life in the Bush of Ghosts

The Palm-Wine Drinkard

and

My Life in the Bush of Ghosts

Amos Tutuola

Grove Press
New York

Printed in the United States of America

Library of Congress Cataloging-in-Publication Data

Tutuola, Amos.
  [Palm-wine drinkard]
  The palm-wine drinkard; and, My life in the bush of ghosts / Amos
Tutuola.
    ISBN 978-0-8021-3363-2
    1. Yoruba (African people)—Folklore—Fiction. 2. Folklore—Nigeria—
Fiction. I. Tutuola, Amos. My life in the bush of ghosts. 1994. II. Title:
Palm-wine drinkard. III. Title: My life in the bush of ghosts.
  PR387.9.T8P3   1994   823—dc20   93-32520

Grove Press
an imprint of Grove Atlantic
154 West 14th Street
New York, NY 10011

Distributed by Publishers Group West

groveatlantic.com

21 22 23 24 25   24 23 22 21 20

Contents

My Life in
the Bush of Ghosts

with a foreword
by
The Rev. Geoffrey Parrinder, D.D., Ph.D.
Lecturer at University College, Ibadan,
Nigeria

Contents

7

Contents

Foreword

When Amos Tutuola's first novel, *The Palm-Wine Drinkard*, was published in 1952 it was presented to the public without introduction and made its way purely on its merit. Considerable interest was aroused by this unusual book, and inquiries have been made about Tutuola and the background of his ideas. It has been thought well to preface this second novel with a few words about the man and his work, in order that his importance may be appreciated in its proper setting.

Amos Tutuola is a native of Abeokuta, one of the big towns of Nigeria, in West Africa. He is a member of the large Yoruba tribe, which numbers over four million people and is one of the most progressive elements in modern Africa. Abeokuta, whose name means "under the rock", is a large sprawling town situated along the sides of hills which are crowned with masses of granite boulders. It is a medley of old mud huts and new concrete buildings, a mixture of cultures such as the subject-matter of the books would lead us to expect. Alongside the modern mosques and churches are ancient pagan temples, and a cave under the most sacred rock is said to have witnessed a human sacrifice as recently as forty years ago. Twice in the present book the wanderer in the bush of ghosts is to be sacrificed to a god.

Foreword

Amos Tutuola was born in 1920, of Christian parents, and he received elementary education at the Salvation Army school and later at Lagos High School, not more than six years in all. He became a coppersmith, and continued this trade in the Royal Air Force in Nigeria for three years during the war.

Tutuola's writing is original and highly imaginative. His direct style, made more vivid by his use of English as it is spoken in West Africa, is not polished or sophisticated and gives his stories unusual energy. It is a beginning of a new type of Afro-English literature. Tutuola prefers to write in English, rather than Yoruba; it is perhaps fortunate that his schooling ended too early to force his story-telling into a foreign style. His writing is distinct from the correct but rather stiff essays that some more highly educated Africans produce. Tutuola's stories are of the kind, lively, vulgar, frightening, which is common in the traditional Africa of the villages.

This story is truly African. It is a fantasy, shaped by the author's fertile imagination. It has a nightmarish quality of its own, and one feels the bewilderment and fear, repugnance and despair, and also intoxication and exaltation, which one would expect to experience in the company of ghosts. But the stories are genuine African myths, such as are told in countless villages round the fire or in the tropical moonlight. Africans have said to me, "My grandmother used to tell us stories like that." Tutuola has told me how he and his boyhood playmates would listen to such yarns on their farms in the evening.

Amos Tutuola has taken over the traditional mythology

and fitted it into his own pattern. There is an over-riding theme: what happens to a mortal who strays into the world of ghosts. This is a familiar motif. Into this have been worked popular beliefs, such as that in the "Burglar-ghosts" who are children that die in infancy and are reborn again and again, and are really troublesome ghosts come to plague and rob the unhappy parents. Again there is "Lost or Gain Valley", which has to be crossed without clothes, but it is a riddle that might be capable of solution. Elsewhere we find witches meeting to devour a victim provided from the family of one of their company. Yet all these ideas are moulded into the story and are lived over by the author. I realized how deeply he lived in his own narrative when I asked Tutuola the reason for the apparently haphazard order of the towns of the ghosts. He replied, quite simply, "That is the order in which I came to them."

From the second chapter, where the lost boy is beckoned on by the Golden-ghost, the Silverish-ghost, and the Copperish-ghost, captured by the disgusting Smelling-ghost, transformed into a horse and later a cow, and then caught by a Homeless-ghost, one is impelled on through all the bizarre adventures. One goes with the author in his waking nightmare. Fear is present throughout. If anyone doubts that there is fear in African life Tutuola's story should convince him of its reality. The unknown bush with its frightful spirits stretching out their tentacles, like trees in an Arthur Rackham drawing, is a dreadful place. Fairy tales can scare, but this is more terrifying than Grimm as its matter is more serious and is believed in by millions of Africans today.

Foreword

The "Bush" in which the ghosts live is the heart of the tropical forest, the impenetrable thickets that are left even when the rest of the forest is cleared for cultivation. Here, as every hunter and traveller knows, mortals venture at their peril. Nobody dares enter there by day, let alone go near at night. In another manuscript Tutuola says that, in addition to the Reserved and Unreserved Bush specified by the government, there is Native Reserved Bush. "It is strictly out of bounds to both Whites and Blacks, because it is only for dead Ghosts and bad Juju. . . . If you enter into it you cannot know the way out again, and you cannot travel to the end of it for ever."

Readers of *The Palm-Wine Drinkard* will remember Deads' Town, where are the spirits of the departed. The ghosts in the present book are different from those deceased mortals. They are all types of beings who have never lived on earth and are dangerous and mischievous spirits. They are creatures of God but different from men; they never grow old or die. Dead people can indeed live with them, and we meet two such, but these are ones who have died before their time and so can live with the ageless spirits.

At the same time as it relates old themes, the story reflects the situation of Africans under the impact of European ideas and government. The ancient beliefs still prevail in this mythology, but they are impregnated by modern touches. So we find churches, schools and Crown Agents in the 10th Town of Ghosts, and the Rev. Devil giving a baptism of fire and hot water in the 8th Town. Later we have a Television-handed Ghostess, described by a man who has never seen television.

12

Foreword

This book is fascinating from the point of view of pure story. It also has scientific value. The anthropologist and the student of comparative religion will find here much of the unrecorded mythology of West Africa. There are themes running through the book, as to the nature of death, fear and disease. There are discernible stages in the process of initiation into the mysteries of the ghost-world, which link up with the rites of secret societies and religious cults. The wanderer in the bush, after his grim early sufferings, gradually learns the language of ghosts and marries two ghosts. He remains twenty-four years in the bush, until he has almost lost the desire to return.

Further, the work is an interesting example of "culture-contact", which is just as much the student's province today as was the "unspoiled native" yesterday. How far have Christian ideas penetrated? Have they changed or displaced ancient beliefs? This book goes some way towards providing an answer. The student is concerned with the African as he is today, as a human being, to understand whom is as important for an imperial people as it is to understand Russians or Americans. We now know a great deal about African economy, social organization, political structure, and their modification in this century, but how hard it is to understand the thoughts of other races, even of those who resemble us superficially, and much more of those whose traditions have been so widely separated from our own.

Psychologists will find this book interesting, particularly those who follow the teaching of Jung on mythology and the archetypes of the unconscious. The morbid fascination of dirt, blood, snakes, insects, smell, ugliness,

Foreword

deformity, size, and all that is grotesque is everywhere evident in the book. The lost boy undergoes more transformations in size and form than Alice in Wonderland. In the midst of his greatest distress and captivity he is so intoxicated by the fumes of the gigantic tobacco pipe that he is forced to smoke, that "I forgot all my sorrow and started to sing the earthly songs which sorrow prevented me from singing about since I entered this bush." In great danger of pursuit he is so entranced by the exceeding ugliness of a ghostess, that he is impelled to delay and look at her face, "her ugly appearance was so curious to me that I was chasing her as she was running away to see her ugliness clearly to my satisfaction". In the end the boy comes to settle in the ghost world so well that, like Persephone, he is reluctant to leave it; "I did not feel to go to my town again, even I determined that I should not go for ever." When he does at length find the way, the return is easy and immediate. But we are warned that he has premonitory dreams of attendance at the coming centenary of the Secret Society of Ghosts.

My Life in the Bush of Ghosts was written after *The Palm-Wine Drinkard*. It is in no sense a sequel, but a completely new story. It deals not with "Deads", but with the spirits of the wild. These abnormal beings remind one of the creations of Bunyan and Dante. The story is a coherent whole and the closing sentence, "This is what hatred did", links up with the opening chapter wherein are revealed the jealousies of a polygamous household which leave a small boy, who does not know what is "good" or "bad", to face by himself the terrors of the Bush of Ghosts.

Foreword

The book has been edited to remove the grosser mistakes, clear up some ambiguities, and curtail some repetition. But the original flavour of the style has been left to produce its own effect.

University College,   GEOFFREY PARRINDER
Ibadan, Nigeria

The Meaning of
"Bad" and "Good"

I was seven years old before I understood the meaning of "bad" and "good", because it was at that time I noticed carefully that my father married three wives as they were doing in those days, if it is not common nowadays. My mother was the last married among the rest and she only bore two sons but the rest bore only daughters. So by that the two wives who had only daughters hated my mother, brother and myself to excess as they believed that no doubt my brother and myself would be the rulers of our father's house and also all his properties after his death. My brother was eleven years old then and I myself was seven. So it was at this stage I quite understood the meaning of "bad" because of hatred and had not yet known the meaning of "good".

My mother was a petty trader who was going to various markets every day to sell her articles and returning home in the evening, or if the market is very far she would return next day in the evening as she was a hard worker.

In those days of unknown year, because I was too young to keep the number of the year in my mind till this time, so there were many kinds of African wars and some of them are as follows: general wars, tribal wars,

17

The Meaning of "Bad" and "Good"

burglary wars and the slave wars which were very common in every town and village and particularly in famous markets and on main roads of big towns at any time in the day or night. These slave-wars were causing dead luck to both old and young of those days, because if one is captured, he or she would be sold into slavery for foreigners who would carry him or her to unknown destinations to be killed for the buyer's god or to be working for him.

But as my mother was a petty trader who was going here and there, so one morning she went to a market which was about three miles away from our town, she left two slices of cooked yam for us (my brother and myself) as she was usually doing. When it was twelve o'clock p.m. cocks began to crow continuously, then my brother and myself entered into our mother's room in which she kept the two sliced or cut yams safely for us, so that it might not be poisoned by the two wives who hated us, then my brother took one of the yams and I took the other one and began to eat it at the same time. But as we were eating the yam inside our mother's room, these two wives who hated us heard information before us that war was nearly breaking into the town, so both of them and their daughters ran away from the town without informing us or taking us along with themselves and all of them knew already that our mother was out of the town.

Even as we were very young to know the meaning of "bad" and "good" both of us were dancing to the noises of the enemies' guns which were reverberating into the room in which we were eating the yam as the big trees and many hills with deep holes on them entirely surrounded the town and they changed the fearful noises of the enemies' guns to a lofty one for us, and we were dancing for these lofty noises of the enemies' guns.

But as these enemies were more approaching the town the lofty noises of their guns became fearful for us because every place was shaking at that moment. So when we could not bear it then we left our mother's room for thé veranda, but we met nobody there, and then we ran from there to the portico of the house, but the town was also empty except the domestic animals as sheep, pigs, goats and fowls and also some of the bush animals as monkeys, wolves, deer and lions who were driven from the bush that surrounded the town to the town by the fearful noises of the enemies' guns. All these animals were running and crying bitterly up and down in the town in searching for their keepers. Immediately we saw that there was nobody in the town again we stepped down from the door to the outside as all the while we stood at the door looking at every part of the town with fearful and doubtful mind.

So first of all we travelled to the north of the town as there was a road which led to the town of our grandmother which was not far away from ours.

But as these animals were giving us much trouble, fear, and disturbing us so at last we left to run to the north and then to the south where there was a large river which crossed the road on which we should travel to some protective place to hide ourselves.

And as the enemies were approaching nearer, we left the river at once and when we went further on this road we reached a kind of African fruit tree which stood by the road, then we stopped under it to find a shelter, but as we were hastily turning round this tree perhaps we would see a shelter there, two ripe fruits fell down on it, then my brother took both and put them into his pocket and started to carry or lift me along on this road as I was too young to run as fast as he could. But as he himself was too young to lift or carry such weight like me, so by that he was unable to lift me to a distance of about ten feet before he would fall down four times or more.

When he tried all his power for several times and failed and again at that moment the smell of the gunpowder of the enemies' guns which were shooting repeatedly was rushing to our noses by the breeze and this made us fear more, so my brother lifted me again a very short distance, but when I saw that he was falling several times, then I told him to leave me on the road and run away for his life perhaps he might be safe so that he would be taking care of our mother as she had no other sons more than both of us and I told him that if God saves my life too then we should meet again, but if God does not save my life we should meet in heaven.

But as I was telling him these sorrowful words both his eyes were shedding tears repeatedly, of course I did not shed tears at all on my eyes as I put hope that no doubt I would be easily captured or killed. And it was that day I believed that if fear is overmuch, a person would not fear for anything again. But as the smoke of the enemies' guns was rushing to our view, then my brother left me on that road with sorrow, and then he stopped and put his hand into his pocket and brought out the fruits which fell down from the tree under which we were about to hide ourselves before; he gave me both fruits instead of one. After that he started to run as fast as he could along this road towards the enemies unnoticed and he was still looking at me as he was running away.

So after I saw him no more on the road I put both fruits into my pocket and then got back to that fruit tree under which we picked them and I stood there only to shelter myself from the sun. But when the enemies were at a distance of about an eighth of a mile to that place where I stood I was unable to hear again because of the noises of the enemies' guns and as I was too young to hear such fearful noises and wait, so I entered into the bush under this fruit tree. This fruit tree was a "SIGN" for me and it was on that day I called it—THE "FUTURE SIGN".

Now it remained me alone in the bush, because no brother, mother, father or other defender could save me or direct me if and whenever any danger is imminent. But as these enemies had approached us closely before my brother left because of me he was captured within fifteen minutes that he left me, but he was only captured as a slave and not killed, because I heard his voice when he shouted louder for help.

In the Bush of Ghosts

At the same time as I entered into the bush I could not stop in one place as the noises of the guns were driving me farther and farther until I travelled about sixteen miles away from the road on which my brother left me. After I had travelled sixteen miles and was still running further for the fearful noises, I did not know the time that I entered into a dreadful bush which is called the "Bush of Ghosts", because I was very young to understand the meaning of "bad" and "good". This "Bush of Ghosts" was so dreadful so that no superior earthly person ever entered it.

But as the noises of the enemies' guns drove me very far until I entered into the "Bush of Ghosts" unnoticed, because I was too young to know that it was a dreadful bush or it was banned to be entered by any earthly person, so that immediately I entered it I stopped and ate both fruits which my brother gave me before we left each other, because I was very hungry before I reached there. After I ate it then I started to wander about in this bush both day and night until I reached a rising ground which was almost covered with thick bush and weeds which made the place very dark both day and night. Every part of this small hill was very clean as if somebody was sweeping it. But as I was very tired of roaming about

22

before I reached there, so I bent down to see the hill clearly, because my aim was to sleep there. Yet I could not see it clearly as I bent down, but when I had lain down flatly then I saw clearly that it had an entrance with which to enter into it.

The entrance resembled the door of a house and it had a portico which was sparkling as if it was polished with brasso at all moments. The portico was also made of golden plate. But as I was too young to know "bad" and "good" I thought that it was an old man's house who was expelled from a town for an offence, then I entered it and went inside it until I reached a junction of three passages which each led to a room as there were three rooms.

One of these rooms had golden surroundings, the second had silverish surroundings and the third had copperish. But as I stood at the junction of these passages with confusion three kinds of sweet smells were rushing out to me from each of these three rooms, but as I was hungry and also starving before I entered into this hole, so I began to sniff the best smell so that I might enter the right room at once from which the best sweet smell was rushing out. Of course as I stood on this junction I noticed through my nose that the smell which was rushing out of the room which had golden surroundings was just as if the inhabitant of it was baking bread and roasting fowl, and when I sniffed again the smell of the room which had copperish surroundings was just as if the inhabitant of that was cooking rice, potatoes and other African food with very sweet soup, and then the room which had silverish surroundings was just as if the inhabitant was frying yam, roasting fowl and baking cakes. But I thought in my

mind to go direct to the room from which the smell of
the African food was rushing out to me, as I prefer my
native food most. But I did not know that all that I was
thinking in mind was going to the hearing of the inhabitants of these three rooms, so at the same moment
that I wanted to move my body to go to the room from
which the smell of the African's food was rushing to me
(the room which had copperish surroundings) there I saw
that these three rooms which had no doors and windows
opened unexpectedly and three kinds of ghosts peeped at
me, every one of them pointed his finger to me to come
to him.

These ghosts were so old and weary that it is hard to
believe that they were living creatures. Then I stood at
this junction with my right foot which I dangled with
fear and looking at them. But as I was looking at each of
them surprisingly I noticed that the inhabitant of the
room which had golden surroundings was a golden ghost
in appearance, then the second room which had copperish
surroundings was a copperish ghost and also the third
was a silverish ghost.

As every one of them pointed his finger to me to come
to him I preferred most to go direct to the copperish-
ghost from whose room the smell of African's food was
rushing out to me, but when the golden ghost saw my
movement which showed that I wanted to go to the
copperish-ghost, so at the same time he lighted the golden
flood of light all over my body to persuade me not to go
to the copperish-ghost, as every one of them wanted me
to be his servant. So as he lighted the flood of golden
light on my body and when I looked at myself I thought

that I became gold as it was shining on my body, so at
this time I preferred most to go to him because of his
golden light. But as I moved forward a little bit to go to
him then the copperish-ghost lighted the flood of his own
copperish light on my body too, which persuaded me again
to go to the golden-ghost as my body was changing
to every colour that copper has, and my body was then
so bright so that I was unable to touch it. And again as
I preferred this copperish light more than the golden-
light then I started to go to him, but at this stage I was
prevented again to go to him by the silverish-light which
shone on to my body at that moment unexpectedly. This
silverish-light was as bright as snow so that it trans-
parented every part of my body and it was this day I
knew the number of the bones of my body. But immediately I started to count them these three ghosts shone the
three kinds of their lights on my body at the same time
in such a way that I could not move to and fro because
of these lights. But as these three old ghosts shone their
lights on me at the same time so I began to move round
as a wheel at this junction, as I appreciated these lights
as the same.

But as I was staggering about on this junction for
about half an hour because of these lights, the copperish-
ghost was wiser than the rest, he quenched his own
copperish-light from my body, so at this time I had a
little chance to go to the rest. Of course, when the golden-
ghost saw that I could not run two races at a blow successfully, so he quenched his own light too from my body,
and at this time I had chance to run a single race to the
silverish-ghost. But when I nearly reached his room then

the copperish-ghost and the golden-ghost were lighting their lights on me as signals and at the same moment the silverish-ghost joined them to use his own light as signal to me as well, because I was disturbed by the other two ghosts. Then I stopped again and looking at every one of them how he was shining his own lights on me at two or three seconds' interval as signal.

Although I appreciated or recognized these lights as the same, but I appreciated one thing more which is food, and this food is my native food which was cooked by the copperish-ghost, but as I was very hungry so I entered into his room, and when he saw that it was his room I entered he was exceedingly glad so that he gave me the food which was the same colour with copper. But as every one of these three old ghosts wanted me to be his servant, so that the other two ghosts who were the golden-ghost and the silverish-ghost did not like me to be servant for the copperish-ghost who gave me the food that I preferred most, and both entered into the room of the copperish-ghost, all of them started to argue. At last all of them held me tightly in such a way that I could not breathe in or out. But as they held me with argument for about three hours, so when I was nearly cut into three as they were pulling me about in the room I started to cry louder so that all the ghosts and ghostesses of that area came to their house and within twenty minutes this house could not contain the ghosts who heard information and came to settle the misunderstanding. But when they came and met them how they were pulling me about in the room with much argument then they told them to leave me and they left me at once.

26

In the Bush of Ghosts

After that all the ghosts who came to settle the matter arranged these three old ghosts in a single line and then they told me to choose one of them for myself to be my master so that there would be no more misunderstanding between themselves. So I stood before them and looking at every one of them with my heart which was throbbing hastily to the hearing of all of them, in such a way that the whole of the ghosts who came to settle the matter rushed to me to listen well to what my heart was saying. But as these wonderful creatures understood what my heart was saying they warned me not to choose any one of them with my mouth, because they thought it would speak partiality against one of these three ghosts, as my heart was throbbing repeatedly as if a telegraphist is sending messages by telegraph.

As a matter of fact my heart first told me to choose the silverish-ghost who stood at the extreme right and if to say I would choose by mouth I would only choose the copperish-ghost who had the African's food and that was partiality, and it was at this time I noticed carefully all the ghosts who came to settle the matter that many of them had no hands and some had no fingers, some had no feet and arms but jumped instead of walking. Some had heads without eyes and ears, but I was very surprised to see them walking about both day and night without missing their way and also it was this day I had ever seen ghosts without clothes on their bodies and they were not ashamed of their nakedness.

Uncountable numbers of them stood before me and looked at me as dolls with great surprise as they had no heads or eyes. But as they forced me to choose the silverish-ghost as he was the ghost that my heart throbbed out to their hearing to choose, when I chose him, he was exceedingly glad and ran to me, then he took me on his shoulder and then to his room. But still the other two were not satisfied with the judgement of the settlers and both ran to his room and started to fight again. This fight was so fearful and serious that all the creatures in that bush with big trees stood still on the same place that they were, even breezes could not blow at this time and these three old ghosts were still fighting on fiercely until a fearful ghost who was almost covered with all kinds of insects which represented his clothes entered their house when hearing their noises from a long distance.

The Smelling-Ghost

All kinds of snakes, centipedes and flies were living on every part of his body. Bees, wasps and uncountable mosquitoes were also flying round him and it was hard to see him plainly because of these flies and insects. But immediately this dreadful ghost came inside this house from heaven-knows-where his smell and also the smell of his body first drove us to a long distance before we came back after a few minutes, but still the smell did not let every one of the settlers stand still as all his body was full of excreta, urine, and also wet with the rotten blood of all the animals that he was killing for his food. His mouth which was always opening, his nose and eyes were very hard to look at as they were very dirty and smelling. His name is "Smelling-ghost". But what made me surprised and fear most was that this "smelling-ghost" wore many scorpions on his fingers as rings and all were alive, many poisonous snakes were also on his neck as beads and he belted his leathern trousers with a very big and long boa constrictor which was still alive.

Of course at first I did not know that he was the king of all the smelling-ghosts in the 7th town of ghosts. Immediately he entered this house, they (golden-ghost, silverish-ghost and copperish-ghost) stopped fighting at once. After that he called them out of the room in which

29

they were fighting, when they came out and stood before him, then he asked for the matter, but when they told him he called me out of the room in which I hid myself for his bad smell with his fearful appearance which I was dreaming of, without sleeping. When they called me to come to him and when I stood before him I closed my eyes, mouth and nose with both my hands because of his smell. Then he told them that he would cut me into three parts and give each part to each of them so that there would be no more misunderstanding. But as I heard from him that he would cut me into three, I fainted more than an hour before my heart came back to normal.

But God is so good these three old ghosts were not satisfied with his judgement at all, and after they had rested for a few minutes, they started fighting again.

So I was very lucky as they did not agree for him to cut me for them and when he saw that they did not agree but were still fighting, then he gripped me with his hands which were very hot and put me into the big bag which he hung on his left shoulder and kept going away at the same time. But when he threw me into the bag I was totally covered with the rotten blood of the animals which he was killing in the bush. This bag was so smelling and full of mosquitoes, small snakes with centipedes which did not let me rest for a moment. This is how I left the golden-ghost, silverish-ghost and copperish-ghost and it was from their house I started my punishment in this "Bush of Ghosts". After he left these three ghosts and travelled till the evening, then he stopped suddenly, thinking within himself with a loud voice either to eat me or to eat half of me and reserve the other half till night. Because as he was taking me along in the bush he was trying all his best to kill a bush animal to eat as food, as he could not reach his town which is the 7th town of smelling-ghosts on that day.

Although as he was carrying me along in the bush he was trying his best to kill the animals, his bad smell was suspecting him that he was coming so they were running away before he could reach them. He could not kill an animal unless it sleeps. But as I was hearing him when he was discussing either to eat me, luckily an animal was passing at that time, then he started to chase it until he saw a half-dead animal which was totally helpless, so he stopped there and began to eat it voraciously and to my surprise he was also cutting some of the animal into pieces and giving them to all the snakes etc. which were on every part of his body. After he was satisfied with this animal, then he put the rest together with its blood into the bag and it fell on to my head as a heavy load. After that he got up and kept going. But as he was travelling along in the bush and as all the snakes on his body were not satisfied with the meat before him they were rushing to the inside of the bag and eating the meat which he threw into the bag and then rushing out at the same time so that he might not suspect them. Sometimes they were mistakenly biting me several times as they could not hesitate for suspicion of their boss who might punish them for stealing. But once I heard from him when discussing within himself whether to eat me before an animal was passing I planned to stretch my hand out from the bag and hold the branch of a gravity tree, as he was sometimes creeping under the lower bush to a

31

distance of a mile or more; this plan means to escape from him.

But after he had travelled for two hours, I noticed that it was very dark, then I got up from the bag to peep out and hold the branch of a gravity tree, because if I jumped right out from the bag he would suspect or remember that I was inside the bag, as I thought that perhaps he had forgotten me there and perhaps if he catches me again at that time he would remember to eat me. Harder to stay in the bag and hardest to come out of it because when it was very dark I got up to peep out and look for the branch of a tree to hold as he was going on, but as these snakes were always rushing in and out of this bag so that at the same time that they saw me they wanted to eat me too as the meat, then I cast down inside the bag at the same moment, and after a few minutes later I peeped out again and they drove me back again, even I could not wait and breathe in fresh air.

So they disallowed me to do as I planned until he reached a place where other kinds of ghosts were in conference, then he stopped and sat with them, but he sat on me as there was no more stool.

As they were discussing some important matters for some hours, he got up on me and took out the rest meat from the bag, he put it before the ghosts that he met there and the whole of them started to eat it together. At that time I was praying not to remember to present me to these ghosts as that meat, until a lower rank ghost brought a very big animal and gave them as a present. But as he sat on me it was hard for me to breathe in or out and if it was not for the boa constrictor with which he belted his trousers which was made with the skin of an animal, I would die for his weight as I could not raise him up or lift him up at all. When it was about two o'clock in the midnight their meeting closed and then every one of them started to go to his town. After the meeting had closed he got up from me and hung the bag back on his shoulder and then kept going to his town. But as he was going hastily along in the bush all the animals were running very far away for his bad smell whenever he met them. If he was at a distance of four miles from a creature it would suspect him through his powerful smell. I was still inside this bag until he reached his town which is 7th town of ghosts on the third day.

My Life in the
7th Town of Ghosts

When he reached his town and entered his house then he took me out of the bag and I saw clearly that all his family were also smelling, and his house was smelling so that immediately he took me out from the bag I was unable to breathe out for thirty minutes. The most wonderful thing I noticed carefully in this smelling town was that all the babies born the same day were also smelling as a dead animal. This smelling town was separated and very far away from all other towns of ghosts. If any one of these smelling-ghosts touched anything it would become a bad smell at the same moment and it is bad luck for any ghost who is not a native of smelling-ghosts to meet a smelling-ghost on the way when going somewhere. It is also very bad luck for a smelling-ghost if he meets any other kind of ghosts on the way if his bad smell does not drive them very far away. At the same time as he took me out of the bag he gave me food which I was unable to eat as it was smelling badly. But as I was unable to eat this food I asked for water as I never drank water since I left my brother or since I entered into the "Bush of Ghosts", but they gave me urine as it was their water which they were storing in a big pot, of course I refused to drink it as well. There I noticed in this house

34

that mosquitoes, wasps, flies of all kinds and all kinds of poisonous snakes were disturbing them from walking easily about and it was as dark in the day as in the night, so this darkness enabled uncountable snakes to fill up there as if they were taming or keeping them.

It was in this town I saw that they had an "Exhibition of Smells". All the ghosts of this town and environs were assembling yearly and having a special "Exhibition of Smells" and the highest prizes were given to one who had the worst smells and would be recognized as a king since that day as all of them were appreciating dirt more than clean things.

When it was night he pushed me with all his power into one of the rooms which were in his house, and I met uncountable flies, snakes and all other kinds of pest creatures which drove me back at the same time as he pushed me in, but as these pest creatures drove me back to him, then he pushed me to them again and closed the door of the room. Immediately he pushed me back to them and closed the door I was covered by these pest creatures and it was hard for me to move about in this room. When I laid down to sleep on the floor without a mat I asked for a cover-cloth to cover my body, perhaps the smells would allow me to sleep or to breathe, but when all of them heard cover-cloth, they exclaimed: what is called—"cover-cloth". Of course, when they said so, I remembered that I was not with my mother or in my town. I could not sleep or rest for a minute till morning because of these pest creatures, and also the bad smells which were blowing from everywhere to this room or house. But when I got out from this room in the morning to the veranda I met over two thousand smelling-ghosts who came from various provinces of this 7th town of ghosts which was the capital to greet him for his good luck, because it was good luck for my boss as he brought me to his house or town.

Immediately I got out from the room they told me to sit down in their middle as they sat down in a circle, so all of them surrounded me closely and looking at me with much astonishment as I was breathing once a minute because of their smells which they themselves were enjoying as perfume or lavender.

In the presence of these guests, my boss was changing me to some kinds of creatures. First of all he changed me to a monkey, then I began to climb fruit trees and pluck fruits down for them. After that he changed me to a lion, then to a horse, to a camel, to a cow or bull with horns on its head and at last to my former form. Having finished that, his wives who were all the while cooking all kinds of food brought the food to them together with ghosts' drinks at the same place that they sat, and looking at me as dolls, because none of them had ever seen an earthly person in his or her life. None of them talked a single word, as looking at me motionless as dolls and all these food and drinks were also smelling badly, and at the same time that they brought them it was hard to see what sort of food and drinks because of flies which almost covered them. After all of them had eaten and drunk to their entire satisfaction then they were dancing the ghosts' dance round me and beating drums, clapping hands on me and singing the song of ghosts with gladness until a late hour in the night before every one of them who came from various provinces of this 7th town returned to his or her province and those who came from this 7th town returned to their houses. But he was still receiving uncountable messages, congratulations with many presents from those who were too old or in difficulties to present themselves at this "good luck ceremony".

After the fourth day that he had performed the "lucky-ceremony", his oldest son, who had only an arm and had no teeth in his mouth, with a bare head which was sparkling as if it was polished, took me out of the house to the front house. After that his father came and performed a juju which changed me to a horse unexpectedly, then he put reins into my mouth and tied me on a stump with a thick rope, after this he went back to the house and dressed in a big cloth which was made with a kind of ghosts' leaves which was the most expensive and he was only entitled to use such an expensive cloth as he is the king of all the smelling-ghosts, but all these smelling-ghosts did not appreciate earthly clothes as anything. After a while he came out with two of his attendants who were following him to wherever he wanted to go. Then the attendants loosened me from the stump, so he mounted me and the two attendants were following him with whips in their hands and flogging me along in the bush. As he was dressed with these leaves and mounted me mercilessly I felt as if he was half a ton weight.

Then he was riding me to the towns of those who attended and who were unable to attend his "lucky-ceremony" to greet them and whenever he reached a house he would get down off me and enter the house to greet the owner of it who came and enjoyed the "lucky-ceremony" with him or who sent him presents. But within an hour that he entered and left the attendants with me all the rest of the young ghosts and old ghosts of that area would surround me and look at me with great surprise. Sometimes these young or children ghosts would be touching my eyes with their fingers or sticks, so that perhaps I would feel it or cry and they would hear how my voice would be. He spent almost one hour in any house he was entering, because he would eat and drink together with everyone that he was visiting to their satisfaction before the whole of them would come out and look at me for about half an hour. After that he would mount me mercilessly and both his attendants would start to flog me in such a way that all the ghosts and ghostesses of that town would shout at me as a thief. But if they shouted at me like that my boss would jump and kick me mercilessly, with gladness in the presence of these bystanders until he would leave that town.

When it was two o'clock in the midday, he reached a village which also belonged to the smelling-town, he got down from me and entered the largest and finest house which belonged to the head of this village, and after a few minutes that he had entered the house a fearful ghost who was speaking with his nose and whose belly was on his thighs brought horse's food in which guinea corn and many leaves were included to me. But as I had never eaten anything since my boss took me from the three old ghosts so by that I ate the corn which I had never tasted since I was born, but I was unable to eat the leaves as I am not really a horse. Having finished the

38

corn another terrible ghost whose eyes were watering all over his body and his large mouth faced his back brought urine which was mixed with limestone to me to drink as they were not using ordinary water there because it is too clean for them. But as I was all the while tied in the sun which was shining severely on me, then I tasted it as I was exceedingly feeling thirsty, although I took off my mouth at once when I discovered that it was urine and limestone. And the worst part of these punishments was that as I was tied in the sun all the young ghosts of this village were mounting me and getting down as if I am a tree as they were very surprised to see me as a horse.

When it was about eight o'clock in the night my boss came out from that house together with some prominent ghosts of the village and after they looked at me for some minutes he hung all the presents given to him on me and then mounted me. As it was very dark at that time, so I was staggering or dashing into trees along the way when he was returning to his town, and it was almost one o'clock midnight before we reached his town. Having reached his home he was unable to change me to my former form that night, but his attendants simply tied me on a stump outside as he drank too much. So the whole of them left me there and I was totally covered by mosquitoes until morning but had no hands to drive them away. But he came in the morning and changed me to my former form.

After some minutes he gave me their smelling food which I was unable to eat satisfactorily. But after I ate some of this food he changed me again to the form of a

camel and then his sons were using me as transport to
carry heavy loads to long distances of about twenty or
forty miles. But when the rest of the smelling-ghosts
noticed that I was useful for such purpose then the whole
of them were hiring me from my boss to carry loads to
long distances and returning again in the evening with
heavier loads. But as I could not satisfy all of them at a
time so they shared me, half of them would use me from
morning till night, then the rest would use me from the
night till morning. At this stage I had no chance to rest
for a minute for all the periods that I spent with them.

As the news had been spread to many towns of other
kinds of ghosts, and as all of them wanted to see me as a
horse, so they invited my boss to a conference so that
they might see how he would ride me to their town where
the conference would be held, because ghosts like to be
in conference at all times. But as he ought to change me
from the camel to a horse, because the camel is useful
only to carry loads so by that he changed me to a person
as I was all the while in form of a camel. After he changed
me to a person then he went away to take the reins which
he would put into my mouth when he changed me to a
horse, but as soon as he went away I saw where he hid
the juju which he was using to change me to any animal
or creature that he likes, so I took it and put it into my
pocket so that he might not change me to anything again.
God is so good, he did not remember to take the juju when
he came out from the house, he thought that he had
already put it inside the pocket of his leathern trousers
which he was always belting with a big boa constrictor,
because he would not change me to a horse until he

climbed a mountain which was at a distance of about six miles from his town and his aim was that he would change me to a horse after he had climbed the mountain and ride me from there to the town in which he was invited to the conference.

When he came back from the house he simply threw me inside the big bag which he hung on his shoulder, because he could not go anywhere without this bag, as it is a uniform for every king that reigns in this 7th town of ghosts which belongs only to smelling-ghosts. Immediately he put me inside the bag then he kept going to the town that they invited him to. But when he climbed the mountain to the top he branched to his right then he bent down and started to pass excreta. But as I was inside the bag I was thinking how I could escape from him, and after a while I remembered that I had taken the juju which he would use before he could change me to any creature that he likes and at this time he has no power to change me to a horse again. So I jumped right out from the bag to the ground and without hesitation I started to run away inside the bush for my life and immediately he saw me running away he got up and started to chase me, saying thus with loud voice: "Ah! the earthly person is running away, how can I catch him now, oh! what can I ride on to the conference today, as all the ghosts who invited me are waiting to see me on a horse. Oh! if I had known I should have changed him to a horse before I left home. But if my head helps me and I catch him now I will change him from today to a permanent horse for ever. Ah! how can I catch him now?" But as he was chasing me fiercely and saying like that, I myself was also saying thus: "Ah! how can I save myself from this smelling-ghost who wants to catch me and change me to a permanent horse for ever, and if he catches me now it means I would not return to my town or I will not see my mother for ever?"

But as any ghost could run faster than any earthly person, so that I became tired before him, and when he was about to catch me or when his hand was touching my head slightly to catch it, then I used the juju which I took from the hidden place that he kept it in before we left his house. And at the same moment that I used it, it changed me to a cow with horns on its head instead of a horse, but I forgot before I used it that I would not be able to change back to the earthly person again, because I did not know another juju which he was using before changing me back to an earthly person. Of course as I had changed to a cow I became more powerful and started to run faster than him, but still, he was chasing me fiercely until he became tired. And when he was about to go back from me I met a lion again who was hunting up and down in the bush at that time for his prey as he was very hungry, and without hesitation the lion was also chasing me to kill for his prey, but when he chased me to a distance of about two miles I fell into the cow-men's hands who caught me at once as one of their cows which had been lost from them for a long time, then the lion got back from me at once for the fearful noise of these cow-men. After that they put me among their cows which were eating grass at that time. They thought I was one of their lost cows and put me among the cows as I was unable to change myself to a person again.

42

My Life with Cows

As I was among these cows I was illtreated as a wild or stubborn cow by these cow-men and always given double punishments which should only be given to the cows. At night they would put the whole of us in the yard and locked the door so that we might not escape. But as these cows were not persons and also more powerful, several times they would be scratching me with their horns and hoofs and jumping on me in the same place that I was cast down, and thinking that no doubt one day I should be killed or sold to a butcher who would kill me as an ordinary cow. The aim of these cows was to kick or scratch me with their horns until I would stand up and be doing as they themselves were doing. They were not sleeping, resting or tired of making fearful noises once till the day would break, especially if the rain comes at night and starts to beat us they would enjoy it to their satisfaction and then begin to kick themselves and dash at everything without mercy, because the yard was uncovered.

Every early morning the cow-men would come and take the whole of us to a wide pasture, and at the same time these cows would scatter on this pasture which was in the centre of the sun and start to eat the grasses voraciously, but I alone would cast myself down on the

43

same place as I could not eat the grasses because I am not a real cow. Of course as a stream crossed the road on which we were travelling to this pasture so I was drinking the water from it when going early in the morning and also when returning in the evening and I was feeding only on this water as food. As I was unable to explain to these cow-men that I am not really a cow, so I was showing them in my attitude several times that I am a person, because whenever they were roasting yams in the fire and when eating it I would approach them and start to eat the crumbs of the yams which were falling down by mistake from their hands and whenever they were discussing some important matter with arguments within themselves I would be giving signs with my head which was showing them the right and wrong points on which they were arguing.

But one day, when they noticed that I was always standing or cast down in the same place and not eating the grasses or roaming about as other cows were doing, then they started to flog me with heavy clubs and also illtreat me as they were treating wild or stubborn cows, so I was feeling much pain and still I was unable to eat the grasses or to be doing as other cows were doing. Their aim was that if they flog me I would eat the grasses and do as other cows, but after they had tried all their efforts and failed then they thought that I was sick.

After the third day that they thought so, they took me to a market for sale, but unfortunately nobody bought me until the evening that the market closed, then they took me back home. Again, two days later they took me to this market for the second time for sale, but the butchers bought all the rest cows in the market and left me alone; everyone of them was telling these cow-men that if they take me back home they must kill me at once otherwise I would die unexpectedly. These butchers thought that I would die very soon as I could not do as other cows and also was very lean for want of food and again from illtreatment. So when these cow-men were returning to their town in the evening with me as no one bought me on that market day again, they were abusing and clubbing me repeatedly along the homeway. They were also thinking within themselves that if they take me to the market for the third time and if butchers refuse to buy me, then they would kill me unfailingly on that day for their food as I was not useful for them. But when the third market day arrived I was taken to the market for the third time, luckily I was bought by an old woman when it was about two o'clock p.m. The reason why she bought me was that her daughter's eyes were totally blinded for a long time and when she went to a fortune-teller, she was told that she must go to the market and buy a cow and kill it for a certain god which was in her town, then undoubtedly her daughter's eyes would see clearly as before. So when this old woman heard this from the fortune-teller then she came to the market and bought me very cheap as I was very lean, then she took me to her town where she would kill me for the god of her town as told.

When she reached her house, she tied me to a pillar which was on the front of her house, but this pillar was exposed to the sun or anything which might come down from the sky. Having tied me to this pillar she entered

into the house and after half an hour she brought plenty
of cooked yams back to me and I ate to my satisfaction as
it was cooked. But when it was night she did not attempt
to put me inside the house or a protected place for any
dangerous creature which might attack me in the mid-
night. It was not yet eight o'clock in the night before
everybody slept in this town, and again when it was ten
o'clock a heavy rain came and beat me till the morning,
and also the mosquitoes which were as big as flies did
not let me rest once till the morning, but I had no hands
to be driving them away from my body, although it is
only in this "Bush of Ghosts" such big mosquitoes could
be found, and as I was in the rain throughout the night
I was feeling the cold so that I was shaking together with
my voice, but had no fire to warm my body.

A Cola Saved Me

When it was twelve o'clock p.m. prompt the whole people of this town gathered at the front of the house of this old woman who bought me. After that four of them loosened me from the pillar and took me to their god which was outside the town. Having reached there I saw clearly that over fifty of these people held daggers or sharp knives, spears, cutlasses and axes which were as sharp as swords. The first ceremony which they performed for this god was that the whole of them laid me down flat and close before the god. At this stage I wanted to speak to them that I am not a real cow but a person. But all of this was in vain, because if my heart speaks as a person my mouth would speak out the words in the cow's voice which was fearful to them and also was not clear to them. As they laid me down before this god, all of them danced round me three times and this was the first ceremony to be performed. After that they were praying which was the second ceremony to be performed. But as the word "COLA" should be mentioned in a part of the prayer, and again the "COLA" should be produced at this point by the old woman as it must be included in this sacrifice before they could kill me before this god, so at this stage they asked the old woman to produce the "COLA". Then she searched her handbag which she brought there, but when she searched the bag there was no "COLA", she had forgotten it at home, then she told them that she would run home and bring it.

But after she left a joke-man was joking funnily about me as I had become a laughing-stock for them, that he would eat cow meat today until he would nearly die, because he had eaten cow's meat for long time. And when a risible man who was among the four men who held me tightly before this god heard what the joke-man was saying then he started to laugh, so when the rest started to laugh together, the four men who held me before the god did not know the time that their hands slackened on me, then I sprang up unexpectedly with all my power to a distance of about ninety yards away. So this made them frightened as there were horns on my head, and before they could start to chase me I ran into a thick bush which was about a mile from them or that god. But after they tried all their efforts to catch me and failed, then the whole of them ran back to the town to take guns, bows and arrows. And before they could come back to chase me again, as I was running helter-skelter in that bush for my life I mistakenly fell into a very deep pond which was full of water as it was in the rainy season and also covered by the weeds which disallowed me from seeing that there was a pond. But to my surprise, immediately I saw my shadow in this water that I was a cow in form I changed to a person as before I used the smelling-ghost's juju which changed me so. Of course if I had known that if I see myself in water that I am a cow I would change to a person I should have done so immediately the cow-men caught me and before they sold me to the old woman whose daughter's eyes were blinded.

But as I had been changed to a person before these people came with guns, I asked them personally what they were looking for, but they replied that they were looking for a cow which was just escaped from them, then I said—"Oh! I saw it now when running far into the bush, better follow this way, you will see it very soon if you follow my advice." And the whole of them followed the direction that I showed them because they thought I was one of them. Then I left that area immediately they left me and I started to find the way to my home town.

But when it was about three months that I left them or changed from a cow to a person, one night, as I was wandering about in the bush I saw a dead wood which was about six feet long and three feet in diameter and there was a large hole inside it which was not through to the second end, which means it has only one entrance. So I entered the hole through this entrance, then I slept there as I did not sleep since I was among the cows before they sold me and again it was in the rainy season which was beating me about both day and night. But I did not wake until a "homeless-ghost" who was only wandering about since he was born by an unknown mother came and entered into the hole of this dead wood as he was also looking for such a dry place to sleep. But when he entered and met me there, he did nothing but got out cautiously and corked tightly the only entrance of this hole. After that he put it on his head while I was inside the hole, then he carried this wood about together with me, and he had carried it very far away before I woke inside this

49

wood as ghosts were very smart to trek either short or long distances.

But when I woke and noticed that I was carried away by an unknown ghost or creature to an unknown destination, so I began to suggest in my mind that perhaps the creature who is carrying me away now is going to throw the wood into a big fire or is going to throw it into a deep river. After I thought so, then I began to cry with a lower voice, not knowing that there was already a big snake inside this hole before I entered it. But at the same moment that the snake heard my voice when crying which was fearful to him, so he was coiled round me instead of running out of the hole as the entrance had been corked before by this "homeless-ghost" who was carrying it about. But as this snake was also fearful to me too, then I was crying louder than before, and when the "homeless-ghost" was hearing my voice inside this wood, it was a lofty music for him, then he started to dance the ghosts' dance and staggering here and there in the bush as if he was intoxicated by a kind of their drink which was the strongest of all their drinks and which was drunk only by "His Majesty" the king of the "Bush of Ghosts", the royal and prominent ghosts. The homeless-ghost who was carrying the wood away thought that it was this wood which he was carrying away that was playing the lofty music. But as he was carrying the wood away, dancing and staggering on, he met over a million "homeless-ghosts" of his kind who were listening to my cry as a radio. Whenever these ghosts met him and listened to my cry which was a lofty music for a few minutes, if they could not bear the music and stand still

.ıen the whole of them would start to dance at the same time as a madman. All these "homeless-ghosts" so appreciated my cry that all would dance to a distance of about a mile away from the carrier of the wood and then dance back to him again. And as all the ghosts that they met were joining them to dance, so all of them danced for three days and nights without eating, resting or being tired once until the news had spread to many towns of ghosts.

So at this time the homeless-ghost who was carrying the wood was invited by several prominent ghosts who had special occasions to perform. But whenever he reached the town that he was called to, first of all they would eat and drink to their most entire satisfaction, after that he would knock the wood as a sign, and when the snake heard it he would be running to and fro inside the wood in searching the way to go out and when doing that he would be also coiling me round in such a fearful way which would make me to cry more bitterly, and when hearing my cry then the whole of the ghosts of that town would be dancing till a late hour in the night as both day and night were the same for all ghosts.

But as a person could not cry from morning till the late hour in the night without stopping or eating once so if I stopped to rest for a moment or if my voice had become stiffness, then he would put this wood near the fire and if the wood started to heat, then I would start to cry louder by force, and the snake would be also dashing to every part of the hole as if ten persons are beating different kinds of drums to my cry, so they would continue at once to dance again.

51

At a Ghost Mother's
Birthday Function

As this "homeless-ghost" was then famous and well known to every prominent ghost because of my cry which was a very lofty music for them, so one day, a famous ghost whose mother had died when all the eyes of all the creatures were still on their knees invited all the ghosts of his kind to his house as all the same kinds of ghosts are living in the same town and called the homeless-ghost to hear the music which would be the most important part for the ceremony of his mother's birthday. But after all the invitees had gathered to his house, and ate and drank to their satisfaction, then the homeless-ghost knocked the wood as a sign, so I started to cry from that morning till the evening, but as I never eat or drink since the night he had corked me inside the hole, then my voice was entirely stiffened or dead. I was unable to cry any more, and as all these invitees had eaten and drunk to excess, and still eager to hear my cry, so after the whole of them with the "homeless-ghost" who carried me to that town had tried all their efforts to make me cry and failed, then he started to split the wood into two with an axe. Luckily when the wood was half broken the snake first found his way out as he was thinner than me and when visible to these ghosts unexpectedly all of them ran furiously to the house of the famous ghost who invited them and hid there. But as the wood had already nearly broken into two, so I tried my best and found my way out as well and without hesitation I ran into a far bush and hid there before they came back and it was already empty, so it was this time they knew that it was a person crying in it.

This is how I escaped from the "homeless-ghost" who was carrying me about, and before the dawn I had travelled very far away from that town and then entered into another town and started a new life with new ghosts. Immediately I entered this town I went round it and saw a ghost who only resembled earthly people among all ghosts who were living there. Then I entered his house, I saluted him with respect and he answered me exactly as an earthly person. He gave me a seat at once. After that I asked him to give me food as I did not eat anything since I escaped from the "homeless-ghost" who was carrying me about, but as he was a kind ghost he gave me the food without any question.

After I ate the food to my satisfaction and rested for some minutes, then I asked him whether he is an earthly person as I was doubting, he replied thus—"I am and I am not." But as I did not know which is to be held as the truth in these two answers, so I told him that I do not understand what he means by "I am and I am not." When heard so from me he started his story and also the story of that town as follows:

"You see, the whole of us in this town are burglars

At a Ghost Mother's Birthday Function

and we have burgled uncountable earthly women in every earthly town, country and village. You earthly person, listen to me well, I shall tell you how we are burgling earthly women today. If an earthly woman conceives we would choose one of us to go to her at night and after the woman has slept then he would use his invisible power to change himself to the good baby that the woman would be delivered of whenever it is time. But after he has driven out the good baby and entered into the woman's womb, he would remain there and when it is time the woman would deliver him instead of the good baby which had been driven out; and the wonderful secret which all the earthly persons do not understand is that before two or three months that the woman bore him, he would develop rapidly as a year and an half old baby and would be very attractive to everyone, particularly the woman who bore him, as a good or superior baby. Having developed to that attractive state he would start to pretend to be sick continuously, but as he is very attractive to this woman, then she will be spending a lot of money on him to heal the sickness and also sacrificing to all kinds of gods. As this inferior baby has invisible power or supernatural power, so all the money spent on him and also the sacrifices would be his own and all would be stored into a secret place with the help of his invisible power.

But after the woman has spent all she has and become poor, then one night he would pretend as if he has died, so the woman who bore him as a superior baby, her family and other sympathisers would be saying thus: "Ah! that fine baby dies", but they do not know that he is not a superior baby. They would bury him as a dead baby,

54

but the earthly persons do not know that he does not die
but simply stops breath. But after he is buried, then he
would come out of the grave at midnight, then he would
go direct to the secret place where all the moneys and the
sacrifices as sheep, goats, pigeons and fowls, all would be
alive and are stored by his invisible power, and he would
carry them to this town. So you earthly person, if you
reach your earthly town and if you hear that a woman is
delivering babies who die always or continuously, then
believe, we are those babies and all the earthly people are
calling such a baby "born and die". But if you do not
believe this story if a "born and die" baby dies from a
woman, after he is buried, watch the grave in which he
is buried and after the second day try and go to that grave
and dig it out; you would be very surprised that he
would not be found there any more, but he has come back
to this town. We have no other work to perform more
than this in this town, so the whole of us in this town are
called "Burglar-ghosts". But after he told me the story
of their town and also about the "born and die babies" I
was very impressed and surprised. He told me too that
the whole of them are feeding on anything that earthly
people have and said further that this is the meaning of
"I am and I am not" when I first asked him whether he
is an earthly person, because they were living as earthly
persons and also as ghosts.

After he related the secret of the "born and die babies",
then he asked me whether I should be living with him in
that town and I said "yes", so he gave me a separate
room in his house. But as I was living with this "burglar-
ghost" and he was taking great care of me as if he was

my father and mother, so one day, he told me that I should take care of everything in the house and said that he would go to a certain town which belongs to earthly people tonight, he said that he would return in ten months' time. Because he had told me before that he would try the wonderful invisible power once in my presence before I would leave him to believe all his saying. Of course as he told me like that I did not believe him at all and I did not know what he was going to do in that earthly town and also I did not know the name of the right earthly town he was going to. So when it was about one o'clock in the midnight he became invisible to me, because I did not see him walk out from the house on foot, so it remained me alone at home. But after he became invisible or gone away, I was playing about in this town as I could not stay at home always, but as it is not hard or very easy for a young boy to get a friend of his rank, by that I became a tight friend with a young ghost whose father was a rich ghost and also a native of that town when I was playing around the town. This young ghost taught me how to speak some simple ghosts' language. Of course I was unable to speak it fluently at that time. Both of us were playing about in the town in such a way that I did not remember to start to find the way to my home town again. But one night at about one o'clock in the midnight when I slept I heard somebody knocking the door of that house, when I opened this door which was a heavy flat stone it was this burglar-ghost who had gone ten months ago. Then he entered with bales of sewn clothes, sheep, goats, pigeons, fowls, all were still alive and moneys with all other used expensive articles.

At a Ghost Mother's Birthday Function

But when he loosened these bales of clothes there I saw plainly many clothes which belonged to my friends and my mother in my town that were among these clothes and was also surprised to see many clothes which my mother just bought for me and my brother before the war scattered all of us. After the second day that he came we killed all the fowls, pigeons, goats and sheep for the rest burglar-ghosts of this town for his good luck as he returned safely with many expensive articles. And when I saw all that he brought and also my own and my brother's properties, then I believed his story which he told me before he went away. Of course I could not ask him how he managed to get the clothes which belonged to me and my brother as I was too young to ask him such questions, so I left them for him and he sold all to another kind of ghosts who had no invisible power to do such work, but I ate those animals with them.

As I had already become tight friends with that young ghost before he returned from the earthly town, so one day this my young ghost friend told me to accompany him to his mother's town which was about twenty miles away from that burglar-ghosts' town, his mother was born and bred in this town which is the 8th town of ghosts. Having reached there his mother gave us food and drinks, and when we ate and drank to our satisfaction, then we were playing all about in the town with the other young ghosts of our ranks that we met there, but as we were playing about there I saw a very beautiful young ghostess, then I told my friend that I want to marry her, so my friend told her and also recommended me highly to her, so by that she agreed at the same time,

At a Ghost Mother's Birthday Function

but as her father was famous and prominent in that town, so he arranged the wedding day for the ghosts' next wedding day which was about nine days to come at that time as all the ghosts have a special day for marriage.

My First Wedding Day
in the Bush of Ghosts

Before the wedding day was reached my friend had chosen one of the most fearful ghosts for me as my "best man" who was always speaking evil words, even he was punished in the fire of hell more than fifty years for these evil talks and cruelties, but was still growing rapidly in bad habits, then he was expelled from hell to the "Bush of Ghosts" to remain there until the judgement day as he was unable to change his evil habits at all. When the wedding day arrived all the ghosts and ghostesses of this town, together with the father of the lady whom I wanted to marry, my friend and his mother, my best man and myself went to the church at about ten o'clock, but it was the ghosts' clock said so. When we reached their church I saw that the Reverend who preached or performed the wedding ceremony was the "Devil". But as he was preaching he reached the point that I should tell them my name which is an earthly person's name and when they heard the name the whole of them in that church exclaimed at the same time— "Ah! you will be baptized in this church again before you will marry this lady."

When I heard so from them I agreed, not knowing that

My First Wedding Day in the Bush of Ghosts

Rev. Devil was going to baptize me with fire and hot water as they were baptizing for themselves there. When I was baptized on that day, I was crying loudly so that a person who is at a distance of two miles would not listen before hearing my voice, and within a few minutes every part of my body was scratched by this hot water and fire, but before Rev. Devil could finish the baptism I regretted it. Then I told him to let me go away from their church and I do not want to marry again, because I could not bear to be baptized with fire and hot water any longer, but when all of them heard so, they shouted, "Since you have entered this church you are to be baptized with fire and hot water before you will go out of the church, willing or not you ought to wait and complete the baptism." But when I heard so from them again, I exclaimed with a terrible voice that—"I will die in their church." So all of them exclaimed again that— "you may die if you like, nobody knows you here."

But as ghosts do not know the place or time which is possible to ask questions, so at this stage one of them got up from the seat and asked me—"by the way, how did you manage to enter into the 'Bush of Ghosts', the bush which is on the second side of the world between the heaven and earth and which is strictly banned to every earthly person to be entered, and again you have the privilege to marry in this bush as well?" So as these ghosts have no arrangements for anything at the right time and right place, then I answered that I was too young to know which is "bad" and "good" before I mistakenly entered this bush and since that time or year I am trying my best to find out the right way back to my

My First Wedding Day in the Bush of Ghosts

home town until I reached the town of "burglary-ghosts" from where I came with my friend to this town. After I explained as above, then the questioner stood up again and asked me whether I could show them my friend whom I followed to that town. Of course as my friend was faithful, before I could say anything, he and his mother whom we came to visit got up at the same time and said that I am living with a burglar-ghost in the town of the burglar-ghosts. But when my friend and his mother confirmed all that I said and as all the rest of the ghosts are respecting all the burglar-ghosts most because they were supplying them the earthly properties, so they overlooked my offence, then Rev. Devil continued the baptism with hot water and fire.

After the baptism, then the same Rev. Devil preached again for a few minutes, while "Traitor" read the lesson. All the members of this church were "evil-doers". They sang the song of evils with evils' melodious tune, then "Judas" closed the service.

Even "Evil of evils" who was the ruler of all the evils and who was always seeking evils about, evil-joking, evil-walking, evil-playing, evil-laughing, evil-talking, evil-dressing, evil-moving, worshipping evils in the church of evils and living in the evil-house with his evil family, everything he does is evil, attended the service too, but he was late before he arrived and when he shook hands with me on that day, I was shocked as if I touch a "live electric wire", but my friend was signalling to me with his eyes not to shake hands with him to avoid the shock but I did not understand.

Having finished the marriage service, all of us went

61

to my in-laws' house where everybody was served with a variety of food and all kinds of ghosts' drinks. After that all the ghost and ghostess dancers started to dance. Also all the terrible-creatures sent their representatives as "Skulls", "Long-white creatures", "Invincible and invisible Pawn" or "Give and take" who fought and won the Red people in the Red-town for the "Palm-Wine Drinker'; "Mountain-creatures", "Spirit of prey" whose eye's flood of light suffocated Palm-Wine Drinker's wife and also the "hungry-creature" who swallowed Palm-Wine Drinker together with his wife when returning from Deads'-town came and saluted my wife's father and they were served immediately they arrived. But at last "Skull" who came from "Skull family's town" reported "Spirit of prey" to my wife's father who was chief secretary to all the terrible and curious creatures in all dangerous bushes, that the spirit of prey stole his meat which the skull put at the edge of the plate in which both were eating as both were served together with one plate, because plates were not sufficient to serve each of them with a plate. But before my wife's father who was their chief secretary could have a chance to come and settle the matter for them, both of them started to fight fiercely so that all the ghosts and all the other representatives came nearer and surrounded them, clapping hands on them in such a way that if one of these fighters surrenders or gives up it would be very shameful to him.

Some of these scene-lookers were clapping, and an old Ape who was a slave and inherited by my wife's father from his first generation since uncountable years was beating a big tree under which both these terrible crea-

62

tures were fighting as a drum which had a very large sound. But as this old slave ape was beating the tree as a drum in such a way that all the scene-lookers who stood round them could not bear the lofty sound of the tree which was beaten as a drum and wait or stand still in one place, so all the ghosts, evils, terrible creatures, my friend, my wife and her father and myself started to dance at the same time. But as I was intoxicated by the strong drinks which I drank on that day, so I mistakenly smashed a small ghost to death who came from the "9th town of ghosts" to enjoy the merriment of the marriage with us as I was staggering about.

At last I was summoned to the court of evil for wilfully killing a small ghost, but as a little mistake is a serious offence as well as big offence in the "Bush of Ghosts", so the "Evil judge" judged the case at one o'clock of the judgement day and luckily I was freed by a kind lawyer whose mother was the native of the "Bottomless Ravine's town", the town which belongs to only "triplet ghosts and ghostesses". But if it was not far this incognito lawyer who was very kind to me without knowing him elsewhere I would be imprisoned for fifty years as this is the shortest years for a slightest offence.

After I freed the case then I returned to my in-laws' town and lived there with my wife for a period of about three months and some days before I remembered my mother and brother again, because I did not remember them again when I married the lady. So one morning, I told the father of my wife that I want to leave his town for another one, but I did not tell him frankly that I want to continue to find the way to my home town which I

My First Wedding Day in the Bush of Ghosts

left since I was seven years old. So I told him that I should leave with his daughter who was my wife, he allowed me to go or to leave, but disallowed his daughter to go with me. Of course, when I thought over within myself that however an earthly person might love ghosts, ghosts could not like him heartily in any respect, then I alone left his town in the evening after I went round the town and bade goodbye to the prominent ghosts.

On my Way to the
9th Town of Ghosts

As I left the town of my wife's father late in the evening, the town which is the 8th town of ghosts in which I was baptized with fire and hot water, so I travelled from bush to bush till a late hour in the night, perhaps I would see the way of my home town, but when I believed that I could not see it or I could not reach the 9th town of ghosts on that night, then I stopped under a tree and climbed to the top. I laid down on its branch which had plenty of leaves that covered me as a cloth from the cold of that night and also from the wind which was blowing the tree to and fro, with dew which was dropping as light rain on everything on the ground. But as I was troubled too much on the way to this tree by the ghost children, because I was very curious to them, so it was not more than five minutes before I fell asleep. And when it was about an hour and half that I was enjoying this sleep to my satisfaction, then I felt suddenly that somebody was knocking the tree at the bottom as if somebody is knocking a door, so I woke alert or with fear and when I bent downward and looked at the foot of this tree, there I saw a very short ghost who was not more than three feet high but very corpulent as a pregnant woman who would deliver either today or tomorrow. He was waving his hand to me to come down to him, but as I was looking at him all the while or for some minutes then I saw clearly that he had one arm, both his legs were twisted as rope and both feet faced sharply left and right, he had an eye on his forehead which was exactly like a moon, this eye was as big as a full moon and had a cover or socket which could be easily opening and closing at any time that he likes, no single hairs on his head and it was sparkling as polished ebony furniture.

When he noticed that I did not want to come down to him then he raised the cover of the eye off and at the same moment every part of this bush was as clear as daytime, and then I saw through this light that there were uncountable of the same kinds of these ghosts already surrounding the tree. All of them were waiting for me to come down to them, but as their attitude showed that they got ready to catch me, so by that I feared them.

But after they waited for a few minutes and believed that I stayed on this tree for their dreadful appearance then the whole of them came nearer to the tree and started to shake it with all their power, but when they nearly rooted out this tree then I fell on to their hands unexpectedly. I noticed carefully at this stage that if they are breathing in I would hear the cry of frogs, toads, pigs' cry, the crowing of cocks, the noises of birds and as if uncountable dogs are barking at the same time, and when they breathe out again there would be another cry of fearful creatures as well. But as the whole of them seized me by violence or rape at the same time, then I began to beg them with a lower or cool voice, because I thought that they were going to eat me alive and they did not listen to me until they took me to their town which is the 9th town of ghosts.

Having reached their town, they put me in a very dark room which was under the ground, as such rooms are very common in the "Bush of Ghosts". After a while they changed me to a blind man and then rubbed my body with their palms which were sharp as sand paper and were slightly scraping me as dulled sand paper. Having left that they were cutting the flesh of my body with their sharp finger-nails which were long at about four inches, so I was crying bitterly for much pain. Again after a little while they left that and then my eyes opened as before, but I saw nobody there with me in this doorless room who was ill-treating me like that. Immediately my eyes opened there I saw about a thousand snakes which almost covered me, although they did not attempt to bite me at all. It was in this doorless room which is in underground I first saw in my life that the biggest and longest among these snakes which was acting as a director for the rest vomited a kind of coloured lights from his mouth on to the floor of this room. These lights shone to every part of the room and also to my eyes, and after all of the snakes saw me clearly through the lights then they disappeared at once with the lights and then the room became dark as before.

After a few minutes later that these snakes disappeared, there I saw that this doorless room changed to a pitcher and unexpectedly I found myself inside this pitcher and at the same moment my neck was about three feet long and very thick, and again my head was so big so that my long neck was unable to carry it upright as it was very stiff as a dried stick. Another two eyes which were as big and round as a football formed and appeared on this head and both eyes could be easily turning anywhere that I liked to look or see and I did not know where my normal eyes which were on my head before went. But as I was in this pitcher then all of these ghosts were visible to me and at the same time all were knocking the big head with sticks, but I had no hands to defend it because only my head and neck appeared out from the pitcher.

After some minutes they left knocking the big head, but I began to feel hunger as if I had not eaten anything for a year, so when I could not bear this hunger I started to cry out—"I want to eat." And immediately I was saying so there I saw on my front the food which I like most or which was exactly the same as the kind that my mother was always cooking for me in my town before we left. But as it was on my front my head could not reach it as my neck could not bend anywhere as a dried stick, of course when I tried my best and overturned the pitcher the head fell a little distance from this food instead of touching it, but as the neck was unable to bend or move the head, and the head was also too big for the neck to lift up, I tried all my power to touch the food more than thirty minutes before my mouth could reach the food and when I was about to start to eat it my mouth changed again to the beak of a small bird unexpectedly, but the food was still in front with its good flavour. When this beak disturbed me eating the food then I wanted to cry because I was feeling hunger as if I would die soon, but I cried out like a small bird instead of a man and when

68

all these ghosts that surrounded and looked at me as I was trying all the while to eat the food heard my cry as a small bird's cry all laughed at me at the same time.

So after I had tried all my efforts on everything and failed, then I was thinking in my mind that it is better for me to die now than to be in punishment like this, so immediately I finished these thoughts the beak disappeared together with the food and there was a mouth as usual and without hesitation I was moving together with the pitcher along the floor of this doorless room, but I saw nobody who was pushing me on and also all these ghosts which surrounded me disappeared unnoticed. At last I found myself where several roads meet together, the place was about one-third of a mile distant from their town, but all these roads were foot paths. After I moved to the centre of these roads by an invisible mover then I stopped. It was an open place, except the bush which spread on it. There I remained till the morning without seeing a single creature.

When it was about eight o'clock in the morning all the ghosts and ghostesses with their children of that town came to me with two sheep and two goats and also with some fowls. Having reached there the first thing they did was that the whole of them surrounded me, then all were singing, beating drums, clapping hands, ringing bells and dancing round me for a few minutes before they killed all the domestic animals which they brought before me and poured the blood of these animals on to my head which ran to the long neck and then into the pitcher in which the rest of my body was. After that the flesh of these animals was cooked and put all near to touch my mouth and I was easily eating it. So all these ghosts were coming every third day and worshipping me there as their god. But the worst part of it was the bells which they were beating with big rods whenever they came, and when sounding it would cause a head-ache, and again the blood of all the animals pouring on to my head was also smelling very bad when rotten. They were spending about four hours with me whenever they were coming to worship me, so I did not feel hunger again as I was eating all the sacrifices they were bringing to me.

Ah! nobody would enter into the "Bush of Ghosts" without much trouble and severe punishment, because as I was repeatedly beaten by rain and scourged by the sun on the centre of these roads as I was unable to move myself anywhere, so at night the bush animals, and other kinds of reptiles would come and stand before me and then looking at me with great surprise for my fearful appearance. And if all of them looked at me for so many hours, then the boa would come to me and start to swallow my head which appeared from the pitcher, but when it swallowed it to the larger part of the pitcher it would disturb him from swallowing the whole of me or the pitcher, and when disturbed then he would vomit me out again and I would not be allowed to sleep or rest for a minute throughout the nights because of the troubles given me by these animals. And if the day breaks again, all the sheep, goats, fowls, pigs and dogs would come again from that town. All would stand and look at me with much astonishment as I was curious and very dreadful to them, even to any person who might see me at this time. If these domestic animals look at me for some hours

70

attentively, motionless or crying once, then all the dogs who were among them would be barking at me and coming to me slowly until they would reach me and then they would start to eat the remaining sacrifice which I could not finish, and before they would finish that the goats and sheep would come to me and start to kick me on the head but I had no hands to drive them away. Again all these dogs would be licking all the blood poured on to my head with their tongues, and as they were doing like this all the ghosts would come again and then all these domestic animals would run back to the town, so by that I had no chance to sleep or rest both day and night.

Within a few months that I was at the centre of these roads in the pitcher news had reached every other town of ghosts of that area and all of them were trying their best to steal me for their towns as they thought that I am really a god.

River-Ghosts
Gala-day under the River

One night at about two o'clock, I saw many ghosts
who came to me and put me inside a big bag which they
brought. After that one of them put me on his head and
then from there to their town which was under a big
river, because they are "River-Ghosts". Which means
they stole me from this centre of the roads to their town.
Having reached their town they took me to their chief
ancestor who sat down on an idle chair before a fearful
god which they supposed to be the most powerful among
their gods which they were worshipping in this town.
Then they put me down before him as he was the one
who ordered them to go and steal me from the centre of
the roads when they heard information about me. Immediately I was presented to him he sent for a ram, then
he killed it before me and poured its blood on to my big
head which was as big as an elephant's head and also
fearful to look at. After, they cooked the flesh of this ram
and put the best fleshy parts of it before me to eat. But
as I started to eat it the whole of them were very surprised and were also exceedingly glad as all their gods
that I met there could not eat, breathe, or make any sign.
But as these river ghosts or sceptical ghosts hate the

72

heavenly God most and love earthly gods most, anything they wanted to do the chief ancestor would ask me first and if I made a sign with my head which would show him that the request should be done then he would tell the rest that I favoured them to do the requests, but if the sign showed that their requests should not be done then he would tell the rest that the requests are not granted by me, so therefore the requests would be cancelled at the same time. The chief ancestor was my interpreter as he only was permitted by his highest title to approach me at any time.

As I was so highly recognized by these river ghosts or sceptical ghosts so they built a one-roomed house and put me inside it and all of them were coming there to worship and sacrifice to me there as well. I was feeding on any sacrifice that I wanted and drinking the blood of the animals which they were killing and pouring on me as water, because they were not giving me water to drink. But as the blood was always pouring on me, so it was attracting flies which were covering me totally all the time and I had no hands to drive them away. Even sometime if the chief ancestor came in to visit me, he would not be able to discover me among these flies unless he first drove them away with a broom before he could see me.

When it was a week that they had brought me to their town the whole of them gathered together. First of all they opened the room in which they put me, after that the chief ancestor who only is permitted to approach me or to talk to me washed my head with my long stiff neck as only both appeared out from the pitcher, after this,

73

he put a small red hand sewn cloth on the long neck which made it more ugly; after this, he put a kind of ghost's face cap on this my big head which made it more fearful to see. After that he put a kind of smoking pipe which was about six feet long into my mouth. This smoking pipe could contain half a ton of tobacco at a time, then he chose one ghost to be loading this pipe with tobacco whenever it discharged fire. When he lit the pipe with fire then the whole of the ghosts and ghostesses were dancing round me set by set. They were singing, clapping hands, ringing bells and their ancestral drummers were beating the drums in such a way that all the dancers were jumping up with gladness. But whenever the smoke of the pipe was rushing out from my mouth as if smoke is rushing from a big boiler, then all of them would laugh at me so that a person two miles away would hear them clearly, and whenever the tobacco inside the pipe is near to finish then the ghost who was chosen to be loading it would load it again with fresh tobacco as it was about three feet deep and four feet diameter.

After some hours that I was smoking this pipe I was intoxicated by the gas of the tobacco as if I drank much hard drink, because it was only ghosts could smoke such tobacco and it was only in the "Bush of Ghosts" such tobacco could be found.

So at this time I forgot all my sorrow and started to sing the earthly songs which sorrow prevented me from singing about since I entered this bush. But when all these ghosts were hearing the song, they were dancing from me to a distance of about five thousand feet and then dancing back to me again as they were much

74

appreciating the song and also to hear my voice was curious to them. After a while all of them surrounded me closely, opened their mouths downward and looked at me with surprise. But as I was more intoxicated by the gas of the tobacco and also as the pipe was loaded continuously with fresh tobacco by the ghost who was specially chosen to be loading it, so by that I could not stop or tire of singing, and again my town's songs were then rushing to my heart at that time. So as they bent, their mouths which opened with great surprise downward onto my head the spit of these mouths was dropping on me and wet me as if I bathed with water, the spit was smelling so badly so that it was hard for me to breathe out or in.

After they listened to my songs for about half an hour, the chief ancestor took me out of this room which was specially built for me, then he rooted out a tall coconut tree which was about three hundred feet long, after that he put me on the top of this tree, then another ghost who was next in rank to him put the tree on his head upright which means I was on the topmost of it, after that he jumped together with the tree on to the chief ancestor's head so the chief ancestor, the one on his head who was next in rank to him, the tree and myself on this tree with all the rest ghosts and ghostesses were dancing together. But as I was intoxicated more and more by the gas of the tobacco which I was smoking in the pipe and also as the ghost who was loading it with fresh tobacco was so busy in loading it so that he could not see or talk to anybody at all at that time, so I was singing other earthly melodious songs which sorrow prevented me singing since

75

River-Ghosts. Gala-day under the River

I entered into this bush, in such a way that all the ghosts or every creature of this town were dancing, singing and shouting with joy and running warmly up and down in the town.

But as this "Gala-day" was so highly recognized with the new earthly songs which I was singing, so the King of the Bush of Ghosts whose seat is at the 20th town of ghosts, which is the capital for all the towns of ghosts sent an invisible message to the chief ancestor to bring me to him when he heard the information. But as the 20th town was very far away and again the invisible message was very urgent, so as all of these ghosts, together with the coconut tree were dancing up and down in the town as a crazy man, there I saw unexpectedly that one quill appeared on each side of the pitcher in which I was on the top of the coconut tree, after that one quill appeared on each side of the coconut tree as well, then ordinary feathers appeared on both arms of the ghosts, but the quills which appeared on the chief ancestor's arms were the largest and strongest because he would be the one who would carry the coconut tree together with me.

After that the whole of us flew by air to the 20th town the seat of H.M. the King of the Bush of Ghosts.

In the 20th Town of Ghosts

Within two hours in the air we reached the 20th town, but before we reached there millions of ghosts have been waiting and looking in the air for us. Immediately we appeared to them and they saw me at the front with the long pipe in my mouth with the smoke which was rushing out as from a big boiler, then the whole of them were shouting at me, pointing their hands at me and then rushing here and there to the King's palace. But when the palace could not contain all of them, then they rushed to their field which was about nine miles in diameter, then we landed on the centre of the field. It was very surprising to see over twenty thousand children smashed to death before we reached the field. Immediately we landed I started to sing and dance together with the tree, the ghost who carried the tree and the chief ancestor who carried us. When all the ghosts of this 20th town with H.M. the King could not bear to hear my earthly songs and also see my dance and sit down or to stand up motionless, then they joined us to dance, and again the smoke of the pipe was rushing out of my mouth continuously, because the ghost who was specially chosen to be loading it with the fresh tobacco did not neglect his duty at all.

But after the whole of them danced with me till the late hour in the night, then the chief ancestor commanded that the whole of us should stop and we did so but hardly as none of us were tired or satisfied. After that he commanded the coconut tree to stand still on the ground with a magical commandment, and at the same moment it stood on the ground as if it was planted there, then he commanded it again to bend down and it did so at once, after that he took me from the top of it and put me on the ground, again he commanded it to stand upright as it was and it did so.

They took me from this field to the palace. Having reached there they built a special doorless house which had only one room in this palace for me and put me inside it so that other kinds of ghosts might not steal me away before the day would break, because it was that day they specially arranged for "Gala-day" in the 20th town as the first one was a hint. After they put me inside this doorless house they also put uncut roasted sheep before me to eat, after that everyone went to his or her house to be preparing for tomorrow on which the "Gala-day" would be celebrated throughout.

Immediately they put this roasted sheep before me I was eating it greedily as I was very hungry in respect of the smoke of the tobacco which was intoxicating me like hard drink. But as I was eating it greedily and when it was one o'clock midnight the wall of this house split into two suddenly and there I saw another kind of ghost enter through that space. I looked at him with fear as he was not a native of the 20th town, then he came to me cautiously with a big coil of rags of cloth on his head.

In the 20th Town of Ghosts

The first thing he did, he sat down and started to eat the meat and within a minute he finished it. For this reason I was so frightened and also his exceedingly fearful appearance with his harmful attitude, so I tried to run away but the pitcher did not allow me at all.

Having finished the meat, without hesitation he put me on his head, he got out of the palace cautiously and then kept going in the town to an unknown place. But as this 20th town is a large town he travelled for about two hours before he reached the gate of the town. As the gate is watched both day and night so he met the gate-keeper at the gate. When the gate-keeper saw me on his head he challenged him that where he was carrying me to, but instead of answering the gate-keeper's question he was only telling him to open the gate for him to pass. But when the gate-keeper insisted and after both argued for a few minutes, then he put me down closely to him, after that both were fighting fiercely so that all the other creatures who were living at the back of the gate woke up from sleep and came nearer to the scene, they were looking and laughing at them, as the gate-keeper was struggling to take me from him and return me to the palace and the ghost who was carrying me away was also struggling violently to take me away to his town.

After they were fighting fiercely for about two hours so as the gate-keeper has seven of the same kind of juju which he could use to change the night to day seven times, because he has no power at night but only in the day, and again the ghost who was taking me away has eight jujus which could change the day to the night as well because he has no power in the day, so the gate-keeper first threw down one of his seven jujus on the ground and at the same moment night changed to the day, so he become more powerful than the one who was carrying me away as he has no power in the day. Then he too threw one of his eight jujus on the ground and that day became night at once and then he became more powerful than the gate-keeper. Both of them were using their juju like this until the gate-keeper had used all his own, but the ghost who was carrying me away still had one. At last he used the one which still remained with him, it changed that day to the night at the same time, so he had more power, then he started to fight the gate-keeper who had been already powerless. But as the gate-keeper received heavy blows from him, so he fell down suddenly, but the ghost who carried me to that place laid down on the gate-keeper and beat him greedily. So the ghost who carried me to that gate kicked the pitcher in which I was unnoticed and it broke into pieces, so immediately my body touched the ground then I changed at once to my former form before they put me in the pitcher. But as both of them were still fighting fiercely and did not know that the pitcher had been broken and I have come out of it, so without hesitation I took to my heels and left them there.

Immediately I came out from the pitcher, and then running away in the bush at that night uncountable flies which were following me along nearly made me suspected, because all the blood of all the animals which were poured on me as sacrifice was rotten on my body as black paint and was smelling so bad so that it collected these flies from the hidden place that they slept, even the cloth which my mother wove for me before I entered this Bush of Ghosts had torn into rags by the rotten blood.

Of course as I did not stop once so I ran far away from that gate before the dawn so that I might not be recaptured by the ghosts of the 20th town. When it was dawn I stopped and rested for some hours. After that I started to wander about searching for the way to my home town as usual. But as I was wandering about in this bush I saw a dead animal's skin which had been killed for long time by an unknown creature, so I took its skin and still went on, because it was very stiff to wear at that time. A few hours later I travelled to a pond, the water of this pond was as clean as if it was filtering every hour, it was under a bush which was not thick but big trees covered it like a roof and prevented the sun shining on it, so by that its water was always as cool as ice. I met many pieces of the ghost's soap at the bank nearly falling inside the water, so this showed me that the users of this pond were not so far from that place.

Immediately I discovered it, first I listened attentively for some minutes perhaps I would hear the noises of the creatures or ghosts who might be coming to draw water at that time or perhaps a town of ghosts would be near there, but when there was no noise or voice of any creature heard, even a bird did not cry near that place at all, then I put the skin down at the bank and entered this pond. I drank the water to my satisfaction as I never tasted either fresh or dirty water since I was in the pitcher, except the blood of the animals poured on me as sacrifice with the spit of their mouths which was dropping on to my head when opening them and looking at me with much surprise as I was singing the earthly songs which were newly born into the town of the aquatic ghosts and also in the 20th town which is the capital.

After that I washed away the rotten blood off my body, then I washed the skin of the animal as a cloth, after that I looked round this pond and saw a place where the sun reached the ground, so I went there and spread this skin there to dry, having done that I went to a thick bush which was as a roof, I hid under it and hastily looked at my back, my front, my left and right and also up and down with a doubtful mind perhaps a ghost or a harmful creature might be coming at that time to catch me.

But as the bush which surrounded this pond was very quiet without any noise of a creature whatever it might be so I began to feel much cold without being cold, and when my heart was not at rest for the quietness of that place then I went to the place that I spread the skin in the sun and began to warm myself in this sun perhaps my body would be at rest, but when there was no change at all until the skin was dried then I took it and left that area as quickly as possible. So I wore it as a cloth, of course, it could only reach from my knees to the waist, so I was going on with it like that. It was on this day I believed that if there is no noise of a creature in a bush or if a bush is too quiet there would be fear without seeing a fearful creature.

After I had travelled to a short distance from the pond I stopped under a tree as it was then in the evening, then I started to think what I could eat because there was

nothing more edible than the small fruits which had
fallen down from this tree where I sat at its foot, although
I did not know the name of the fruits or its tree as they
belonged only to ghosts of that area. When I tasted them,
they were very sour, though I ate them like that as
there was no other food or any edible thing there for me
again. Having finished these fruits at about eight o'clock
I was looking for a safe place to sleep. After a few minutes
I saw a large tree which was near that place and there
was a huge hole in its body which could contain a person.
Not knowing that this hole was the home of an armless
ghost who had been expelled from his town which
belonged only to all the armless ghosts. When I entered
this hole I travelled to a part of it which contained me,
but it still went further, so I laid down and fell asleep at
the same time, because I had no chance to sleep or rest
once for all the time that I spent inside that pitcher. But
when it was about twelve o'clock in the midnight this
armless ghost who was the owner of the hole wanted to
go out, of course, I did not know that somebody was living
there before I entered.

As he could only go out at night to fetch his food, so
when he reached the place that I slept he stumbled on
me and fell down unexpectedly, because he did not know
that somebody was there already and also the hole was
very dark, so some part of his body was wounded as he
was armless to defend himself. I woke up unexpectedly
as he fell down on me suddenly, after a few minutes he
tried his best and got up with pain, then he asked with
rage—"Who is that?" Of course, as my friend the young
ghost in the town of the ghost burglars had taught me

some of the ghosts' language, so I replied—"I am an earthly person."

But when he heard the words of "earthly person" from me, he exclaimed—"Oh you are the one who is always coming here and stealing all my property whenever I go out, I will catch you this night, just hold on for a minute." Having said so he cried out louder to the other ghosts who are his partners to come and help him to grip me as he is armless. But before his partners could reach there I jumped down from the hole to the outside, and without any ado I started to run away that night for my life. Immediately I jumped down and ran away I met over one thousand ghosts who were rushing to his hole to help him, but at the same time that they met me all of them did not go to him direct to hear what he called for, instead of that all were chasing me as I was running away as fast as I could. When they chased me to a short distance to catch me and failed then they got back from me to the armless ghost to hear what he called them for. But I was still running away, I did not stop, as I thought within myself that perhaps if I stop to rest for a few minutes they might come again to catch me, so by that I was still running away faster until I stepped into a part of the ground of this bush. But to my surprise at the same moment that I put my left foot on it to be still running away it was saying thus with a loud voice—"Don't smash me! oh don't smash me, don't walk on me, go back to those who are chasing you to kill you, it is paining me too much as you are smashing me."

When I heard this so suddenly, I was so frightened so that I withdrew my foot back at once and I heard no voice again. After that I turned to another part and smashed it with the same foot as well, perhaps that part would not cry out—"don't smash me." But I heard the same caution suddenly with louder voice, so I withdrew my foot from it, then I stopped there and asked myself this question—"can land talk like a human being, or can land feel pain if somebody smashes it?" After I asked myself this question with a dead voice, as there was nobody to ask and explain it to me, so I turned back at once to look for where is possible to travel or run in this bush without any noise, but I saw more than one thousand of the armless ghost's partners that were hunting for me up and down in this bush to catch me and kill me, after they heard from the armless ghost what I had done to him. When they nearly traced me out and I believed that if they caught me no doubt they would kill me instantaneously, so without hesitation I jumped onto this "talking-land", running away as fast as I could. Then it started to speak as before, of course, I did not listen to what it was saying, I was only running on faster to leave that "talking-area" in time to the "talkless-area" to hide myself in a safe "talkless-place", because this "talking-land" was showing the place that I was reaching in the bush to these ghosts. But as I was still running on fiercely and with fear I did not know the time I mistakenly entered into another bush which was more dreadful than the "talking-land".

Immediately I entered it every part of it was blowing alarm, which was very fearful to hear and remain there, because it was blowing as if enemies are approaching a town. Then I stopped suddenly behind a tree as the noises of these alarms were so curious and too fearful for me. To my surprise immediately I stopped all the alarms stopped blowing at once, but there I saw a very young ghostess who hid herself under a small bush which covered the bottom of this tree. She ran out unexpectedly and when she ran out I saw her clearly that she was very ugly so that she could not live in any town of ghosts, except to be hiding herself about in the bush both day and night for her ugly appearance. But her ugly appearance was so curious to me that I was chasing her as she was running away to see her ugliness clearly to my satisfaction, because I had never seen such a very ugly creature as this since I was born and since entered the Bush of Ghosts.

Again, at the same moment that I left the place that I stood behind this tree the alarms started to blow according to how I was chasing this ugly ghostess and I was unable to stop in one place so that the alarms might stop, my aim was only to see the ugliness of this ugly ghostess clearly, because as she was running away so that I might not see her ugliness it was so she was laughing louder at her ugliness and I was also laughing louder at the ugliness. As I was chasing her to and fro to look at her ugliness it was so this bush was blowing various fearful alarms and this was pointing out how I was running and how far reaching in the bush to the ghosts who were chasing me at the back to kill me. This young ghostess was so ugly that if she hid under a bush and if she looked at her ugly body she would burst suddenly into a great laugh which would last more than one hour and this was detecting her out of the hidden place she might hide herself. She could not live with any ghost or other kind of creature because of her ugly appearance. As I was chasing her fiercely to and fro for a long time it was so those ghosts who were chasing me to kill me were approaching nearer, because these alarms were blowing repeatedly and showing what I was doing. This ugly ghostess did not allow me to look at her ugliness as she was running and laughing with all her power and full speed until I was seeing all these ghosts slightly and they were also seeing me slightly before I hid behind a tree, but at the same moment that I stood on a place it was so all these alarms stopped blowing, which means this bush wanted me to be in one place until these ghosts would come and kill me there.

Having rested for a few minutes then I remembered again the ugliness of this ugly ghostess, but at that time I was seeing these ghosts clearly and they were also seeing me clearly. But as I determined to see or to look at the ugliness of this ghostess to my satisfaction and said— "It is better for me to die than to leave this ugly ghostess and run away without seeing her ugliness clearly to my entire satisfaction.

"This will be a great surprise to everybody to hear that I see something which is more interesting for me than the 'death' which is coming behind to kill me."

Immediately I remembered her ugliness again I started to chase her on, because I did not care for any consequence at that moment at all. But as these ghosts were near to catch me before I started to chase the ugly ghostess for the second time and again these alarms were then blowing with another terrible sound, so I could not chase her so far before the hands of these ghosts were touching me at the back and slightly to grip me. When I believed that this ugly ghostess would not wait or stop for me in a place to look at her ugly appearance to my satisfaction then I branched from her and started to run to another part of this bush.

In the Spider's Web Bush

As these ghosts did not stop in chasing me along so after I ran further in this "alarm-bush" there I saw a bush which was almost covered with spiders' webs in front at a distance of about eighty yards, then I pretended to stop and not to run to it, but when these ghosts nearly gripped me I ran to this "spider web bush" unnoticed, of course they were banned from entering it. And after I ran to a distance of seven feet in this "spider web bush" and when I was stopped from running along by this thick web, so I turned sharply at once back to come out of it, and instead of coming out easily I was simply wrapped as a chrysalis by the web, at the same time I was held up by it and dangled to and fro by the breeze as a dried leaf. Immediately I was held up and dangling all these ghosts went back as they were strictly banned from entering it, because it belonged only to a kind of ghosts who are "spider eating ghosts". This "spider web bush" was totally covered with spiders' web as a fog in a season. There was no single tree, bush, refuse, or plants which are usually found in other bushes, but only the spiders and their web represented them. The town of these "spider eating ghosts" is separated from all other kinds of ghosts. They were fond of eating spiders which were the most important food for them, so therefore no other kinds of ghosts should enter there. I was so wrapped that I was hardly able to breathe out easily, even it so straightened me that I could not bend anywhere as a dried stick and I could not cry out for help, because it corked my mouth as a bottle and I could not see anywhere whether any danger or harmful creature was coming there to kill me.

So I remained there helplessly, except the breeze or wind which was blowing me to and fro. When it was about seven hours that I was wrapped and held up there a heavy rain came, beating me till the third day that one of the "spider eating ghosts" came to eat the spiders. This rain beat me so that the web which wrapped me tightly soaked my body as if I was bathed with water. As he came to eat the spiders on this day and as he was going round there searching for the spider and when he saw me dangling to and fro he stopped suddenly at a little distance from me and looking at me for some minutes before he came to me then he pressed every part of my body with his hands, although I did not see him with my eyes but was hearing his foot noise and also feeling on my body that he was pressing it with his hands. Having pressed it for a few minutes then he was saying thus—"Oh! I thank God almighty today, I discover my father whom I had been looking for, many years ago, and I do not know that it is here he died when he came to eat the spiders so I shall take him to the town for burial and the other ceremony. Ah! I thank God today." He was exceedingly glad as he discovered me as the dead body of his father, then he took me on his head and kept going to the town at once with joy, he did not wait and eat the spiders on this day at all.

In the Spider's Web Bush

When he carried me and appeared in the town all his town's ghosts asked him that what sort of heavy load he was carrying and sweating as if he bathed in water like this, so he replied that it was the dead body of his father who died in the "spider web bush" when he went there to eat the spiders. But when his town's ghosts and ghostesses heard so, they were shouting with joy and following him to his house. Having reached his house and when his family saw me how I swelled up as a pregnant woman who would deliver either today or tomorrow they thought that it was true I was the dead body of their father, so they performed the ceremony which is to be performed for deads at once. After that all the ghosts of this town were dancing the native dance of the "spider eating ghosts" round me, because all the rest of the ghosts of this town also thought I am his father and again this father could eat spiders more than the rest.

Then they told a ghost who is a carpenter among them to make a solid coffin. Within an hour he brought it, but when I heard about the coffin it was at that time I believed that they wanted to bury me alive, then I was trying my best to tell them that I am not his dead father, but I was unable to talk at all as the web corked my mouth hard and I was unable to shake my body to show them that I am still alive, it was in vain. So after the carpenter brought the coffin, then they put me inside it and also put more spiders inside it before they sealed it at once, they said that I would be eating the spiders which they put inside this coffin along the heaven's road, because they thought that if somebody died he would be eating along the heaven's road before he would reach

91

heaven. After that they dug a deep hole as a grave in the back yard and buried me there as a dead man.

As I was inside this grave in the coffin I was thinking within myself that—"Can I be saved from this grave or is there anybody to save me out of this?" then I said— "I shall put hope on God that He shall save me out of the coffin and out of the grave." But luckily at last my thoughts became the truth, so when it was one o'clock in the midnight a resurrectionist who was present when they buried me there came and dug out the coffin, then he broke it and took me out of it. He put me on his head and kept going to another far bush again. His aim was to eat the spiders which were on the web that wrapped me and also to eat me. As he stole me from the grave and went hastily along in the bush that night he was meeting several ghosts of his kind in the bush, and whenever they met him and asked what he carried like this, he would answer that it is the dead body of his father who died yesterday. He would tell them further that he is going to bury him very far into the bush so that he might not be smelling to anybody in the town when decayed. He would not tell them the truth that he stole me from the grave and he is going to eat me. Whenever he was explaining to them like this they would be sorry for him and then he kept going on his way. It was that night I believed that thieves are giving themselves much severe punishment whenever they steal important things, because as he was talking to those whom he was meeting on the way his voice was trembling with fear and his body was also shaking and looking here and there per- haps somebody was chasing him to catch the thief of the dead body, he was unable to wait and attend to them satisfactorily before he would leave them unnoticed and keep going.

As he was going hastily zigzag in the bush it was so he was dashing at both trees and hills and always mistakenly falling into the deep holes, and several times he would jump on thorns unnoticed, but he would not be able to wait and take care of himself, as he was thinking that they were chasing him from the town to catch as a thief. Having gone very far into the bush he reached a place which was cleared some time ago by an unknown creature, then he put me down and without hesitation he gathered some dried sticks and prepared the fire in which he would roast me and eat me as meat. But immediately he put me inside this fire the spider web which wrapped me could not catch fire as it was very wet from the rains which were beating me repeatedly in the "spider web bush" before I was taken to the town for burial. Again the fire was insufficient to burn the web away from my body before I could be roasted, because the dried sticks were very scarce near there. But at the same time that he put me on this fire about twelve ghosts of his kind appeared and came to him, then they asked him what he wanted to do in that place. He replied that it was the dead body of a "spider eating" ghost's father, he stole from the grave to roast and eat. But as all these ghosts heard so from him they were jumping up with gladness, they told him that they would eat me with him. He was very annoyed when he heard so, as he alone wanted to eat me.

As the fire which had been prepared before these

ghosts appeared to him was insufficient to roast me and luckily as the dried sticks were very scarce to get near there, so he sent two of these ghosts to go for the dried sticks, but these two selected ghosts refused totally to go, unless the whole of them would go, because they were thinking that it was a trick, so the rest would eat me before they would come back when fetching the dried sticks. When these two selected ghosts refused to go unless the whole of them would go together, then he told them to go together, but the whole of them said again unless he would follow them as well before they would go. After they argued for some minutes then all of them together with the one who brought me there went to fetch the dried sticks. But after they went away and left me there and as this fire was yet half quenched, so I tried my best and laid my body on it. After some minutes the web became half-dried and caught the fire which was slowly burning the web, then I found my way out by force from the web, of course, it burnt some parts of my body slightly. Without any ado I took to my heels and before they could return from the place that they went for the sticks I had gone very far into another bush which did not belong to them. This is how I was saved from the spider-eating ghosts who buried me alive. Immediately I escaped then I travelled to the south-east of this bush perhaps I would see the way to my town and perhaps I might see something to eat as I was feeling hunger.

At that moment a heavy rain with a very strong wind came. This wind was blowing here and there so that many trees were falling down unexpectedly, so I stopped

and looked for a safe place to shelter myself from the rain
and to save my life from all the trees which were falling
down here and there by the strong wind. But as I was
looking for such a place there I discovered a place which
was close to a big tree with props and I thought that the
place was refuse of dried leaves which were heaped
together closely to this tree, because it was so dark at that
time so that I could not see everything clearly, even I
could not see myself as well. So I laid down and crept into
it, not knowing that it was inside the pouch of a kind of
the animal who has a big pouch or bag under his belly,
I entered as he had already sheltered himself there before
me. So I simply entered it. But as it was warm slightly
like a room I fell asleep in it within a minute. But when
the rain with the strong wind were too heavy or too much
for him to bear and remain there, he left that place and
looked about for another place to shelter himself, and
did not discover such a place until he reached a bush
which belongs to the 13th town, which only belongs to
short ghosts, but I did not wake at all in his pouch as he
was carrying me about until he reached this bush.

The Short Ghosts and their Flash-eyed Mother

As all the short ghosts of this 13th town were not doing other work more than to go to bush to hunt for bush animals, to kill them and to bring them to the "flash-eyed mother" who is their ruler, so this animal fell into their hands at about nine o'clock in the morning. They shot him to death at once with guns, after that all of them started to drag him to their town as he was too heavy for them to carry on their heads. But I did not wake as they were doing all these things. Having reached the town, all the rest of the short ghosts of this town gathered together round this curious animal. All were looking at him with much surprise as this kind of animal was so scarce to get or see frequently in their bush. But as the hair on his body should be first scraped off carefully and kept in a safe place, as it is very precious to all of them, so at first they scraped the hair on the first part of his body and when they were scraping the hair inside the pouch in which I slept, so the scrapers or knives which they were using mistakenly touched one of my feet suddenly, then I woke inside the pouch, but as I shook my body to left and right to come out as I did not know that it was inside the pouch of an animal I slept, I thought

96

The Short Ghosts and their Flash-eyed Mother

I was inside a room. So as I shook, the pouch shook as well in their view and immediately all of them took their guns ready to shoot the pouch; they thought that the animal became alive again. But as one of them was wiser, he noticed carefully that only the inside or a part of the pouch was shaking, then he expanded it and saw me there. Having discovered me he held both my feet and dragged me out unexpectedly and I simply found myself in the centre of them.

The first thing I did immediately I got out was to run away to save my life, but I was not allowed. All of them were looking at me with their terrible eyes for about half an hour. They did not talk or shake their bodies as a dummy. As they were too terrible for me to look at or to stand with, then I was running away for the second time, perhaps I would be safe from them. But all of them gripped me violently and took me before an old woman who is the "flash-eyed mother" the ruler of that 13th town and she was the only woman in this town. As I stood before her on this critical day and when I saw her clearly, I closed my eyes tightly at the same moment, I could not open it till I was forced to open it by these short ghosts who escorted me before her and still I was unable to open it in full, because of her fearful, dreadful, terrible, curious, wonderful and dirty appearance.

This "flash-eyed mother" sat on the ground in the centre of the town permanently. She did not stand up or move to anywhere at all, she was all the time beaten there by both rain and sun, both day and night. There was no single house built in this town as she alone filled the town as a round vast hill, it was hard for the rest inhabitants to move about or to sleep in the town. This town is about six miles in circumference, it was as clean as a football field. All these short ghosts were just exactly a year and an half old babies, but very strong as iron and clever while doing everything, all of them had no other work more than to be killing the bush animals with short guns like pistols which were given to them by the "flash-eyed mother" and whenever an animal is killed they would bring it to her in the same place that she sat. Millions of heads which were just like a baby's head appeared on her body, all circulated set by set. Each of these heads had two very short hands which were used to hold their food or anything that they want to take, each of them had two eyes which were shining both day and night like fire-flies, one small mouth with numerous sharp teeth, the head was full of long dirty hair, two small ears like a rat's ears appeared on each side of the head. If they are talking, their voices would be sounding as if somebody strikes an iron or the church bell which sound would last more than ten minutes before stopping. If all of them are talking together at a time it would be as a big market's noises, they were arguing, flogging and reporting themselves to their mother. They could not move about or from the body of their mother to another place. Their mother had a special long and huge head which she was using to talk and to feed herself, it was above everything in the town and it showed her out from a distance of about four miles from this town. She had a large mouth which could swallow an elephant uncut. The two fearful large eyes which were on the front of her head were always flashing or bringing out fire

98

whenever she was opening them, and this is why all the rest ghosts and ghostesses with all other creatures gave her the name of "flash-eyed mother". There were over a thousand thick teeth in this mouth, each was about two feet long and brown in colour, both upper and lower lips were unable to cover the teeth. The hair on her head was just as bush, all could weigh more than a ton if cut and put on a scale, each was thicker than a quarter of an inch and almost covered her head, except the face. All these hairs were giving shelter to her whenever it was raining and whenever the sun was scorching her as she was not walking to anywhere. Both her hands were used in stirring soup on the fire like spoons as she did not feel the pain of fire or heat, her finger nails were just like shovels and she had two very short feet under her body, she sat on them as a stool, these feet were as thick as a pillar. She never bathed at all.

It was these eyes which were bringing out splashes of fire all the time and were used to bring out fire on the firewood whenever she wanted to cook food and the flash of fire of these eyes was so strong that it would catch the firewood at the same moment like petrol or other inflammable spirit or gunpowder, and also use it at night as a flood of light in lighting the whole town as electricity lights, so by that, they were not using other lights except the flash fire of her eyes. Whenever one or more of the short ghosts who were serving her as their mother offended her, both eyes would be flashing out fire on to the body who offends her, and the fire would be burning the body at the same moment as fluffy things or rags. She was using it as a whip to flog any other of her offenders as it could be flashed to a long distance. For this reason she was very fearful to other creatures coming to her town without special reason, even H.M. the King of the Bush of Ghosts could not say—"Who is she?" She was using all kinds of animal skins as clothes which made her more fearful, ugly and dreadful to see or look at. As she was not standing up or moving about so all the short ghosts of this town who were under her flag were killing the bush animals and bringing them to her, although all of them were feeding on these animals as well.

I was escorted before her on this day and stood before her as if I had been dissolved into vapour or no more alive and also dreaming of her terrible, dreadful, ugly, dirty appearance without sleeping. She asked the short ghosts whether I am the son of the animal from whose pouch they took me out, all of them replied that they could not say definitely. After she heard so from them, then she flashed the fire of both her eyes on to my body and it burnt the animal skin which I wore as a cloth and also burnt some part of my body as well at the same time, because she wanted to know whether I could talk or not, but as my body caught fire and I cried suddenly with a loud voice, so when they heard my sorrowful voice the whole of them burst into a great laugh at a time as if uncountable cannons fired together, and her own laugh among the rest was just as if a bomb explodes, and as her own voice was louder in a very queer way, terrible and dreadful, so some of the big trees on hills around this town fell down, and I myself nearly sank into the ground to half of my body before some of these short ghosts pulled me out of the ground. But after she heard my voice she believed that I am an earthly person, but she did not know how I managed to be in the Bush of Ghosts.

Having believed that I am an earthly person then she asked me whether I would live with her, so I replied— "yes". But she did not ask whether I escaped from somewhere or offended somebody before I reached there. After I agreed to her request she ordered the short ghosts to give me a short gun to be hunting with them. These short ghost hunters taught me how to kill the bush animals. Having qualified as a hunter, then I followed them to the bush. Whenever we were killing an animal we would bring it to "flash-eyed mother" who was supposed to be our mother or guardian, so she would take it from us and cook it at the same time in the same place that she sat permanently like a stump. Having cooked it, the first thing she was doing was to serve the fleshy part of the animal to all the heads that surrounded her body, after that she would serve the rest fleshy part to herself and then the bony part to all the short ghosts. If all the heads and herself were eating at the same time their mouths would be making noises as if one hundred winches are working together. Within a minute all the heads would finish their own, then would be asking for more immediately as they were not satisfied with small food, so for this reason the mother was not serving us with enough food so that it might be sufficient for them. All of them would be fighting, arguing and flogging themselves while eating the food greedily and also the biggest head which belongs to their mother would be settling their misunderstandings for them several times before they would finish the food. As she added the dirt as her beauty, so she was not checking all the heads from passing urine, excreta and spitting on her body which would wet all over her body.

One day when we went to the bush since morning it was hard for us before we killed a very small animal at about 4.30 p.m., then we brought it to her. Having cooked it, she served very little to every one of the heads in such a way that the remainder would reach every one of us, but all these heads protested because the "flash-eyed mother" served us out of it, they wanted to eat all, of course when their mother noticed that they protested she took all that she served to every one of us back from us and then shared it for them, because she did not want them to be hungry at any time, so all of us slept that night with empty stomachs. But when it was early in the morning all of us struck going to the bush to hunt. When she noticed that we struck she called the whole of us before her, she asked us to bring the animal which we killed for food that morning, but we said none, we told her further that we did not go to bush at all that day. Immediately she heard so from us, she was exceedingly annoyed and started to flash the fire of her eyes on to us with all her power, so that the skins of the animals that every one of us wore caught fire at once as by petrol and this means she was flogging us. As she was flogging us with the fire all the heads on her body were also abusing, scorning and cursing us badly.

After that she ordered us to go to bush at once and we must not come back without an animal, otherwise all of us would be burnt to ashes willing or not, she concluded. Then all of us went to the bush at the same time. Having

reached the bush God is so good, within an hour we killed
a kind of ghosts' animal which had plenty of fat like a
pig, then we brought it to her. Having cooked it she
served all the heads to their entire satisfaction, after that
she served herself to her satisfaction and then served us
last according to the rule and regulation given to her by
the heads. So the whole of us ate this animal to our entire
satisfaction, because this animal was as big as an elephant
and also fatty.

She had a kind of a terrible alarm which was in a
hidden part of her body, but it was not visible to us,
except those heads and herself. It was this alarm she was
blowing every early in the morning to wake us up, but
it would be after she had cooked a kind of short ghosts'
pap before it would be blowing repeatedly with a terrible
sound. Whenever we heard it, every one of us would be
in a single line before her as soldiers and as every one of us
had his own small basin or cup which were made by
them, then she would be serving us one by one with the
pap which would be poured into the cups; it would reach
the half. It was like this we were receiving it as when
soldiers are receiving their rations before an officer and
all the heads had their own cups as well, but all the times
that their mother was serving us all of them would be
telling her seriously and repeatedly that she was serving
us with much food. These heads were always making
noises and all of them were not sleeping at the same time
at night, because if some of them sleep, the rest would be
talking until those who were sleeping would wake. Some
times they would be abusing their mother whenever she
was sleeping and also snoring or snorting as if a sea is

roaring with great power as follows:— "Hear our 'flash-eyed mother' who is snoring like strong wind." But if she woke at that moment they would tell her with louder voice—"Take away your flash eyes from us."

Barbing Day in the
Town of Short Ghosts

As all the heads which were on the body of "flash-eyed mother" and also all short ghosts' heads were full of much thick and dirty hair like weeds, so they were only barbing once in a century when the "Secret Society of Ghosts" festival is near.

So that a special full day is reserved for barbing their heads and their barber is one of the "fire creatures" who was qualified for barbing heads with the clippers and knife of fire. But when it was announced by the "flash-eyed mother" that the barbing day would be tomorrow I thought our heads would be barbed with the ordinary clippers, scissors and knives as in my home town, so I was jumping up with gladness because I was never barbed once since about fourteen years that I entered the Bush of Ghosts. So when the day was reached all of us were bound to be in one spot. After a few minutes there I saw a creature who was fire and held the clippers of fire which were blazing with the flame of fire. First, he started to barb for those heads as everything must first start from them. But I was very surprised to see that all of these heads were shouting with joy as these clippers of fire were touching their heads instead of crying. Again

Barbing Day in the Town of Short Ghosts

it was this day I noticed carefully that uncountable beetles, bees, wasps and many other kinds of biting insects were living inside the hair of these heads as their homes and also their mother's head was full up with numerous small birds which built their nests inside the hair of her head as on the trees. Having barbed all the heads and their mother then he started barbing for the short ghosts. But after he barbed half of them all the heads reported to their mother that they were feeling hungry, then she ordered those half who had been already barbed to go and kill an animal from the bush, so at this stage I had a chance and mixed with those who had been already barbed as if I had barbed my own too. So it was this way I saved myself from barbing my head with the clippers of fire.

One day, when I was seriously sick, I was detailed to be at home by the short ghosts to be serving the mother with anything that she wanted to do. I was greatly surprised to say that it was that day I knew that she was selling the flash fire of her eyes to other kinds of ghosts who were coming from the various towns to buy it, and a flash was worth a heavy amount of ghosts' money.

I become an
Aggressor for Ghosts

The very day that I completed three years in this town, the "flash-eyed mother" got a letter and warrant about me from the town that I escaped to her.

But when the mother received the letter she was very annoyed and replied with passion that—"I am ready for war or for any consequence." Then both parties arranged the day that they would meet on their battle-field for seven days to come at that time. But before the day arrived "flash-eyed mother" had sent for all the soldiers of "Wraith-Island" who were uncountable in numbers and also sent for the following wonderful and curious creatures:— "Spirit of prey" who is fighting with the flood of light of his single eyes, "Invisible and invincible Pawn" who fought and won the "Red- creatures" in the "Red-town" for the "Palm-Wine Drinker" when he was living in the "Red-town", and all the fearful and harmful prominent creatures as:— White long creatures, Hungry creature, Shapeless-creatures, and also the "Palm wine tapster", who is living in the Deads' town, who gave the wonderful egg to the Palm-Wine Drinker came too. So all of them had gathered in this town (13th town) before the day came. When the day arrived "flash-eyed

107

mother" gave a wonderful short gun to every one of the
heads of her body, then to the other creatures, after that
to all the short ghosts and me as well, and she took the
biggest gun for herself and also gave a sword to every one
of us in addition.

After this the whole of us were going to the battle-
field, so she was following us as a commander. It was this
day I first saw her stand up and walk away from the
same place that I met her since the three years I came
there, and it was this day I noticed that over four thousand more heads were still hid under her body and all
were exceedingly glad when they were exposed to the
fresh air since the last century when the "Secret Society
of Ghosts" celebrated last. So as the whole of us were
marching hastily to the battle-field that morning because
we had kept late, all these heads were making various
fearful noises with louder voices along the way, even the
rest of us could not hear any other creatures' voices
except their own which nearly made us become deaf.

Before we reached the field the other party had reached
there before us. But immediately we reached there we
started to shoot guns at the enemies and using the swords,
and they were also shooting us. As this fight was so
serious nobody could eat, sleep or rest for three days and
nights. But when we were hiding in a hiding-place at
night or at any time from the enemies all these heads
would not stop making noises until the enemies would
suspect us and then start to shoot us to death. And as it
was a powerful war, so, through the noises of these heads
all the hero-ghosts who were fighting the enemies with
us were killed and also many of the heads were cut away

from their mother's body with swords, except their mother who was fighting on fiercely with her big gun until the "Invisible and Invincible Pawn" who had disappeared for a little while came and killed some of the enemies until the rest escaped to their town. After that he woke up all the hero-ghosts with all the short ghosts who had been killed by the enemies. But to my surprise as all these heads had been cut down to the ground all were still crying to their mother. Of course, the "Invisible and Invincible Pawn" replaced them back on their mother's body, and this means the 13th town won the victory.

After we won the war the whole of us were gladly marching to the town. But as the "Invisible and Invincible Pawn" woke up all the dead soldiers and replaced their heads which were cut off by the enemies to their necks and as my own was cut off as well, so he mistakenly put a ghost's head on my neck instead of mine. But as every ghost is talkative, so this head was always making various noises both day and night and also smelling badly. Whether I was talking or not it would be talking out the words which I did not mean in my mind and was telling out all my secret aims which I was planning in mind whether to escape from there to another town or to start to find the way to my home town as usual. All these secret thoughts were speaking out by this inferior head whenever I stood before "flash-eyed mother" and also telling lies against me every time that I am abusing her because I did not understand the language of the short ghosts. At the same time that I discovered that it was not my own head which was

109

mistakenly put on my neck, so I reported the matter to the mother, but she simply replied—"Every head is a head and there is no head which is not suitable for any creature." So I was carrying the earthly body with the head of a ghost about until the "faithful mother", the inhabitant of the "white-tree", who is faithful to all creatures came and settled the misunderstandings between the two parties when she heard information that there was a war between them, but it was very late before she heard about this war. Having settled the misunderstanding for them I begged her respectfully to replace my own head back on my neck instead of this one which belongs to a ghost. So she agreed and interchanged it for my original head at once, if not I should be still carrying the head of a ghost about throughout my life time. But at the same time she had settled the misunderstanding for both parties (12th town and 13th town) then she went back to her "white-tree" with the "faithful-hand" who accompanied her as a guard and she inspected the "guard of honour" which was specially arranged for her by the "flash-eyed mother" before she went away.

It was this day I knew that this "flash-eyed mother" is the mother of the "Invisible and invincible Pawn" who is the ruler of all the animal creatures and non-living creatures which he could command to become alive in all bushes of the curious creatures, and it was also this day he washed his mother who warmed the water with which to wash her body with the flash fire of her eyes as the water was too cold for her. Having washed his mother he went back to his bush which is near the "Red-town" which had been ruined long ago when the "Palm-

I become an Aggressor for Ghosts

Wine Drinker" was living there with the "Red-creatures".

After the war was over all the short ghosts and I continued our usual work as hunters. At this time I was illtreated by all these short ghosts with the "flash-eyed mother" and also all the heads of her body as I was the aggressor of the war which ruined some of them and their opponents as well. So by that my mind was not at rest to live there any longer except to continue to look for the way to my home town which I had left for about eighteen years, as I was remembering my mother at this time always. But as I was at that time near to become a full ghost and did not care for any ghost again, because I had seen many of their secrets except the "Secret Society of Ghosts" which is celebrating or performing every century, so whenever I was following the short ghosts to the bush in which we were killing the animals, I would go farther than them.

The Super Lady

One day, I travelled to every part of this bush if
perhaps I might see the way to my town, but instead of
seeing the way I saw an antelope. When I was about to
shoot him with the gun, he was running away and I myself
was chasing him to kill him until he reached a big tree
then he ran to the other side of it which debarred me
from seeing him, but as I was a little distance from this
tree I thought within myself to approach it before I
would shoot him. Having approached the tree before I
could touch the trigger of my gun there appeared a very
beautiful lady and as I was startled immediately I saw
that it was that antelope changed to this lady, then I
stopped suddenly and looked at her with doubtful and
fearful mind that perhaps it was the "flash-eyed mother"
changed like this, so that I might not escape from her as
I was thinking in my mind. But as I stood and trembled
in the place she was waving her right hand as a signal
to throw the gun down and I did so at the same moment
because of fear. Although if she did not give such sign I
would not be able to shoot her at all as an animal. Though
it was clear to me that she was an antelope in form at the
first time that I saw her when running to that tree.
Again I was greatly surprised that it was in my presence

she took away the antelope skin from her body and hid it inside a hole which was at the foot of that tree.

Having thrown the gun down then she was waving the hand again to me to come to her at the same place that she stood. Of course, when she was doing so I refused to go, I told her—"No, I cannot come to you, because you are a wonderful and terrible antelope who changed to a lady in my presence."

After that she came to me for herself and asked—"Will you marry me?" but I replied—"Not at all!" Then she held both my hands by force and looking at my face which was nearly touching her own which was as fresh as an angel's face, and she asked again with a lofty smiling face and solemn voice—"Why do you dislike marrying me?" But I replied that I am an earthly person. When she heard so she said—"I prefer to marry an earthly person more than the other creatures." After she said so, she told me to follow her and I followed her at a very low walking speed, because she was fearful to me, but she did not leave my hands because perhaps I might run away from her, and it is truth.

Within a few minutes when I noticed that she was not a harmful ghostess, then I thought within myself to follow her to her town, perhaps if I begged her to show me the way to my town she would agree. But having travelled with her to a distance of about one and an half miles we entered a town, and immediately we entered there I asked her for the name of the town, she replied that it is a nameless town. After a while we reached her house and then entered it, but there was nobody living with her.

In the Nameless-town

So immediately we entered the house she swept every part of it and then decorated it. After that she put water in the bath-room, then I went to bathe and before I finished she had put down clothes. Having taken off the animal skin which I wore she took it and hid it in an unknown place and I wore the clothes, but when I looked at myself in a big mirror which was in the parlour I could not identify myself again for the beauty that the clothes added to me and it was this day I believed that clothes are very important for the body, because as I wore it my appearance looked as fresh as an earthly person. Then I asked her where she got the clothes, as all the ghosts are not using earthly clothes, she replied that she got them from the earthly witches who are coming to her father's town for "witch-meetings". Having decorated the house or all the rooms, she went to the kitchen at once and cooked the food which was exactly the same as the earthly food. But I could comb my hair finish before she had put the food on the table in the dining room, then we ate it together. As this food was prepared in the method which earthly people prepare their food, so I ate it to my entire satisfaction, because it was that day I first ate the food which was prepared as good as this since I entered the Bush of Ghosts. Having finished with this food, we went to the parlour and then she brought drinks of all kinds, then both of us started to drink them, and then she started to tell me her story as follows:—

"My mother is a lame ghostess who can only creep about instead of walking. She is born and bred in the 7th town of ghosts and my father is also a native of the 6th town of ghosts which is about two hundred miles distance from this Nameless-town. He is the most powerful wizard among all the wizards in both the Bush of Ghosts and in the earthly towns. And my mother is also the most powerful of all the witches in both the Bush of Ghosts and in the earthly towns. Therefore, for this reason, both are selected by all witches and wizards to be their heads and to be giving orders to every one of them. So by that all of them are coming from every town of ghosts and from every earthly town as well every Saturday to my father's house where there is a special big hall which is built for this meeting. But as both my mother and father are their heads, so we shall prepare all kinds of food and drinks before their arrival at my father's town every Saturday.

"After they eat and drink, they will start to sing the song of witches and wizards, after this they will pray the prayer of the wizards and witches, then the meeting will start, but the most important of their discussions are on those who are not their members as how to rob and wreck them and to lodge the complaints of those who have offended them before my father and mother who will either give them the order to kill their offenders or not. Of course, they will wait and hear the last order from them before going back to their various towns. But if my father and mother do not order them to do any harm to those who they bring the complaint of, they must not do any harm to them, but if both give them the order to harm or kill them so immediately they return to their towns they will kill them.

"One day, when I sat down with my father discussing a matter with him, to my surprise, there I saw an earthly old woman who is a witch or one of their members come to my father and started to lodge complaints:— 'One of my neighbours who is depending on her only son called me a "witch" which is an insult to us, but for this I will kill her only son who is taking care of her as a revenge, so that she will not get anyone to assist her in her need and she will have nobody to look after her again, and she shall be in sorrow and hunger throughout her life.' Having finished the complaint, then she hesitated and expected which order will be given her by my mother and father. So my father and mother decided the complaint in their minds within themselves for some minutes then both ordered the complainant to go and kill the only son of the woman who offended her and without hesitation she disappeared. But as this was a great surprise to me immediately she disappeared I told my father that—'this is a sin' and I reminded him again that— 'you ordered her to go and kill the son on whom his mother depends?' But he replied—'Yes, I do believe before you say that it is a sin, even it is more than a sin or worse, because I am living on such evil works and you are living on it as well through me and I do not care for any kind of punishment which God might give me about it, because I prefer evil works more than godly works and

I am sure that I shall go direct to the everlasting fire which is the most hot and the most severe punishment. Even these evil works will appear as well on my "Will" that you are the one who have the right to inherit it after my death.' But when he said that I will inherit all his evil works whenever he dies, I told him at once that—'I shall not do any evil work throughout my life-time in this Bush of Ghosts.'

"Again, one night, my father and mother entered into a private room which is in a dark corner of the house, then both were discussing within themselves with a low voice whether to kill me next week for their wizard and witch meeting which is very near, because it is our turn to prepare food for our members who will attend the meeting according to our rule, as they have no other daughter or son who is to be killed and cooked and presented to our members, because every one of them will do so whenever it is his or her turn and it is not fair enough to depart away from this rule because of their daughter. So, therefore, as from this night they would not allow me to go anywhere and not to hear about this 'secret arrangement' at all, so that I may not run away from home. But as the time that both of them were discussing this matter within themselves was dark so they did not know that I hid near them and heard all their sayings and also heard the very day that they will kill me. But when the day that they arranged within themselves remained three days, all the wizards and witches were arriving in large number to my father's house from all the towns of ghosts and from all the earthly towns.

"But my grandmother, who is the native of the

'Hopeless-town' which is the 5th town of ghosts and who is at present in the everlasting fire, had given me the power of a 'Superlady' before she was imprisoned in that fire for a little mistake she did to H.M. the King of ghosts. So through this power I had the opportunity to change to an invisible bird early in the morning that my father and mother would kill me, then I packed all my belongings, after that I bade both of them invisibly 'good-bye' and then I came to live permanently in this Nameless-town, which belongs only to women, and since that day I am not appearing to them personally but changing to a kind of a creature, because they would kill me as they are still looking for me to kill, because they have no other son or daughter to kill for their members, as it is a great pain to them if they cannot fulfil the order made for themselves and this rule cannot be cancelled, as uncountable members have killed their sons or daughters when it was their turn.

"Now, my earthly husband, I have the wonderful power to change to any form of creature as I sit with you on the same chair in this parlour." But when she said so, I told her to change to some form at that moment to let me see. Then she said—"look at me carefully." First, she became an antelope with two short horns on its head, secondly a lioness and roared at me several times so that I nearly died for fear, thirdly, a big boa constrictor which made me fear most when she was coiling round my body, especially when it opened the mouth very wide as if it wanted to swallow me, and after this a tigress and jumped on me at the same time, after this she jumped away from my head and was jumping from room to room, having stopped jumping about in the rooms and house, then without hesitation she jumped outside the town, she was chasing fowls about in the town. After some minutes she killed two of the fowls and brought them by mouth to the house, then she came back to me on the same chair that I sat on, after that she changed to a lady as usual, and to my surprise she was on the same chair as before she started to use her supernatural powers and also held the two fowls which she killed outside with her hands.

Then she started another conversation with me for a few minutes before she went to the kitchen with the two fowls, she roasted both, after that she brought them to me with tea and bread. So we ate them together. But before we finished with all these things it was about ten o'clock in the night. Having rested for about an hour and when she noticed that I was feeling sleepy, then she went to the bedroom, she stretched many costly clothes on the bed, after that she called me to enter the room, but when I dangled one of my feet on the door of this room as a step and when I looked how this room was decorated and also how the bed was decorated and then looked at the bed itself how it was made with the finest and most attractive patterns which could be found in this Bush of Ghosts so I insisted on entering the room, but I was simply suggesting in my mind that—"Is this for me? Am I going to sleep on this fine bed on which only a king can sleep?" Because I was afraid to enter this room as it was beautified by all kinds of costly decorations, as all of them could be only made with supernatural power, because an ordinary creature could not make them attractively like that. But after she called me for several times to come inside the room to sleep on the bed, but I stayed at the door looking at both bed and decorations with much surprise, then she came to me and held my hand as smooth as a delicate thing and then drew me very gently and gradually into the room. Then I hesitated again to touch or to sleep on this bed, but when she saw that I did not attempt to sleep on it, so she pushed me on it for herself very gently as a breakable article. As I lay my body on this bed and felt how it was very easy for me, so I sprang up suddenly to go out of the room.

But at the same time that she saw me that I wanted to get down and go out of this room she pressed me on it with all her power for about one hour before my body and mind became at rest, and it was at that night I believed that—"clean places are driving a dirty person away as if it will hurt him." But still I was unable to sleep as I was always thinking in mind how she had been changing herself to various fearful animals and also thinking that perhaps—"She may change again to another form and kill me in the midnight." But having watched her for some hours and believed that she had no such harmful aim in mind at all, then I fell asleep unnoticed. Again to my great surprise there were "all-coloured lights" which lighted and shone as diamonds on to every part of this house, even I tried my best to find out from where the lights were coming, but it was in vain, because it was not quenched both day and night. As it surprised me greatly I asked her about it, she replied —"the power of lights is among my supernatural powers."

In the Nameless-town

This is how I married for the second time in the Bush of Ghosts, but I was not baptized with fire and hot water as I was in the 8th town of ghosts when I married for the first time, and this was easier than that, because we did not go to any church, but she is a "super-lady" who has the power to do everything. So I was unable to tell her some of my stories before I slept that night.

Before she woke me up early in the morning, she had put out the water, and soap which had a sweet and lofty smell; of course, it is in the Bush of Ghosts such soap could be found, even it is only from this "supèr-lady" it could be found, as it belongs only to her, then the sponge which was as fluffy as cotton, she put them in the bath-room which was as clean as a food plate. After that she woke me up, because if not I would not be able to wake for myself as this bed was so easy for me. Having taken my bath, then I went to the dressing room where she combed my hair for me, she powdered my face and also rubbed my body with a kind of sweet smelling oil. Then from there to the dining-room, so we drank tea together. After we drank the tea, she brought some cold drinks. When I was drinking it she left me there and went away, after a few minutes she returned with two maids who would be helping her to do all the housework. Having given them work to do, then she came to me in the parlour and sat down on the chair which was touching my own which was an easy-chair with cushions. Then she told me with a very cool lofty voice and smiling face to tell her my story which I related very shortly.

After this, one of the maids or servants came and called us for chop which was rice, etc. Having finished with the food, we drank some of the cold drinks which were always in the ice, after this, both of us went all round the town and also to a village which is not more than two miles away from the Nameless-town.

Where Woman Marries Woman

When we went round this Nameless-town before we went to the village, there I noticed carefully that all the inhabitants are ladies and women, no single man is living there or coming there at all and to my surprise all these ladies and women have long brown moustaches which resemble that of he-goats, the moustaches are under their lower jaws, so every woman married a lady, because there are no men to marry them. But when I asked the "Super-lady" or my wife—"Why all the ladies and women have moustaches in this town like he-goats?" she replied—"those women with moustaches had been betrayed by their husbands after their marriage, but now none of them could marry any male again except to marry ladies as husbands." After we took a stroll round the village and saw many terrible and wonderful things for some hours, then we came back home. Having rested and drank some drinks as a refreshment, then we slept till the evening.

When I completed the period of eight months with her I told her that I want to know her father and mother who are wizard and witch and also her grandmother's town who is the native of the Hopeless-town. After a few weeks that I had advised her like this, we left home and there remained only those two maids at home. But we travelled for a week before we saw the town of her father at a distance of five miles, then she told me to stop, so both of us stopped near a tree whose leaves were shaking with powerful speed. Then she told me that she wanted to change herself to a goat and said furthermore that if she appeared personally to her father and mother they would catch her to be killed for their "witch and wizard members", because both of them had promised to kill her for them. After a few minutes she used her supernatural power and changed at once to a goat with a strong rope on its neck, then she told me to hold the rope and pull her along the way. She was directing me whenever I wanted to miss the way and I understood all her sayings as she was changed to the goat, but nobody could hear her voice, except me.

When we reached the town she directed me to her father's house in which we met over three thousand witches and wizards members who were holding an important meeting at that time, then we stood near them and looked at every one of the members. Of course we did not enter the house because she only showed them to me. I saw her father and mother sat on the higher chairs in the centre of these members talking to them. To my surprise I saw many old men and women of my home town who were tight friends to my father and I was greatly surprised to see them in this meeting, because I did not know how they managed to be there, but I did not let them see me. After a while she told me in the same voice to let us go, so we left there for her grandmother's town. Having left that town at a distance of about a mile, then she changed to the lady as before,

124

after that she started to tell me the story of some of the wizard and witch members' witchcrafts and wizardcrafts, that they can travel all round the whole world within a minute and they have power on everything and furthermore all of them have no good thoughts except evil thoughts both day and night, even those who are worshipping the heavenly God are also their enemies. But she did not change to any form again until we entered the town of her grandmother.

Hopeless-town

Having entered this wonderful town which is the Hopeless-town, we went straight to her grandmother's house in which we met many ghosts and ghostesses who received us with gladness because they are her family. But I did not see her grandmother, because she had been imprisoned inside the everlasting fire. When we entered this Hopeless-town, she warned me seriously three times thus—"You must not speak any word with your mouth but with a shrug of your shoulders. Whenever you are talking to any ghost in this town you must not raise up or down your eyelids and also your mouth must not open at all. If you mistakenly or wilfully break any of these warnings it would result in a severe punishment for you." Having warned me like this, I told her that—"I do not think that I will return without any punishment, because I shall forget to comply with the whole warnings." Having warned me like this, she herself stopped talking with her mouth and I too.

As a matter of fact I noticed well that nobody is talking by mouth in this town, even if a baby is born on the same day, he or she would not talk by mouth and also all their domestic animals as sheep, goats, fowls or all creatures that are living there are not talking with their mouths but with the shrug of their shoulders.

126

Hopeless-town

One day, when my wife with her sister went to visit their grandmother in the everlasting fire in which she was imprisoned over two hundred years, as I remained alone at home I thought within myself to go as far as the centre of this town as a stroll. Having travelled to the centre of the town I stopped and I was gloating at a curious creature whose body was full of large eyes, but as a ghost was passing closely to me, he mistakenly smashed my foot unexpectedly with his heavy foot which had long nails of about half a foot. But as he smashed me, I cried out louder suddenly—"Oh", and those who stood by heard my voice which was very strange to them, because there is no noise of any creature, every part of the town is always calm as if there is nobody living there at all. So as I cried out which is against their law, those who stood by came and held me as a thief, then they took me to their king who sat on a fearful idol which was moulded with yellow and red clay or mud, because it is on such a seat that the king of this town must be sitting whenever he wants to judge a very serious case. Then he was asking me these questions with a shrug of his shoulders as follows:— "Who are you?" But as I did not understand what he was asking me with the shrug of the shoulders, so to set myself free from the punishment I began to reply as well with my own shrug of the shoulders as he was doing, which means to him—"you are a bastard king." And again, on the same spot that I stood before him I mistakenly raised up and down the lids of my eyes which means—"you are fool," and this is contrary to the law of this town. Again I mistakenly opened down my mouth at the same moment, and this means to

them—"I shun you away." But when all the ghosts and
ghostesses who stood by saw this again, all were shouting
with the shrug of their shoulders in such a way that the
shoulders were nearly cut off, this means—"Ah! you are
abusing the king."

So as these three rules are very important offences for
them in this town, and also all the three are not pardon-
able as my wife had already told me before we entered
the town, so the king ordered those who brought me to
him to take me to the purgatory which is near the town
to throw me inside it as a punishment. But as these
ghosts were dragging me mercilessly along the road to
the purgatory instead of letting me walk with my feet,
so, luckily, at that time, my wife with her sister were
returning from the place that they had gone to visit their
grandmother and it was on this road they were travelling
along to the town. Immediately both of them met these
ghosts dragging me along, they knew already that I had
made mistakes, so both started to beg these ghosts not to
put me inside the purgatory, and bribed them with some
amount before I was released. But at the same time that
I was released, my wife and myself did not return to that
town again, except her sister. So we started from there
to return to our Nameless-town, but it was a queer road
we took instead of the one on which we travelled to that
town. If my wife and her sister had not met these ghosts
on the way as they were dragging me to the purgatory,
I should have perished before she would know. This is
how we left the Hopeless-town.

On the Queer Way to Homeward

On our queer way to homeward we visited many towns and villages. But this queer way is farther than the way on which we travelled when going to the town of my wife's father and her grandmother's town and also we spent more time before we reached our Nameless-town than when going. We visited the towns and villages as follows:— We first visited a village which is near the 26th country of ghosts. All the inhabitants of this village were not more than forty thousand ghosts and ghostesses. All of them were in peace and in pleasure always. They were harmless to either earthly persons or to other kinds of creatures. We reached there at about ten o'clock in the night and yet they received us with gladness. Before an hour that we reached there they had cooked food and brought it to us with drinks, after that, all of them sat round us outside, then merriment began in which jokes, dance, clapping and the drums of ghosts were included.

None of them sleep till the morning but amused us throughout, especially the "jocose-ghostess" who was among them, she was joking in such a way that if a sick man is hearing her jokes he would be healed at once without using any medicine. As all of them were wealthy in corn, sheep, fowls and foxes, so they gave us one fowl, a fox, some quantity of corn and a lamb which was not more than five months old as gifts, because my wife informed them that I am her husband and all of them were pleased to be so. After these gifts then we went round to their houses and thanked them greatly for their kindness.

Then we left there at about nine o'clock in the morning and all of them led us to a short distance as if we are a king before they returned to their village. But having travelled to a distance of seven miles away from that village we reached a wide river which crossed our way.

Lost or Gain Valley

Having crossed the river we travelled to a distance of four miles from that river till we reached a deep valley which is crossed this queer way. A very slender stick was put across it with which to be crossed by everyone, but there was no other single stick near that area. But when we reached this "Lost or Gain Valley" we saw a notice-board on which all these warnings are written in the ghosts' language as follows:—"Put all the clothes on your body with loads down here before climbing this valley." And I did not understand it. But as this slender stick was so slender, so we tried all our best to climb it with clothes on our bodies and failed before we understood what is written on the board, then my wife took all the clothes off her body and put them down, then she first crossed it. This means the slender stick was not strong enough for a person to climb it with clothes on their body. After my wife crossed it easily without clothes on her body, then I did as she did and I crossed it easily as well. All of our dress cost more than £100. Not knowing that the meaning of the name of this valley which is— "Lost or Gain Valley" means as we put all our clothes down at this first edge before crossing it, it is so for those who are travelling towards us from the opposite direction who should put down all the clothes off their bodies at

131

the second edge as well before they could climb it and after climbing it then they will take any clothes that they meet there and wear them instead of their own which they leave before climbed it. Perhaps the clothes that they might meet there might cost more than their own, so it is their gain and if the one that they meet there are not worth their own it is also their loss.

So having made ourselves naked and climbed to the second edge, then we stopped there and waited, perhaps a cloth-seller might come to pass at that time, so that we might buy some clothes from him or her to wear at that spot and then to continue our journey, because we did not meet any clothes at this second edge and we could not travel along the road without clothes on our bodies. But after some hours that we had been waiting there for a cloth-seller, a couplet ghosts, wife and husband, came. They wanted to climb this valley to the other edge. But as both are the natives of that area so they knew how they are climbing it every time and without hesitation they took away all the animal skins that they wore from their bodies and put them down there, then both of them climbed the valley to the second edge. Having reached there they did not waste time, but the husband wore my costly clothes as trousers, shirt, tie, socks, shoes, hat, golden ring with my costly wrist-watch. After this his wife wore my wife's clothes as—underwear, gown, golden beads, rings, hat, shoes, wrist-watch, after that she handled her (my wife's) lofty hand-bag, and then both of them went away without hesitation. But when they did so and went away then we quite understood what we should do. So we wore their own as well. But it is a great pity and loss that their own were only the animal skins which were worth nothing and the worst part of it, it was just a baby's clothes on our bodies, because it was not the size for us at all and also made us more ugly and fearful to any creature to meet us on the way. So it was our loss and it was their gain. And it was after we left that area we heard that no stranger would cross this valley without loss, because all the ghosts and ghostesses of that area are very poor and only living on this kind of exchange.

Then we kept going as usual with our shameful appearance which did not make us feel happy as before. But I am not satisfied as somebody told us that those ghost etc. of that area could not lose but gain. So I am still eager to find out the right way of how to cross this "Lost or Gain Valley" without any loss except gain. "Do you know?" After we had travelled again on this "queer-way" to about two miles in that valley, then we entered into a town at about eight o'clock in the night, because we had wasted much time at the valley, but as we were totally tired, so we went to a ghost's house who is well-known to my wife, and we slept there till the morning. But as we wanted to spend a few days there to rest, so we cooked our food early in the morning, then we ate it to our satisfaction.

Having left there we did not branch again to any town but straight to our Nameless-town. Immediately we reached home we ate the food which had been prepared for us by the two maids who deputed for us at home. After that we left the dining-room for the parlour and then started to drink and also tell my wife some of the earthly news which she is always interested to hear every time.

133

Son Divides Us

When I completed the period of a year with her, then she conceived and some months later she delivered a male baby who resembled me with half of his body and the rest his body resembled his mother. The naming ceremony of this baby was performed after the third day he was born according to the ghosts' custom. All the prominent ghosts with ghostesses came in large numbers for this grand ceremony. They gave him the ghosts' name which I could not write or pronounce, of course, I myself gave him an earthly name which is—"OKOLE-BAMIDELE", the meaning is—"you cannot follow me to my home." I gave him this name according to his nature which is half ghostess and half earthly person.

Within six months that he was born he had grown up to the height of four feet and some inches. He could do everything in the house. But the worst part of it is that whenever I talked to him to do something, he would do it in the half method that ghosts are doing all their things and then in the half method that the earthly persons are doing everything. So I hated him for this habit, because I wanted him to do everything completely in the method that the earthly persons are doing everything and also his mother hated him for the half method that he was doing everything, because she wanted him

134

to do everything in the full way that ghosts are doing their own things. She wanted him to be acting as a full ghost as herself and I myself wanted him to be acting as a full earthly person as I am. So by this reason the love which was between ourselves was vanishing away gradually until when I completed the period of four years with her.

One night I was joking with her that—"earthly people are superior to the ghosts and ghostesses or all other creatures." But when she heard this from me she was extremely annoyed. Without asking me the reason about what I said, she simply went to an unknown place that she kept the animal skin which was on my body when she met me. But as she had taken it from me and hid it in an unknown place at the time I followed her from the bush to her house on the day she met me in the bush, so she brought it and took away all the clothes that she gave me from my body and then gave me my animal skin to wear. But when I saw her rude attitude I was greatly annoyed as well, then I took it from her and wore it as before I met her. After that she drove me away from that town. Which means I come back to my former condition. So I left there at two o'clock in the midnight to an unknown place, because I did not know any part of that area or to hear any news about any town which is near there to go direct and shelter myself throughout that night from any dangerous ghost or creature.

Having left her and travelled in the bush to a short distance then I remembered to continue to be looking for the way to my home town as I had forgotten that for a while, because of love. So this is how I left the "Superlady" who was my wife because of our son. After the fifth month that I had left her and roamed about in the bush both day and night, and nobody could identify me again that I am not a ghost, because I was then nearly become a full ghost and was doing everything that ghosts are doing and also speaking the language of ghosts fluently as if I was born in the Bush of Ghosts, so through this language that I could speak and understand I was always protected from uncountable merciless ghosts as it was hard for some of them to believe that I am an earthly person.

One night, at about eleven o'clock there I entered a town unnoticed. All the inhabitants of this town had slept very early, because it was in the rainy season, again it was raining from morning of that day till the evening, as this is always happening in the Bush of Ghosts. But when I went as far as to the centre of this town perhaps I might discover the fire in which to roast a very small *j*am which a ghost gave me after he slapped my ear warmly ten times before giving it to me, because yams were very scarce to get in some parts of the Bush of Ghosts. Having given me this yam he mounted me and rode me about for three days and nights before he released me.

So as I was roaming up and down in this town to get the fire I was easily arrested as a burglar. Because many of their houses had been burgled a week previously before I entered there, so the guard-ghosts who arrested me thought that I was one of the burglars or coming to burgle another house again and furthermore, when they saw the small yam which I wanted to roast in the fire some of them held me tightly for the rest who were beating me repeatedly with clubs in respect of this yam alone. After that they took me to their guard-room to keep me safely till the morning before they would put the case in the court. I was very surprised to see that I was totally covered by mosquitoes in this guard-room so that nobody could see many parts of my body and it was in this town I saw that mosquitoes are worshipped, kept or tamed and regarded as their god, they are respecting them as their doctors and none of them could live in any town where there are no mosquitoes as they are recognising them purifying their blood to the good state. There I noticed as well that they have several special shrines in which they are worshipping them and scheduled the term of festival two times in a year. But if they discover in any year that mosquitoes are less than previous years it would be bad luck for them and at once they would make a special sacrifice in these shrines to increase mosquitoes in abundance so that they would fill everywhere in the town.

So it was not yet eight o'clock in the morning before I was taken to the court which was specially arranged for my case and the judge did not ask me any question before he judged it and then sentenced me to sixteen years' imprisonment with hard labour. Then I was taken to their prison yard in which all kinds of severe punishments are always awaiting offenders. Immediately I was taken there and handed to one of the chief warders who are in charge of the yard, then two junior warders were preparing fire inside a big oven in which I would spend the sentence passed on me. I would be entering inside this oven from five o'clock every morning and coming out at seven o'clock every evening till the term would be expired. But as it was hard labour, so instead of resting for some time till I would enter it again at five o'clock in the morning I would be collecting charcoal into this oven again with which to make another fire. So by that I would have no rest for a minute until the term would be expired. I was very surprised that all ghosts are thinking that earthly persons could not die as they themselves could not die. Because to imprison themselves and other creatures in the fire are very common in the Bush of Ghosts.

Immediately these two warders had prepared the fire and told me to be getting ready to enter inside it and when I was preparing to enter it, luckily, it was that day their king should come to visit the yard and he entered it at that time without noticing all the warders, so he saw me stand closely before the oven or fire with my eyes which were as wild as a wild animal's eyes when chasing his prey with hunger and much difficulty. So he approached me at the same moment he saw me and asked whether I knew him. But I replied—"I did not." Then he said— "I am your son and your wife who is 'Superlady' is my mother." Then I knew him very well after he had explained himself to me. After that, he ordered some of the warders to lead me to his palace and they did so. So I was very glad that this king is my son and also saved me entering the fire. Having inspected the prison yard all round, then he came back to the palace, he told his attendants to give me food with all kinds of drinks.

Having spent some years with him, then I told him to

tell me the right way to my home town. But as none of
the ghosts is too young to persuade he told me—"Yes,
I know the right way to your town, but to tell you such
a thing is against our rule in this Bush of Ghosts."
When he said so, I explained that if he tells me the way
and if I go, I will be spending only a few days in my
town before I will be coming back to visit him regularly,
but yet he insisted on the first point that he raised. When
it was a week later after he refused to tell me the way,
then I told him that I want to continue to find out the
way. Of course, when heard so, he begged me not to
leave him, but I myself refused totally to stay with him
as he refused to tell me the way. So I left him and started
to find the way.

After the eighth month that I had left him there I
reached the 4th town of ghosts at about twelve o'clock
midnight. But I did not enter it at that time so that the
guard ghosts might not catch me there as a thief as in
the town in which my son is the king. When it was eight
o'clock in the morning then I entered the town and went
direct to the king, I reported that I am a foreigner in his
town, because at that time I could explain myself fully
before any ghost as I said that before I left my wife or
the "Superlady" she taught me the language of the
ghosts. So by that I explained before this king that:—
it is disgraceful to hear that the earthly people are
always abusing all the ghosts and now I volunteer myself
to go to their towns to warn them of this abuse and I shall
be glad if he will tell me the right way to any of the
nearest earthly towns. After I explained to him like this,
he waited for half an hour, of course, he could not

identify me that I am not a ghost and he did not understand my trick that I am only to find out the right way from him. Before he started to reply my request he told a ghost to give me food with drinks as he noticed that I was feeling hunger at that time. As I was eating the food, then he was telling me—"I will tell you the right way to the earth to go and warn them if you can volunteer your left arm to me. Because one arm of the most beautiful of all my wives had been cut away before I married her, so that I will fit your own there, because it is our rule in this town that any king who is on the throne must not marry any armless or amputy as wife. And one of the rest of the wives had told this secret to all the chiefs, kingmakers and the prominent ghosts of this town that I married an armless ghostess as wife. The reason why she leaked out the secret is only because I love this armless wife more than the rest of them. All the chiefs, and kingmakers, with the prominent ghosts had come and asked me about the matter in secret whether it is true, but I told them that it is not true, because if I tell them frankly that it is true they will kill me. But when I told them that it is not the truth, then they told me that in five days to come they will come to the palace, then all my wives will come out and sit in a row, after that every one of them will be grinding corn on the stone with two hands in the presence of the chiefs, kingmakers and the prominent ghosts, but if any one of the wives cannot produce two hands or arms to grind the corn, then they will kill me on the same spot, as I am against the rule and now it remains only two days to come for the test." But as he said that if I could volunteer one of my arms to fit on his wife's arm which

140

was cut off, then he would tell me the right way to the
earthly towns, so I was very glad to hear that.

Then I told him to call the armless wife to show me the
arm which had been cut off, when she came and showed
me the arm, so I measured it with a kind of ghosts' rope
in such a way that the measurement was equal with the
one which was not cut. After this, I went to a bush which
is near that palace with this rope, and moulded another
arm with mud which was the same size with the rope,
then I brought it and told this armless wife to stretch the
other half which remained with her, so I let the artificial
arm touch the part that remained with her, after that I
performed a kind of juju which was given to me by a
"triplet ghost". Immediately I performed the juju the
artificial arm joined together with the rest and at the
same time it became exactly the natural arm, even
nobody could believe that it was cut off before, and none
of the wives who hated her knew that she had got complete arms until the day of the inspection was reached
and all of them were still proud that they have complete
arms and were also telling this armless wife in the pro-
verbial way that she is near to be killed with the king
who loved her only.

When the day of this inspection was reached, all the
chiefs, kingmakers, with all the prominent ghosts of this
town came to the palace, all of them sat in the same row,
then they put a flat grinding stone with corn on the
front, after that they called all the king's wives out and
told them to sit down in a row at a little distance from
them and also told the king to sit in the middle. After
that they asked the king again—"Is it true that you

141

married an armless ghostess as a wife?" But he replied
as usual that he did not marry an armless ghostess as
wife at all. Having spoken one of the inspectors started
to command every one of these wives to be grinding that
corn on the stone with two hands so that the wife who
has an arm might be detected. But after all the rest
who had complete hands ground the corn with their
complete hands successfully, they told the one who was
suspected to be armless that it is her turn to grind the
corn. But as she was all the while hiding the hand under
her cloth till the time she was called, so she got up and
approached the stone, but the other wives were still
thinking that she would not be able to grind it. So she
knelt down and ground the corn successfully with two
hands as the other wives. When the rest of the wives
with the chiefs, kingmakers and prominent ghosts who
were inspectors saw her with two complete hands all were
greatly surprised. Then these chiefs, kingmakers and
prominent ghosts or inspectors asked the rest of the
wives—"Why did all of you tell a lie against the king
that he married an armless ghostess as wife?" But when
none of them could answer this question, and only
looked as dummies, then the inspectors killed all of them,
except the one who was supposed to be armless, because
it is their rule as well in this town not to tell lies against
the king. After all have been killed, then the inspectors
went back to their houses. So the beauty of a woman or a
lady among ugly women or many ugly ladies is always
resulting in extreme hatred, and the hatred sometimes
brings good luck to one who is abhorred or hated.
Because it was only this beautiful ghostess was then the

ruler of the palace with the king after the rest of the wives who hated her greatly for her beauty had been killed.

After a week that I had done this wonderful work to this king and also saved his wife, then I asked him to tell me the right way to the earthly towns as he promised before. But instead of telling me the way he said—"I like you to stay here with me for the period of fifteen years, perhaps the arm may be cut unexpectedly, so that you may rejoin it again." Of course, I did not blame him as he told me to wait for fifteen years, because he did not know that I am not a ghost. Although I believed that my trick would not succeed, then I left there at night without his knowledge and continued my journey as usual, until I entered a very clean town which resembled an earthly town, even at first I thought that it is my town.

I meet my Dead Cousin
in the 10th Town of Ghosts

Having entered this 10th town of ghosts all the inhabitants of this town rushed out from their houses to see what happens. Immediately I saw them then I ran directly to one of them who resembled an earthly person among them, but when I approached him he was my dead cousin who had died in my town since I was six and an half years old. Immediately I saw him clearly that he is my dead cousin I ran to his back and held him. After that he told all the inhabitants of this town who came to the scene that I am his junior brother. But when they heard so from him all of them shouted with gladness at a time. After this, I followed him to his house with some of the ghosts to greet him at home. Because all of the inhabitants of this town were respecting him as he is the one who brought Christianity to their town. Having reached home, he told one of his servants to give me food and drinks at once, again many of the prominent ghosts of this town were sending a variety of food and drinks through him to me for "well come". Furthermore, when it was about eight o'clock in the night all the chiefs and king, with famous and prominent ghosts of this town gathered together at the front house of my cousin, then the whole of us started to drink all kinds of ghosts' drinks, we were also dancing, drumming and singing the song of ghosts until daybreak, and this was the "Well come Function". It was that day I saw that some of these ghosts were dancing in such a way until they cut into halves and again both these halves were also dancing until they joined together as usual.

After this "Well come Merriment" ended and when the day broke all of them went back to their houses, but still my cousin was receiving uncountable letters of congratulation, with presents from various towns and villages which were under this 10th town of ghosts, who were unable to come personally. Having gone back to their houses, I told my cousin that I want to sleep as all of us did not sleep throughout that night, so he opened a reserved room, then I slept on a bed which was specially decorated with expensive clothes. Of course, it is only in the Bush of Ghosts such a bed could be found. I woke up at two o'clock p.m., because I had not slept on such a bed since I left my wife the "Superlady" in the Nameless-town. After that I took my bath, then I ate and drank to my satifaction, because in the Bush of Ghosts whenever you eat drinks must follow. Then my cousin started his story after he died before he came and was established in this 10th town as follows:—

"Immediately I died in our town I went to several towns which perhaps would be suitable to establish the Christianity works, but I could not get such a suitable town until I reached here which is suitable. As you know that before I died I was one of the staunch members of the Methodist Church in our earthly town and I am still

145

praying to God that I shall carry on the services until the last day, which is the 'judgement-day' because I could not die again for the second time until that day. At the same time that I came to live in this town, first of all, I went direct to H.M. the King of the Bush of Ghosts and informed him that I want to establish the Christianity works in this 10th town, so he agreed after several meetings to consider this request with himself and his councillors. After this request was approved, the second thing I did, I went round this town, then I found a suitable ground on which I built the first church and it was 90 × 70 ft., the roof was covered with flat bark of the big trees, because there were no iron sheets or other things to use at that time, and then was written on the upper entrance of the main door as follows— 'THE METHODIST CHURCH OF THE BUSH OF GHOSTS.' It was written in bold letters with the white juice of a tree, because there was no paint at that time and also the wall which is mud was painted inside and out with a kind of leaves which yielded the grey colour when ground and mixed with water. Of course, as I was all the while sub-letting a house with a ghost during the time that I was in activity in building the church, so also after it was been completed, although some ghosts helped me. Then I found another suitable ground again and built this house in which we are at present, but it was three months before it was completed with the help of some young ghosts of this town. After that I went round the town on a Saturday evening with a flat hard wood as a bell and told them what is to be doing in that house.

"On Sunday, which was the 1st Sunday to attend or to

hold the 1st service there, I noticed that only two young ghosts attended with me out of about four million ghosts and ghostesses who are living here. Because all of them did not know anything about God or believe that there is God who created them or believe that no other creature is above them. Though, I preached and encouraged those two who attended with me, after that the service closed at 11 a.m. But I did not attempt to hold the evening service on that Sunday. It was a short dead stump of a big tree which has a large hole inside which was beaten as the toll-bell or church-bell whenever it is time for service, because this dead stump is near the church. On Monday, I formed a campaign, I was preaching from house to house, encouraging and explaining what is God to these ghosts until the second Saturday. On Sunday which was the second Sunday, the attendance showed fifty old, thirty-eight young and forty-five child ghosts respectively who attended and all totalled = 133. So, I was exceedingly glad on that day. After the service closed at 11 a.m. I told them that all the young with children should come for Sunday-school at 2 o'clock or if any of the old who like may come as well. Again, the attendance for the Sunday-school showed fifty-seven. Of course the attendance in the evening service was very poor and was only forty-eight in all, because all ghosts like to go to the farms for their food every evening.

"After the sixth month that the church was opened, I converted it to both church and school. I was teaching ghost children of this town how to read and write and also scripture which is the main subject. But there was no paper, chalk or slates on which to write as in the earthly

147

towns so, instead of that I cut a 4 ft. sq. flat bark of a tree as blackboard and also cut 1 ft. sq. for each of the scholars as slates and all were using coal as chalks. As we were using the church in the ordinary day and also on Sunday as a church, then I built a big separate house as church with the help of both scholars and members of the church, because the scholars are making the former one too rough before Sunday. This second building nearly touched the former one. After some years I have had more than fifty ghost teachers out of these scholars and over nine hundred scholars were attending the school regularly. Having trained many bright scholars as teachers and headmasters, then I built over a thousand churches with schools in all provinces which are under this 10th town. So I am using the 10th town as head-quarters for the rest and also the Synod is held here yearly, because I am the bishop at present. My work after the church services is only to be supervising churches and schools. Although there are many supervisors, directors of education and education officers who are carrying on their tasks according to the rules and regula-tions given them to my satisfaction. In my leisure hours, I taught many scholars who had been passed out from the schools sanitary work, surveying, building, first aid nursery work, but only this 'first aid' nursery work I could teach them, because I am not a qualified doctor.

"After all these students had qualified for these various trades and carrying them on successfully to my entire satisfaction, then I introduced new plans of houses and luckily all the ghosts who are the rulers of this town agreed to follow it. Then new houses were built which made this town to link up as the most beautiful town in the Bush of Ghosts. Though it was only disqualified at that time for the hospital which was not established in the town, although there was provision for it but no qualified doctor who could carry on the works."

The second day my cousin took me round the town and I saw many churches, schools, hospitals and many houses which are built in modern styles. But when I asked him about the hospitals who is acting as a doctor and as nurses or who are treating the patients there as he himself is not a doctor, so he replied—"Do you see my wife?" I said—"Yes." Then he told me in short about her as follows—"She is the native of a town in Zulu country, the town which has now been converted to a big city after she had died there. Before she died, she was a well-educated girl and after she had finished her schooling, her father sent her to a part of England as a doctor student, but after she had qualified as a doctor, she returned to her father's town and in the same week that she arrived home she met with an accident and died suddenly as a result of injuries. Having died she left that town, she was going here and there as a dead young person could not stay in a town which belongs to earthly persons, because that is forbidden for all deads and she was roaming about until she reached this town, then we got married as both of us are deads. But as this town is well improved but only disqualified by the hospitals which were not then in it, so as she is a qualified doctor before she died, she established hospitals in this town and acted as the Director of Medical Services. Having trained several thousands of nurses and medical officers."

149

Again I asked him these questions:— (1) Who ordained you before you came up to the rank of a bishop? (2) Who is supplying you all kinds of medicines and apparatus which you are using in the hospitals? (3) Who are supplying you all the educational books, religious books as bibles, songs books and papers or stationery, as the flat bark of the trees are no more in use by the scholars? (4) From whom are you getting the iron sheets and all the building materials, as all the houses are no more thatched with grasses and flat bark of the trees? Then he replied as follows—"(1) As I am carrying on this Christianity work for many years and faithfully to all creatures and did not doubt once for everything that I am doing, so one night, I dreamed a dream and heard the holy voice from heaven that I am ordained as a bishop from heaven as from this night. When the day broke which was Sunday and I explained this news to all the members they confirmed it since that day. (2) Thank you, we are getting the medicines with apparatus for the hospitals from the dead medicine-makers and hospital apparatus-makers who are expert in such works before dying and living in the Deads' town which belongs only to deads. (3) All deads who are the publishers of religious books, educational books and stationery before they died and went to live in the Deads' town are supplying us from there. (4) Deads are supplying us everything that we need here after we had entered into the agreement with them and they are acting for us as the 'Crown Agent'.

Having answered all the four questions, then we came back to the house. After that he called his four daughters and two sons, after a while his wife who is the Director of Medical Services came back from the hospitals and showed me to them and explained how I am related to him. Those two sons were still attending the school, but the four daughters had passed out from the school and also qualified as nurses and doctors.

After the third day that he had told me his stories, then he told me to give him the home news which went thus—"After you had died and before I myself entered into the Bush of Ghosts none of our family die, but one of them was sick seriously for three weeks before he became well. After the sixth month that you died a war of slavery broke into the town and drove me into this Bush of Ghosts, even I was seven years old before I entered it. At present I could not definitely say anything about their condition at home, because I left there over twenty years ago. So since I left the town my mind does not rest at all at a time except to return and I am still looking for the way until I reached here and instead of seeing the way I was only punished in the bush by the merciless ghosts. So I am exceedingly glad as I meet you in this town and I shall be very glad as well if you will allow me to live with you here for a short period to rest for some time for all the punishment which I had met past and then to continue to find the way as before I reached here or I shall be glad too if you will tell me the right way direct to the town."

After I told him some of my stories in this Bush of Ghosts, then he asked this question—"Have you died before entered this bush?" I replied—"Not at all sir." But at the same moment that this reply came out of my

mouth, he shouted with his loudest voice "Ah!" together
with some ghosts who sat with us at that time. Then he
said—"You will not be able to live with deads, of course,
as you soon become a full ghost and also hear the language
of ghosts, so by that I will teach you until you will
qualify to be a full dead person."

After some weeks he handed me to one of the prin-
cipals of his schools as a new scholar, then I started to
learn how to read and write. In the evening my cousin
would be teaching me how to be acting as a dead man and
within six months I had qualified as a full dead man.
And again as I had a quick brain at that time, so I finished
my schooling after a few years. Then I was sent without
hesitation direct to the Deads' town as a student to learn
how to judge cases, as police and also all the branches of
the court works. Having become expert in this field,
then I returned and started the works. But at the first
time we built police stations, courts and prison yards in
every part of the town, because these works were not yet
established before I reached there. After that I taught
many ghosts who had just passed out from the schools
all these works and later on I was chosen as the chief
judge of the highest court which is the "Assize court".
So I was judging all of the important cases which were
sent to me from the lower courts.

One day my cousin called me to discuss about his four
daughters with the two sons. He asked me who would
marry the four daughters, because they are at the ripe
age to be married, but no earthly man in any part of the
Bush of Ghosts could marry them and again no earthly
ladies for the two sons to marry. When he asked me like

this, I told him to let us advertise them on the earthly newspapers several times, perhaps we would get those who would marry them, he agreed to my suggestion and told me to advertise them on the earthly newspapers. "So do you like to marry one of them? If it is so, please, choose any and only one of these numbers—733, 744, 755, 766 and 777, 788 respectively, so that his or her picture may be sent to you or to come to you personally."

Invisible Magnetic Missive
sent to Me from Home

Having been educated and become the chief judge my mind was then at rest, I did not feel to go to my town again, even I determined that I should not go for ever. But one night, when I slept I dreamed a dream which was just as if I was in my home town and also eating with my mother and brother as we were doing before we left each other and I was also playing with my friends as before entered the Bush of Ghosts. So when I woke up in the morning I remembered all these dreams, then I began to feel to go, but however I was putting my mind away from it. When I slept the following night I dreamed the same dream again, but when I woke up in the morning I felt to go my town more than the first time. And the third time that I dreamed again I was unable to eat, play, or feel happy at all, except to go. Even if I walk to any corner it would seem as if I was with my people, doing everything we were doing before I left them. So at this stage I thought of nothing more than to go, because I could not sleep both day and night any more, and I was always dreaming without sleeping or without closing my eyes. Not knowing that my people at home had gone to an earthly fortune teller and asked him

154

whether I am still alive or dead already, but he told them that I am still alive in a bush, but my aim is not to come back to home any more. He said furthermore that I am living with somebody who is taking great care of me. Although he was unable to tell them the real bush that I was in and he could not tell them the kind of the person that I was living with. As he told them that I am still alive, my people simply told him to call me home with the power of his "Invisible Missive Magnetic Juju" which could bring a lost person back to home from an unknown place, how far it may be, with or without the will of the lost person. So having paid him his workmanship in advance, then he started to send the juju to me at night which was changing my mind or thought every time to go home.

Bad-bye Function

But as I could no longer bear to stay with my cousin except to go, then I told him, but he refused totally at the first time. When I was pressing him every time and telling a lie that I want to go and visit a friend of mine in the 7th town of ghosts, then he allowed me to go, because I was lean as if I should die within a few days. So as I was very popular with all ghosts of this 10th town and environment, when it remained one day for me to leave there I called all the ghosts of this town to my cousin's front house for a special function for this "Bad-bye". But none of them knows that I would not come back again as it was a "secret function" to all of them. This function was so greatly performed so that nobody could sleep till the morning except drinking, dancing various dances, beating drums and singing. But my cousin was so sad that he did not appear.

Immediately the day broke I left them there and started to find the way to my home town as before I met my cousin in this 10th town of ghosts. This is how I left them. But as I did not know the right way straight to my town so this "Magnetic juju" was taking me to every place in either dangerous bush or not, so I started another punishment by ghosts. After the ninth month that I left my dead cousin I reached the 18th town which is about six hundred miles away from the 10th town. Having reached there a ghost whose throat was always sounding with various voices as a motor horn received me to his house with gladness. His house was on a high rock which is above every house in this town, he was the one who was blowing the horn through his throat to all the ghosts of this town in every hour as a clock and this horn was also waking everyone at five o'clock in the morning. After a week that I arrived to his house I noticed that he was too poor to feed me, because he was very old, even he could not feed himself and had nobody to support him. But as I had already become a real ghost before I left the 10th town, so by that a ghost friend of mine taught me the art of magic, because he did not know that I am an earthly person at that time, otherwise he would not teach me to become a magician. So as I was taught this art before I reached this town, one day, when I thought within myself that this old ghost could not feed me unless I would feed him, therefore I went to a village which is near this 18th town, luckily, I met a ghost magician who was displaying his magical power for the head chief of that village at that time. Then I joined him to display my own as well before these chiefs, as a competition. But when I changed the day to the night, so every place became dark at once, then I told him to change it back to the day as usual, but he was unable. After this I changed him to a dog and he started to bark at everybody, then as my power was above his own the chief with all the scene-lookers gave me all the gifts which were to be shared for both of us. After that I changed him from the dog to a ghost as usual. Then I

packed all these gifts and kept going to the 18th town
where I came to that village, I did not give him any of
the gifts.

Having left this village to a distance of a mile this
ghost magician came to me on the way, he asked me to
let both of us share the gifts, but when I refused he
changed to a poisonous snake, he wanted to bite me to
death, so I myself used my magical power and changed to
a long stick at the same moment and started to beat him
repeatedly. When he felt much pain and near to die,
then he changed from the snake to a great fire and burnt
this stick to ashes, after that he started to burn me too.
Without hesitation I myself changed to rain, so I
quenched him at once. Again he controlled the place that
I stood to become a deep well in which I found myself
unexpectedly and without any ado he controlled this
rain to be raining into the well while I was inside.
Within a second the well was full with water. But when
he wanted to close the door of the well so that I might not
be able to come out again or to die inside it, I myself
changed to a big fish to swim out. But at the same
moment he saw the fish he himself changed to a crocodile,
he jumped into the well and came to swallow me, but
before he could swallow me I changed to a bird and also
changed the gifts to a single palm fruit, I held it with my
beak and then flew out of the well straight to the 18th
town. Without any ado he changed himself again to a big
hawk chasing me about in the sky to kill as his prey.
But when I believed that no doubt he would kill me very
soon, then I changed again to the air and blew within a
second to a distance which a person could not travel on

foot for thirty years. But when I changed to my former form at the end of this distance, to my surprise, there I met him already, he had reached there before me and was waiting for me for a long time. Now we appeared personally to ourselves. Then he asked me to bring the gifts, but after both of us struggled for many hours, then I shared the gifts into two parts, I gave him a part, but he insisted to take the whole. However, I gave him all.

Immediately he left me, then I changed to the air again, after I blew far away after him, I stopped on the way on which he would travel to his town, then I changed to a person. Before he could travel to that place I used my magical power. I killed a bush animal, I dug a hole close to this road, after that I cut the head off this animal, I put it upright inside the hole, it faced the road as if it peeped out of the ground alive, having done this, I hid myself near there. After a while he travelled to that place but when he saw this head as it appeared from the ground, he stopped suddenly and looked at it carefully for a few minutes, because it was very curious to him. Then he started to ask this head with fearful mind— "Ah! my lord, here you are?" After that he bowed down respectfully for it for three times, having done so, he was asking it—"Do you want one of these gifts?" But as it did not show any sign of motion, so he threw one of them before it. But as he wanted this head to talk to him, he said again—"Or this is the one you want?" he held the gift, showing it to this head as he was saying so. And threw that as well before it, and it was like this he was doing until he threw all these gifts before it. After that, he laughed louder and ran hastily to his town, he told all the inhabitants with the king that he saw where the "ground has head and eyes" today. Having told them this wonderful news, the king asked him three times—"Are you sure?" he said—"yes, I am sure." And said furthermore that if it is a lie, then they may kill him for telling a lie. Having confirmed it, the whole of them with their king from whose head the smoke was rushing out followed them to the place to witness this ground whether it is true. But as I had removed this head together with all the gifts and went away immediately he left there for the town, so when the whole of them followed him to the place, they did not see where the "ground has head and eyes" as he told them. But as he had been promised that they may kill him for telling a lie, so the king ordered the ghosts to kill him, because they did not see any sign of what he told them. This is how I took all my gifts back from him.

Of course, I did not return to the 18th town again, but started from there to find the way to my home town as usual, because that place was too far from the 18th town.

Television-handed Ghostess

When it was about 2 o'clock p.m. I saw a ghostess who was crying bitterly and coming to me direct in a hut where I laid down enjoying myself. When she entered I noticed that she held a short mat which was woven with dried weeds. She was not more than three feet high. Immediately she entered she went direct to the fire, she spread the mat closely to the fire and then sat down on it without saluting or talking to me. So at this stage I noticed carefully that she was almost covered with sores, even there was no single hair on her head, except sores with uncountable maggots which were dashing here and there on her body. Both her arms were not more than one and an half foot, it had uncountable short fingers. She was crying bitterly and repeatedly as if somebody was stabbing her with knives. Of course, I did not talk to her, but I was looking at her with much astonishment until I saw the water of her eyes that it was near to quench the fire, then I got up with anger and told her to walk out of my hut, because if the water quenches the fire I should not be able to get another again, as there were not matches in the Bush of Ghosts. But instead of walking out as I said she started to cry louder than ever. When I could not bear her cry I asked her—"by the way what are you crying for?" She replied

161

—"I am crying because of you." Then I asked again—"because of me?" She said—"yes" and I said—"What for?" Then she started to relate her story thus—

"I was born over two hundred years ago with sores on my head and all over my body. Since the day that I was born I have no other work more than to find out the doctor who could heal it for me and several of them had tried all their best but failed. Instead of healing or curing it would be spreading wider and then giving me more pains. I have been to many sorcerers to know whether the sore would be healed, but every one of them was telling me that there is an earthly person who had been lost in this Bush of Ghosts, so that if I can be wandering about I might see you one day, and the sorcerers said that if you will be licking the sore every day with your tongue for ten years it would be healed. So that I am very lucky and very glad that I meet you here today and I shall also be exceedingly glad if you will be licking the sore with your tongue every day until the ten years that it will be healed as the sorcerers had told me. And I am also crying bitterly in respect of you because I believe that no doubt you have been struggling for many years in this Bush of Ghosts for the right way to your home town, but you are seeing the way every day and you do not know it, because every earthly person gets eyes but cannot see. Even it is on the right way to your home town that you found this hut and sleep or sit in it every day and night. Although I believe that you will not refuse to lick the sore until it is healed."

Having related her story and said that if I am licking the sore it would be healed as the sorcerers said, so I replied—"I want you to go back to your sorcerers and tell them I refuse to lick the sore." After I told her like this she said again—"It is not a matter of going back to the sorcerers, but if you can do it look at my palm or hand." But when she told me to look at her palm and opened it nearly to touch my face, it was exactly as a television, I saw my town, mother, brother and all my playmates, then she was asking me frequently —"do you agree to be licking the sore with your tongue, tell me, now, yes or no?"

Hard to say "No" and
Hard to say "Yes"

Because when I thought over how the sore was dirty
and smelling badly, especially those maggots which were
dashing here and there all over the sore, so it was hard
for me to say "yes". But as I was seeing my town with
all my people, it was also hard for me to say "No". But
as I was hearing on this television when my mother was
discussing about me with one of her friends with a
sorrowful voice at that time that—"She was told by a
fortune teller that I am still alive in a bush." So as I was
enjoying these discussions the television-handed ghostess
took away the hand from my face and I saw nothing
again except the hand.

After that she asked again whether I would do her
request, of course, I was unable to answer at that moment,
but only thinking about my people whom I saw on the
television and also thinking how to reach the town as
quickly as possible. But as it was just a dream for me, I
told her again to let me look at them once more before
I would answer her request. Immediately she showed it
to me my people appeared again at the same time and
as I was looking at them and also hearing what they were
talking about me which I ought to answer if I was with

them, luckily, a woman brought her baby who had a sore on its foot to my mother at that time to tell her the kind of leaf which could heal the sore. But as my mother knows many kinds of leaves which can heal any sore, so she told this woman to follow her. Having reached a small bush which is near the town, then she cut many leaves on a kind of plant and gave them to this woman, after that she told her that she must warm the leaves in hot water before using it for the sore. But as I was looking at them on the television I knew the kind of leaf and also heard the direction how to use it. After a while this "Television-handed ghostess" took her hand away from my face and I saw nothing again. Then she asked again whether I would do her request, so I said—"Yes, but not with my tongue would I heal the sore." After I said "yes" I got out of the hut and I went round near the hut. God is so good, this kind of leaf or plant were full up there. Then I cut some and came back to the hut, after that I was using it for the sore according to the direction that my mother told the woman who brought her baby to her. It was so I was using these leaves for the sore every day and to my surprise, this sore had been healed within a week. But when this "Television-handed ghostess" saw that she had no more sores again she was exceedingly glad.

Having eaten and drunk to my satisfaction I told her to tell me the right way to my home town as she had promised me before I healed her sore. She agreed, but warned me seriously that I must not attempt to enter into the Bush of Ghosts forever, because 90% of ghosts hate any of the earthly persons to enter this bush, as I myself am aware of it since I have been struggling to find the right way back to my town, but none of the merciless ghosts would show me the way. After the above warning she said further—"Do not tell anybody that I am the 'Television-handed ghostess' who shows you the right way whenever you reach your town." Then she opened her palm as usual, she told me to look at it, but to my surprise, I simply found myself under the fruit tree which is near my home town (the Future-Sign). It was under this fruit tree my brother left me on the road when he was running away from the enemies' guns which were driving me farther and farther until I entered into the Bush of Ghosts, and it was the fruit of this tree I ate first immediately I entered the Bush of Ghosts. This is how I got out of the Bush of Ghosts, which I entered when I was seven years old.

The Future-Sign Tree

A<small>S</small> I simply found myself under this fruit tree I stopped there for more than half an hour, because everything had been changed as before I left them. Of course, I believed that the fruit tree is near my town, otherwise I should not know at all that I am near my town. But as I stood under this fruit tree, thinking with doubtful mind that— "This fruit tree is marked as a 'Future-Sign' before I entered the bush" there I saw that two strong men held both my arms at my back unexpectedly and without hesitation they tied me with rope, then one of them put me on his head and both kept going inside the bush at the same time. They were slave-traders because the slave trade was then still existing.

After some days they reached their town which is foreign to mine. So having taken me to their town I was again sold to a man who took me to his town. But as there was no other transport to carry loads more than by head as now-a-days, so I was carrying heavy loads which three men could not carry at a time to long distances which I would travel for ten days with many other slaves. But as my body was full of sores, so it was debarring my boss getting loads from those who were giving him the job. For this reason he started to wash the sore of my body with a sponge and sand perhaps it would

be healed and also flogging me severely if I cry or shake
while he was washing the sore. Having done this every
day for one month and when it was not healed, then he
sold me again to another man who took me to the slave
market, because I was not useful for any purpose in
respect of the sore. Having reached the market he chained
me to a tree together with the other slaves that we met
there, all of us were in a straight line. But within four
hours all the rest slaves had been sold and nobody buys
me because of the sores. When he waited with me till
about two o'clock and when he believed that no one
could buy me that market day, then he was loosing the
chain from me, and when he was about to return to his
town a rich man came to the market, he looked round
but saw no more slaves except me, because he kept late,
then he came to my boss. He priced me very poor and my
boss agreed, he told him to pay any amount that he likes
to buy me, but when he stood before me and looked at
me for many hours he said—"I cannot buy sores for my
town." Then he went back to his town. But as nobody
buys me and I remained unsold, so my boss was flogging
me repeatedly along the way back to his town.

When he was taking me to this market for several
market days without seeing anybody to buy me, then
he said—"If I take you to the market once more and if
nobody buys you on that market day as well so if I am
returning from the market to the town I will kill you
on the way and throw away your body into the bush,
because you are entirely useless for any purpose, even
I have told several of my friends to take you free of
charge but none of them accepts the offer, because I can

no longer remain with you and your sore which is smelling badly to everybody, even the smell is also disturbing
my friends and all my customers to come to my house
again before I bought you." But when the following
market day was reached, the day he would kill me if there
is nobody to buy me, luckily, this rich man came late
to the market on that day as well, then he came to me
because all the rest slaves had been sold, except me. When
he came he asked from my boss how much he would sell
me, but my boss told him to pay any amount that he
likes. After he heard so, he stood looking at me for about
an hour, then he looked round the market, but saw no
more slaves, except me, then he said—"I will buy you,
because I ought to sacrifice to my god with a slave for
some months to come, so that I may kill you for the god."
Having said so, he paid three shillings and sixpence to
my boss and he received it from him with many thanks
and also thanked God greatly that I leave him.

This is a great pity that I was lost in the Bush of
Ghosts for twenty-four years with punishments and
when I came out of it I am caught and sold again as a
slave, and now a rich man buys me and he is going to
kill me for his god. This is what I said before I was
following him and his follower who followed him to the
market was pushing me along the road to the town. Not
knowing that this rich man is my brother who left me
on the road and ran away before I entered the Bush of
Ghosts. Having reached the town which is my town, they
put me among his slaves in the yard, but the sore of my
body still remained with me. So I was living and working
with the rest slaves, but as this slave yard was far from

his house he was only coming there occasionally to inspect us. But as he hated me more than the rest slaves because of the sore, so he would tell some of the rest slaves to flog me in his presence for many hours as I was not useful and also at that time it was their rule that every useless slave should be severely beaten every day, because every slave buyer recognised slaves as non-living creatures. Of course, I believed that I am in my town and my mother with my brother or my family are there also, but I did not know them again and they did not know me as well.

But in those days a slave is too common to approach his master or any of his master's family to talk or to discuss anything with him or her, so that I had no right to describe myself to my master who is my brother, that I am a native of that town and again it was hard to describe myself to the rest slaves because they were foreigners, I did not understand their language. But one day, when my mind was at rest my brother who is our master came to inspect us in the yard, as he was talking to us I listened to his voice well, and it was the same as before we left each other, again I looked at his forehead carefully which had a small scar before I left him and this scar was there as well, so through these two signs I believed that he is my brother, but still I was unable to talk to him at all, otherwise he would order the rest slaves to kill me on the same spot without hesitation.

One day, when I thought over that I am in my home town, but I could not see my family even I am a slave too in my town, so after a while I remembered the song which my brother and I were singing when we were eating the two slices of cooked yam which our mother left for us before she went to the market on the very day that we left each other, then I was singing this song and mentioning his name in this song several times. But as his name was mentioned, so whenever his wives were hearing the name they would be flogging me, and I did not understand what they were flogging me for. And as I was singing this sorrowful song every day, so one day, they reported me to him that—"Your slave who has sores on the body is mentioning your name whenever he is singing a kind of sorrowful song, hence all the slaves are strictly banned to mention their master's name." Having heard so he told them to go and bring me before him.

When I reached there and stood before him all my body was shaking and my voice was also trembling, because if a slave is selected from many slaves like this no doubt he is going to be killed for a god. Then he told me to repeat the song that I am singing in the yard so that he may hear it. His aim was to kill me on the same spot if I mention his name. But I started to sing this song and before I reached the part that his name should be mentioned he had remembered how we left ourselves on the road under the fruit tree. So at the same moment he shouted with gladness and jumped towards me. After that he told all his wives that I am his brother who had been lost twenty-four years ago. Then the second thing he did he told his orderlies to wash me, after that he brought many costly clothes for me as a king, but the sore of my body still remained there. After this his wives gave me food with drinks, then he sent for our mother and all his friends as well.

171

Gladness becomes Weeping

After a few minutes our mother came, but she did not know me again and I myself did not her as well, and it was this day I believed that "feeling" sometimes proves the same blood if they have left each other for long time that they are the same family, because my brother did not show me to our mother when she came, because he was waiting for his friends to come before he would tell her. So as she sat down behind me she was feeling perhaps I am her son. After a while my brother's friends came, they sat in the form of a circle and I was in the centre. Then my brother told the whole of us to kneel down to pray. After the prayer he told our mother that I am her son who had been lost since I was seven years old. But when our mother with my brother's wives with his friends heard so, all shouted with gladness and held me, but when they looked at my body and saw the sore they burst into a cry which lasted for about an hour before it stopped. And it was this day I believed that if "gladness is too much it sometimes becomes weeping". Having stopped crying our mother started to treat the sore and within a week willy-nilly it has been healed.

After the second day that my brother and mother knew me and I myself knew both of them as well, then he told me how he was captured. Our mother also told me how she was captured when coming home to rescue us immediately she heard from the market that war broke into the town. She said that she was captured and taken to a town of which she did not understand their language until she left there when resold to a lame woman. She said that the work that she was doing for the lame woman was only to be carrying her wherever she was going to, but she spent only four years with her before she sold her again on the way carrying her to somewhere, because she was feeling hunger and had no money to buy the food. So the lame woman gave mother to the food-seller and took food instead of paying her money. After she was exchanged to this food-seller, the food-seller was not feeding mother at all, so if she worked for her from early in the morning till eight o'clock in the night, then she would start to work from that night till dawn for her living, so by that she had no time at all to rest or sleep both day and night and she was doing so every day for years until she had a chance to escape at night, and again she was captured on the way by another man who was the most famous slave-buyer in his town. All his slaves were performing the same kind of work which only men could be performing, but however she was working as hard as a slave man. When her master noticed how she was working as a man, then he set her free after the 8th year that he captured her.

But when she came back to the town she met none of us in the town and was in a sorrowful life until my brother came after he spent many years in various towns. When he came both of us were expecting you every day to come home but it is in vain and they did not know that it was in the Bush of Ghosts you were. Our mother told me as above. But one day when I remembered our dead cousin who I met in the 10th town of ghosts I told them about him that he had resettled down in a town in the Bush of Ghosts. I told them that I was educated from him because he had established schools and churches there. Of course when they heard so they were very surprised. They asked me whether I feared him as he had died in our town here in my presence before I left the town, so I replied that if anybody enters into the Bush of Ghosts he or her would not fear for anything within a week he or she had entered into it, because he or she will see "Fear" personally who bought the "Palm-Wine Drinker's" "fear" before he entered inside the "White-tree" to the "Faithful-mother". I told them further that it is in the Bush of Ghosts the "fears", "sorrows", "difficulties" all kinds of the "punishments" etc. start and there they end.

After that I hinted to them about the "SECRET-SOCIETY OF GHOSTS" which is celebrated once in every century. I told them that as it is near to be celebrated I like to be present there so that I may bring some of its news to them and other people. But when both of them heard so again from me, they said that I will not go to the Bush of Ghosts again in their presence. Of course they said this of their own accord, because I dreamed a dream that I am present when this "Secret Society of Ghosts" is performing and I believe so, because my dream always comes to the truth in future, however it may be. So you will hear about this news in due course.

"This is what hatred did."

The Palm-Wine Drinkard

and his dead Palm-Wine Tapster in the Deads' Town

With an Introduction
by
Michael Thelwell

Introduction

It happened in the Yoruba town of Abeokuta, somewhat more than sixty but less than seventy years ago, on a night just before the second Ogun festival. The sound of singing and joyous cries rose from behind the tall mud walls of the compound of the *Odafin* Odegbami. It was the sound of the midwives praising the gods (*Orishas*) and ancestors and proclaiming the birth of a boy.

The boy's father, the firstborn son of the *Odafin*, known as *Tutuola*—"the gentle one"—received the news calmly (this was not, after all, his first son). He uttered the traditional words of thanksgiving, rewarded the midwives, and then made his way through the complex of rooms and passageways to the *obi* or receiving room of his father where he informed the old man.

The *Odafin*, the spiritual leader of his clan, sub-chief, and administrative ruler of a section of the city of Abeokuta, was a figure of power and authority, as befitted the head of a large and influential compound. His name, Odegbami, meant "Gift from Ogun," or alternately "It was hunting that saved me" for the Yoruba language is subtle and flexible and the same combination of phrases can be variously interpreted. His strong name indicated that the *Odafin* was fa-

177

vored by the great *Orisha* Ogun, lord of fire and iron and therefore father of technology and political power and patron of smiths, warriors and hunters. He was "one of Ogun's children."

Anticipating his son's message, the old man would have had ready to hand kola and palm-wine with which to offer thanks and libation to the ancestors. Then he whispered into his son's ear the name already selected after divination and consultation with the elders. "His name shall be Olatubusun," the old man pronounced gravely. Tutuola thanked him for the name.

At sunrise the *Odafin* and his heir-apparent would go to offer the proper and necessary sacrifice of thanksgiving in the upper room where the great ancestral mask or *egugun,* the visible symbol of the clan's power, resided. Then they would go to the *ile-Orisha,* the house of the *Orishas,* where the images of the gods were enshrined. But for the moment Tutuola took his leave and made his way back to the birth chamber where the grandmother waited to whisper the name and *irike* or birth-poem into the ear of the newborn, thus setting the new spirit in its appropriate place in the world of mankind, society, and history.

If Tutuola was disappointed at the name, he was not surprised. Looked at in one way, the name was almost a cliché. In its most obvious meaning Olatubusun could mean simply "wealth increases," which was, among the Yoruba and all African peoples, true of the birth of any child, particularly a son. He might have wished for a name more powerfully portentous, more resonant with omen. But a birth was not extraordinary in this household. The *Odafin* had six wives and more than twenty children and he himself had three wives and was already the father of a number of sons. Yet, like every father, he would have welcomed a name of unique power and promise, something that would mark even so junior a son for special prominence. Not that there was anything wrong with this name Olatubusun. For all wealth was not the same and no wealth was bad. The boy might be the bringer of a special kind of wealth, perhaps in ways not yet contemplated in the councils of the elders. For was not the world changing before their very eyes? Had not the great oracle under the rock foretold such change? By its very lack of specificity this name could suggest that the boy was specially chosen. This fourthborn son will see things that we have never seen, mused the gentle and thoughtful Tutuola as he went to look upon his son.

According to local legend a small band of refugees, fleeing the destruction of their town during a wave of slave-taking, were guided by a spirit to a cave in the side of a hill that was capped by a spectacular granite formation. There in the cave, "under the rock," or in Yoruba "Abeokuta," they found refuge. The cave became their most sacred shrine——the seat of an oracle——and the place where festivals of sacrifice and thanksgiving, ritual re-enactments of the salvation of the town's founders and the ongoing covenant with the protective spirit, were performed.

Secure in the covenant, the town prospered, and indeed, spread so widely that the king had to appoint surrogates for different sections of the city. These *Odafins*——an appointive rather than a hereditary position——were responsible under the authority of the king for the administration of local government, the collection of taxes, and the observance and enforcement of law and tradition, both religious and secular. To be effective these appointees would have had to be figures of recognized worth; men of substance, respect, probity, and virtue within the terms of the traditional values of the culture.

The fortunes and prominence of the family had reached its zenith with the appointment of the "father," Odegbami, as *Odafin* of their sector. Ironically, this rise in the family fortunes coincided with a serious erosion of the primacy of traditional values and practice. As befitted his civic status and influence, the *Odafin* had taken additional wives and expanded his compound. His son Tutuola, next in succession for head of the clan, did likewise. As was proper, the *Odafin* commissioned the finest artists of Abeokuta to create a new and elaborate *egugun.* This new ancestral mask, ornate and imposing in its awful beauty and authority, was consecrated and enshrined in an upper room specially built for that purpose. The elaborate mask was at once a symbol of the family's spiritual foundation and an expression of its material prosperity. So too was the *ile-ere* of the compound, the large room in which imposing images of important *Orishas—Shango, Oya, Ogun, Obatala*—were carefully tended and ministered to by the *Odafin* himself as part of his responsibility as spiritual head of the household. All of this was no more than what tradition required and was supported for a time by produce from ancestral lands and the revenues and entitlements of office.

What was not anticipated was the way in which the integrity of the indigenous Yoruba institutions of Abeokuta would begin to feel an unprecedented and unassimilable

pressure. This is not to say that the region had been cultur-
ally insulated. At the time of Odegbami's appointment (circa
1900–10), Islam had long been present and mosques were
not unknown in the city. Islamic culture and doctrine and
Yoruba belief and practice co-existed relatively free of tension, for Islam in West Africa went back many centuries and
each system had had time and pressing reason to adjust,
however uneasily, to the peculiar character of the other.

The new pressure came at this time from an intolerant,
bumptious, and vigorously proselytizing European Christianity, a new dispensation that was not to content itself
with the harvesting of souls and the elevation of the spirit,
but which increasingly set itself the task of transforming
societies. The missionaries—courageous and mostly
doomed—frequently brought, or possibly had to bring, to
their civilizing mission that narrow self-righteousness that is
so often the sword and shield of the religious idealist.

More significantly, hard on the heels of their chapels,
mission schools, and hospitals had come new laws and moral
codes which were enforced by native courts, a parallel civil
service buttressed by police and military forces, a mercantile
economy accompanied by a different system of currency, and
a new and mysterious system of land tenure, all of which in
combination represented during the transition first a parallel government and then a superceding one. The cumulative
effect of this challenge on all the traditional institutions of
religion, culture, education, commerce, and government was
the growing devaluation of native conceptions of identity,
authority, and value on civic, moral and personal levels
alike.

It was during this period of transitional confusion—

a chaos of values and moral authority—that the birth of Olatubusun was celebrated according to custom and tradition, in circumstances themselves emblematic of this tension.

The child was born into a powerfully traditional household—to Christian parents. From his earliest memories he recalls that "I met my father and mother as Christians." Though nearly all of his children adopted the new faith, the *Odafin* never did. While he lived, he was master of a traditional household in which all the *Orishas'* festivals were celebrated, ancestral feast days observed, and the spectacular dancing *egugun* regularly received the petitions and offerings of women wanting children. Every Thursday the household awakened to the sound of ritual drumming and the chanting of the *babalawo* or sacred drummer. On Sundays the Christians went to church. But in that house, young Olatubusun remembers, "in a large room I met all the gods, Ogun, god of iron, Shango, god of thunder, Oya, Oshun, Obatala . . . all of them." This was an encounter certain to make a lasting impression on the young boy. As Robert Farris Thompson, our most inspired Africanist, has observed, "A child growing up among the Yoruba is exposed daily to one of the finest traditions of sculpture produced by any people." And the pantheon of gods, the *Orisha* system, was considered by Frobenious to be "richer, more original, more rigorous, and well-preserved than any of the forms coming down to us from classical antiquity."

But the youthful imagination was fed not only by the awesome images looming in the dim, sacred *ile-ere*. Ritual, spectacle, song, dance, drumbeats, mystery, and power surrounded him. Poetry, pageantry, and history combined in the luminous presence of the *egugun* as the ancestor became flesh and danced among his children. The boy was attracted to the art of the storyteller, a tradition of oral literature that had reached a very high level of complexity and diversity among the Yoruba. But to call these expressions of the culture "stories" is reductive. As developed in this culture, their elaborate narrative line incorporated elements of theater, music, mime, ritual, magic, dance, and the linguistic elements of proverb, poetry, riddle, parable, and song. They were not told so much as performed, dramatically reenacted, so that the accomplished taleteller had to be master of a range of skills. He was at once actor, mime, impressionist, singer, dancer, composer, and conductor, using his range of artistic skills and even the audience and environment to create a multidimensional experience that has no obvious equivalent in Western culture. A more elaborate expression of this form—most often with a strictly religious reference, being ritual recreations of sacred myths—was performed by costumed dancers to the accompaniment of religious music, and became known to Western observers as "folk operas."

It was in this dynamic, powerfully dramatic, and evocative, yet extremely *ordered* environment that the boy's formative sensibilities developed. At about fourteen years old, a new Christian, he left the traditional compound for the Salvation Army School, literally a new world. The death of the distinguished grandfather, followed a few years later by that of the father, brought further changes. The family yielded to new realities and Europeanized their name. Mostly in deference to the great man—now a respected ancestor—who had brought them prominence, they took the surname *Odegbami.* Only the boy Olatubusun, junior

183

though he was in the lineage, dissented. He either chose or was given the Christian name Amos for the fierce old prophet of righteousness ("Justice shall come down like a mighty water. . . ."). And with filial loyalty he took his father's name, hence Amos Tutuola.

Change was rapid. The grand household of the *Odafin* could not be maintained. In this transition period, there appear to have been the usual problems of succession, inheritance, entitlement, and questions about which lands belonged to the family (who in any case had now neither the power, prestige, nor revenues of former times) and which to the office. The family dispersed to make their way in the strange world where 2,000 cowries, a substantial sum in traditional exchange, translated to sixpence in British currency. Amos Tutuola attended the Anglican Central School in Abeokuta while his father, now living on some family lands a short distance from Abeokuta, was alive. Upon his death the "junior" son had to end his formal education. He went to Lagos, became apprenticed to a coppersmith, and joined the British army, occupations that must have brought a smile to the face of the dead grandfather since both were under the jurisdiction of his patron *Orisha*, Ogun.

At the war's end he was demobilized with thousands of other young men and thrust upon his own devices to make his way in the world. He secured, in his own words, "this unsatisfactory job" as a messenger in one of the civil service departments in Lagos. There he might have lived and worked in modest circumstances and obscurity save for a fortuitous accident. One of the Commonwealth information journals that the British used to circulate in their colo-

Introduction

nial territories and at home caught the eye of Mr. Tutuola. His attention was attracted to the cover, an impressive full-color reproduction of a sculpture of an *Orisha*. The section on Nigeria contained many such "portraits" of gods, artfully photographed in color, and his mind rushed back to the *ile-ere* of his grandfather's compound. He bought the journal.

Well, it happened that since I was young and I was in the infant school which we call nowadays primary, each time I went to my village I learnt many tales and I was much interested in it so that later when I could read and write I wrote many of them down. And as much as I had great interest in these, I took myself to be one of the best taletellers in the school for the other children. Later, having left the school, one day I bought one magazine. I was working then. I had joined the army and left the army. I was engaged as a messenger by the Department of Labor. One day I got one magazine published by the Government of Nigeria Information Service. It carried all the festivals, Oya, Ogun everything. It was a quarterly magazine, so I bought the magazine and started to read it. It contained very lovely portraits of the gods. When I bought the magazine I read it to a page where books which were published were advertised. Well . . . I had read some of those books when I was at school. Then I saw that one of the books which were advertised here was about our tales, our Yoruba tales. "But Eh! By the way, when I was at school I was a good taleteller! Why, could I not write my own? Ooh, I am very good at this thing." The following day I took up my pen and paper and I started to write The Palm-Wine

Introduction

Drinkard. *Well, I wrote the script of* Palm-Wine *and kept it in the house. I didn't know where to send it to.*

Again, the following quarter I bought another magazine of the same type. Fortunately when I read it, I got to where it advertised "Manuscripts Wanted" overseas. Well then! Immediately I sent my story to the advertiser. When my script got to them they wrote me in about two weeks saying that they did not accept manuscripts which were not concerned with religion, Christian religion. But, they would not return my manuscript. They would find a publisher for me because the story was so strange to them that they would not be happy if they returned it to me. By that I should be patient with them to help me find a publisher. Then a year later I got a letter from Faber & Faber that they got my manuscript from Lutheran World Press. Faber & Faber said that the story . . . uh they were wondering whether I found the story fallen down from somebody because it is very strange to them. They wondered because they were surprised to see such a story . . . they wanted to know whether I had made it up or got it from somebody else . . . and they would be happy if I would leave the story for them to do it as they want. I reply that I didn't know anything about book publishing and so on, so I leave everything for you to do as you see is good. . . . Then after about six months now they publish the book in 1952 and sent a copy to me. That is how I started to write.

What was in my mind? Well. Oh . . . the time I wrote it, what was in my mind was that I noticed that our young men, our young sons and daughters did not pay much attention to our traditional things or culture or customs.

Introduction

*They adopted, they concentrated their minds only on Euro-
pean things. They left our customs, so if I do this they may
change their mind ... to remember our custom, not to leave
it to die. . . . That was my intention.*

Appearing unannounced and without fanfare in the British edition in 1952 and in the Grove Press American edition
in 1953, the book has had the kind of career of which
publishing legends are made. I cannot say to what extent the
lineage's "wealth increased" as a consequence, but certainly
the book has continued in print ever since. It has been
translated into fifteen languages, European and non-Euro-
pean as well. It seems to enjoy a respectable and steady
circulation and to have attracted a loyal following world-
wide. It is frequently to be found on syllabi of university
courses in religion, anthropology, psychology, and even literature and has been followed by *My Life in the Bush of
Ghosts* (1954) and *The Brave African Huntress.*

I shall not speculate—intriguing though that prospect
be—on precisely which chords of modern literary sensibility
are set resonating under the stimulus of *Drinkard*'s unique
vision. Certainly one can see where certain Jungian and
Freudian critics could, with barely compatible assumptions,
find much to engage them in its world. So too can surrealists
and devotees of magical realism find within it hospitable
territory on which to plant their respective standards. It is,
however, more important to attempt to identify the cultural
and intellectual provenance of the material, and to deter-
mine its specific relationship to the traditions that produced
it.

This novel is a cultural hybrid, the child of the clash of

cultures I have been describing. The stories in it are translations—more accurately, transliterations—of conventional folktales into the idiomatic "young English," as Dylan Thomas called it, of the Nigerian masses. It is clear from the reading, and even more so when one listens to the author telling a story, exactly how difficult the translation process really is. This is not simply "young English" but *new* English, an English whose vocabulary is bent and twisted into the service of a different language's nuances, syntax, and interior logic. The result is original and often startling.

Apart from the aesthetic distance between rhetorical devices, linguistic traditions, rhythms, puns, repetitions, cadences, nuances, metaphors, and idioms, the total poetic sensibility of one language and culture and that of another, there is a further consideration. We are looking at only one element of the form. The other inclusive aesthetic dimensions of the tradition—dramatic voice, expression, pantomime, song, and rhythm—are necessarily absent in the purely literary form. To that extent it is a new form. And if the form is new, what survives presumably must be "sensibility."

It is usual to hear that these tales express the "traditional sensibility" of an "African" worldview and offer a window into the inchoate and frightening world of the primitive imagination. So general a statement would be quite misleading. The stories and the narrative and visionary techniques reflect one particular and identifiable aspect of a complex and sophisticated tradition.

The central Yoruba tradition—that of the sacred myth describing the creation, evolution, and jurisdiction of the deities and historical heroes—represents a remarkably rigorous cosmology of intellectual coherence and elegance. It is a universe of elemental forces both natural and social which finds metaphoric expression in a pantheon of deities, whose complicated interrelationships, jurisdictions, and necessities are rationalized into an architectonic system of knowledge. The sophisticated worldview embodied in this myth has as its central value the balancing and harmonizing of powerful forces—natural, numinous, and social.

Out of the interplay of deities, ancestors, and humanity, through a process of mutual obligation expressed in language, ritual, and protocol as handed down by tradition, society became possible. A universe of history, stability, morality, and order was achieved.

But bordering on this system of stability was terra incognita: the evil forest, the bad bush. Here was the home of chaos, where random spirits without name or history, of bizarre forms and malignant intent were to be found. This was the domain of the deformed, the unnatural, and the abominable. The Sunufo, distant cousins of the Yoruba, have a mask that expresses this. It has the snout of an alligator, the tusks of a boar, the horn of a rhinoceros, and the ears of a zebra. It represents an animal that existed before order was imposed on the world.

In the oral tradition the folktale—a moral and cautionary story but clearly recognized as fiction and entertainment—had free range of this random and arbitrary world. Because they were intended for entertainment and instruction, these tales could be as horrific, frightening, and bizarre as the imagination could render them. They required the willing suspension of disbelief.

Many of Tutuola's motifs and even complete tales and

images are drawn from this genre. But the structure and cumulative effect, the vision, is the creation of this sensitive and pensive man. To what extent this overriding vision, one of constant suffering, danger, insecurity, and struggle is the product of the cultural trauma, uncertainty, and psychic alienation through which that generation passed is hard to say.

Amos Tutuola says that he wrote to "tell of my ancestors and how they lived in their days. They lived with immortal creatures of the forest. But now the forests are gone. I believe the immortal creatures must have moved away."

Some years ago he returned to the ancestral compound in order to visit the *ile-Orisha.* The compound was ruinate, the *egugun* had disappeared, and in his words, "The gods had perished."

—Michael Thelwell
April, 1984

I was a palm-wine drinkard since I was a boy of ten years of age. I had no other work more than to drink palm-wine in my life. In those days we did not know other money, except COWRIES, so that everything was very cheap, and my father was the richest man in our town.

My father got eight children and I was the eldest among them, all of the rest were hard workers, but I myself was an expert palm-wine drinkard. I was drinking palm-wine from morning till night and from night till morning. By that time I could not drink ordinary water at all except palm-wine.

But when my father noticed that I could not do any work more than to drink, he engaged an expert palm-wine tapster for me; he had no other work more than to tap palm-wine every day.

So my father gave me a palm-tree farm which was nine miles square and it contained 560,000 palm-trees, and this palm-wine tapster was tapping one hundred and fifty kegs of palm-wine every morning, but before 2 o'clock P.M., I would have drunk all of it; after that he would go and tap another 75 kegs in the evening which I would be drinking till morning. So my friends were uncountable by that time and they were drinking palm-wine with me from morning till a late hour in the night. But when my palm-wine tapster completed the period of 15 years that he was tapping the palm-wine for me, then my father died suddenly, and when it was the 6th month after my father had died, the tapster went to the palm-tree farm on a Sunday evening to tap palm-wine for me. When he reached the farm, he climbed one of the tallest palm-trees in the farm to tap palm-wine but as he was tapping on, he fell down unexpectedly and died at the foot of the palm-tree as a result of injuries. As I was waiting for him to bring the palm-wine, when I saw that he did not return in time, because he was not keeping me long like that before, then I called two of my friends to accompany me to the farm. When we reached the farm, we began to look at every palm-tree, after a while we found him under the palm-tree, where he fell down and died.

But what I did first when we saw him dead there, was that I climbed another palm-tree which was near the spot, after that I tapped palm-wine and drank it to my satisfaction before I came back to the spot. Then both my friends who accompanied me to the farm and I dug a pit under the palm-tree that he fell down as a grave and buried him there, after that we came back to the town.

When it was early in the morning of the next day, I had no palm-wine to drink at all, and throughout that day I felt not so happy as before; I was seriously sat down in my parlour, but when it was the third day that I had no palm-wine at all, all my friends did not come to my house again, they left me there alone, because there was no palm-wine for them to drink.

But when I completed a week in my house without palm-wine, then I went out and I saw one of them in the town, so I saluted him, he answered but he did not approach me at all, he hastily went away.

Then I started to find out another expert palm-wine tapster, but I could not get me one who could tap the palm-wine to my requirement. When there was no palm-wine for me to drink I started to drink ordinary water which I was unable to taste before, but I did not satisfy with it as palm-wine.

When I saw that there was no palm-wine for me again, and nobody could tap it for me, then I thought within myself that old people were saying that the whole people who had died in this world, did not go to heaven directly, but they were living in one place somewhere in this world. So that I said that I would find out where my palm-wine tapster who had died was.

One fine morning, I took all my native juju and also my father's juju with me and I left my father's hometown to find out whereabouts was my tapster who had died.

But in those days, there were many wild animals and every place was covered by thick bushes and forests; again, towns and villages were not near each other as nowadays, and as I was travelling from bushes to bushes and from forests to forests and sleeping inside it for many days and months, I was sleeping on the branches of trees, because spirits etc. were just like partners, and to save my life from them; and again I could spend two or three months before reaching a town or a village. Whenever I reached a town or a village, I would spend almost four months there, to find out my palm-wine tapster from the inhabitants of that town or village and if he did not reach there, then I would leave there and continue my journey to another town or village.

The Palm-Wine Drinkard

After the seventh month that I had left my home town, I
reached a town and went to an old man, this old man was
not a really man, he was a god and he was eating with his
wife when I reached there. When I entered the house I
saluted both of them, they answered me well, although
nobody should enter his house like that as he was a god, but
I myself was a god and juju-man. Then I told the old man
(god) that I am looking for my palm-wine tapster who had
died in my town some time ago, he did not answer to my
question but asked me first what was my name? I replied
that my name was "Father of gods who could do everything
in this world," then he said: "was that true" and I said yes;
after that he told me to go to his native black-smith in an
unknown place, or who was living in another town, and
bring the right thing that he had told the black-smith to
make for him. He said that if I could bring the right thing
that he told the black-smith to make for him, then he would
believe that I was the "Father of gods who could do everything in this world" and he would tell me where my tapster
was.

Immediately this old man told or promised me so, I went
away, but after I had travelled about one mile away then I
used one of my juju and at once I changed into a very big
bird and flew back to the roof of the old man's house; but
as I stood on the roof of his house, many people saw me
there. They came nearer and looked at me on the roof, so
when the old man noticed that many had surrounded his
house and were looking at the roof, he and his wife came out
from the house and when he saw me (bird) on the roof, he
told his wife that if he had not sent me to his native
black-smith to bring the bell that he told the black-smith to

make for him, he would tell me to mention the name of the bird. But at the same time that he said so, I knew what he wanted from the black-smith and I flew away to his black-smith, and when I reached there I told the black-smith that the old man (god) told me to bring his bell which he had told him to make for him. So the black-smith gave me the bell; after that, I returned to the old man with the bell and when he saw me with the bell, he and his wife were surprised and also shocked at that moment.

After that he told his wife to give me food, but after I had eaten the food, he told me again, that there remained another wonderful work to do for him, before he would tell me whereabouts my tapster was. When it was 6.30 A.M. of the following morning, he (god) woke me up, and gave me a wide and strong net which was the same in colour as the ground of that town. He told me to go and bring "Death" from his house with the net. When I left his house or the town about a mile, there I saw a junction of roads and I was doubtful when I reached the junction, I did not know which was Death's road among these roads, and when I thought within myself that as it was the market day, and all the market goers would soon be returning from the market—I lied down on the middle of the roads, I put my head to one of the roads, my left hand to one, right hand to another one, and my both feet to the rest, after that I pretended as I had slept there. But when all the market goers were returning from the market, they saw me lied down there and shouted thus:—"Who was the mother of this fine boy, he slept on the roads and put his head towards Death's road."

Then I began to travel on Death's road, and I spent about eight hours to reach there, but to my surprise I did not meet anybody on this road until I reached there and I was afraid because of that. When I reached his (Death's) house, he was not at home by that time, he was in his yam garden which was very close to his house, and I met a small rolling drum in his verandah, then I beat it to Death as a sign of salutation. But when he (Death) heard the sound of the drum, he said thus:—"Is that man still alive or dead?" Then I replied "I am still alive and I am not a dead man."

But at the same time that he heard so from me, he was greatly annoyed and he commanded the drum with a kind of voice that the strings of the drum should tight me there; as a matter of fact, the strings of the drum tighted me so that I was hardly breathing.

When I felt that these strings did not allow me to breathe and again every part of my body was bleeding too much, then I myself commanded the ropes of the yams in his garden to tight him there, and the yams in his garden to tight him there, and the yam stakes should begin to beat him also. After I had said so and at the same time, all the ropes of the yams in his garden tighted him hardly, and all the yam stakes were beating him repeatedly, so when he (Death) saw that these stakes were beating him repeatedly, then he commanded the strings of the drum which tighted me to release me, and I was released at the same time. But when I saw that I was released, then I myself commanded the ropes of the yams to release him and the yam stakes to stop beating him, and he was released at once. After he was released by the ropes of yams and yam stakes, he came to his house and met me at his verandah, then we shook hands together, and he told me to enter the house, he put me to one of his rooms, and after a while, he brought food to me and

196

we ate it together, after that we started conversations which went thus:——He (Death) asked me from where did I come? I replied that I came from a certain town which was not so far from his place. Then he asked what did I come to do? I told him that I had been hearing about him in my town and all over the world and I thought within myself that one day I should come and visit or to know him personally. After that he replied that his work was only to kill the people of the world, after that he got up and told me to follow him and I did so.

He took me around his house and his yam garden too, he showed me the skeleton bones of human-beings which he had killed since a century ago and showed me many other things also, but there I saw that he was using skeleton bones of human-beings as fuel woods and skull heads of human-beings as his basins, plates and tumblers etc.

Nobody was living near or with him there, he was living lonely, even bush animals and birds were very far away from his house. So when I wanted to sleep at night, he gave me a wide black cover cloth and then gave me a separate room to sleep inside, but when I entered the room, I met a bed which was made with bones of human-beings; but as this bed was terrible to look at or to sleep on it, I slept under it instead, because I knew his trick already. Even as this bed was very terrible, I was unable to sleep under as I lied down there because of fear of the bones of human-beings, but I lied down there awoke. To my surprise was that when it was about two o'clock in the mid-night, there I saw somebody enter into the room cautiously with a heavy club in his hands, he came nearer to the bed on which he had told me to sleep, then he clubbed the bed with all his power, he clubbed the centre of the bed thrice and he returned cautiously, he thought that I slept on that bed and he thought also that he had killed me.

But when it was 6 o'clock early in the morning, I first woke up and went to the room in which he slept, I woke him up, so when he heard my voice, he was frightened, even he could not salute me at all when he got up from his bed, because he thought that he had killed me last night.

But the second day that I slept there, he did not attempt to do anything again, but I woke up by two o'clock of that night, and went to the road which I should follow to the town and I travelled about a quarter of a mile to his house, then I stopped and dug a pit of his (Death's) size on the centre of that road, after that I spread the net which the old man gave me to bring him (Death) with on that pit, then I returned to his house, but he did not wake up as I was playing this trick.

When it was 6 o'clock in the morning, I went to his door and woke him up as usual, then I told him that I wanted to return to my town this morning, so that I wanted him to lead me a short distance; then he got up from his bed and he began to lead me as I told him, but when he led me to the place that I had dug, I told him to sit down, so I myself sat down on the road side, but as he sat down on the net, he fell into the pit, and without any ado I rolled up the net with him and put him on my head and I kept going to the old man's house who told me to go and bring him Death.

As I was carrying him along the road, he was trying all his efforts to escape or to kill me, but I did not give him a chance to do that. When I had travelled about eight hours, then I reached the town and went straight to the old man's house who told me to go and bring Death from his house. When I reached the old man's house, he was inside his room, then I called him and told him that I had brought Death that he told me to go and bring. But immediately he heard from me that I had brought Death and when he saw him on my head, he was greatly terrified and raised alarm that he thought nobody could go and bring Death from his house, then he told me to carry him (Death) back to his house at once, and he (old man) hastily went back to his room and started to close all his doors and windows, but before he could close two or three of his windows, I threw down Death before his door and at the same time that I threw him down, the net cut into pieces and Death found his way out.

Then the old man and his wife escaped through the windows and also the whole people in that town ran away for their lives and left their properties there. (The old man had thought that Death would kill me if I went to his house, because nobody could reach Death's house and return, but I had known the old man's trick already.)

So that since the day that I had brought Death out from his house, he has no permanent place to dwell or stay, and we are hearing his name about in the world. This was how I brought out Death to the old man who told me to go and bring him before he (old man) would tell me whereabouts my palm-wine tapster was that I was looking for before I reached that town and went to the old man.

But the old man who had promised me that if I could go to Death's house and bring him, he would tell me whereabouts my palm-wine tapster was, could not wait and fulfil his promise because he himself and his wife were narrowly escaped from that town.

The Palm-Wine Drinkard

Then I left the town without knowing where my tapster was, and I started another fresh journey.

When it was the fifth month since I had left that town, then I reached another town which was not so big, although there was a large and famous market. At the same time that I entered the town, I went to the house of the head of the town who received me with kindness into his house; after a little while he told one of his wives to give me food and after I had eaten the food, he told his wife to give me palm-wine too; I drank the palm-wine to excess as when I was in my town or as when my tapster was alive. But when I tasted the palm-wine given to me there, I said that I got what I wanted here. After I had eaten the food and drunk the palm-wine to my satisfaction, the head of the town who received me as his guest asked for my name, I told him that my name was called "Father of gods who could do anything in this world." As he heard this from me, he was soon faint with fear. After that he asked me what I came to him for. I replied that I was looking for my palm-wine tapster who had died in my town some time ago. Then he told me that he knew where the tapster was.

After that he told me that if I could help him to find out his daughter who was captured by a curious creature from the market which was in that town, and bring her to him, then he would tell me whereabouts my tapster was.

He said furthermore that as I called myself "Father of gods who could do anything in this world," this would be very easy for me to do; he said so.

I did not know that his daughter was taken away by a curious creature from the market.

I was about to refuse to go and find out his daughter who was taken away from the market by a curious creature, but when I remembered my name I was ashamed to refuse. So I agreed to find out his daughter. There was a big market in this town from where the daughter was captured, and the market-day was fixed for every 5th day and the whole people of that town and from all the villages around the town and also spirits and curious creatures from various bushes and forests were coming to this market every 5th day to sell or buy articles. By 4 o'clock in the evening, the market would close for that day and then everybody would be returning to his or her destination or to where he or she came from. But the daughter of the head of that town was a petty trader and she was due to be married before she was taken away from the market. Before that time, her father was telling her to marry a man but she did not listen to her father; when her father saw that she did not care to marry anybody, he gave her to a man for himself, but this lady refused totally to marry that man who was introduced to her by her father. So that her father left her to herself.

This lady was very beautiful as an angel but no man could convince her for marriage. So, one day she went to the market on a market-day as she was doing before, or to sell her articles as usual; on that market-day, she saw a curious creature in the market, but she did not know where the man came from and never knew him before.

THE DESCRIPTION OF THE CURIOUS CREATURE:—

He was a beautiful "complete" gentleman, he dressed with the finest and most costly clothes, all the parts of his body

were completed, he was a tall man but stout. As this gentleman came to the market on that day, if he had been an
article or animal for sale, he would be sold at least for £2000
(two thousand pounds). As this complete gentleman came to
the market on that day, and at the same time that this lady
saw him in the market, she did nothing more than to ask
him where he was living, but this fine gentleman did not
answer her or approach her at all. But when she noticed that
the fine or complete gentleman did not listen to her, she left
her articles and began to watch the movements of the complete gentleman about in the market and left her articles
unsold.

By and by the market closed for that day then the whole
people in the market were returning to their destinations
etc., and the complete gentleman was returning to his own
too, but as this lady was following him about in the market
all the while, she saw him when he was returning to his
destination as others did, then she was following him (complete gentleman) to an unknown place. But as she was
following the complete gentleman along the road, he was
telling her to go back or not to follow him, but the lady did
not listen to what he was telling her, and when the complete
gentleman had tired of telling her not to follow him or to
go back to her town, he left her to follow him.

DO NOT FOLLOW UNKNOWN MAN'S BEAUTY

But when they had travelled about twelve miles away from
that market, they left the road on which they were travel-

ling and started to travel inside an endless forest in which only all the terrible creatures were living.

RETURN THE PARTS OF BODY TO THE OWNERS; OR HIRED PARTS OF THE COMPLETE GENTLEMAN'S BODY TO BE RETURNED

As they were travelling along in this endless forest then the complete gentleman in the market that the lady was following, began to return the hired parts of his body to the owners and he was paying them the rentage money. When he reached where he hired the left foot, he pulled it out, he gave it to the owner and paid him, and they kept going; when they reached the place where he hired the right foot, he pulled it out and gave it to the owner and paid for the rentage. Now both feet had returned to the owners, so he began to crawl along on the ground, by that time, that lady wanted to go back to her town or her father, but the terrible and curious creature or the complete gentleman did not allow her to return or go back to her town or her father again and the complete gentleman said thus:——"I had told you not to follow me before we branched into this endless forest which belongs to only terrible and curious creatures, but when I became a half-bodied incomplete gentleman you wanted to go back, now that cannot be done, you have failed. Even you have never seen anything yet, just follow me."

When they went furthermore, then they reached where he hired the belly, ribs, chest etc., then he pulled them out and gave them to the owner and paid for the rentage.

Now to this gentleman or terrible creature remained only the head and both arms with neck, by that time he could not crawl as before but only went jumping on as a bull-frog and now this lady was soon faint for this fearful creature whom she was following. But when the lady saw every part of this complete gentleman in the market was spared or hired and he was returning them to the owners, then she began to try all her efforts to return to her father's town, but she was not allowed by this fearful creature at all.

When they reached where he hired both arms, he pulled them out and gave them to the owner, he paid for them; and they were still going on in this endless forest, they reached the place where he hired the neck, he pulled it out and gave it to the owner and paid for it as well.

A FULL-BODIED GENTLEMAN REDUCED TO HEAD

Now this complete gentleman was reduced to head and when they reached where he hired the skin and flesh which covered the head, he returned them, and paid to the owner, now the complete gentleman in the market reduced to a "SKULL" and this lady remained with only "Skull". When the lady saw that she remained with only Skull, she began to say that her father had been telling her to marry a man, but she did not listen to or believe him.

When the lady saw that the gentleman became a Skull, she began to faint, but the Skull told her if she would die she would die and she would follow him to his house. But by the time that he was saying so, he was humming with a terrible voice and also grew very wild and even if there was a person two miles away he would not have to listen before hearing him, so this lady began to run away in that forest for her life, but the Skull chased her and within a few yards, he caught her, because he was very clever and smart as he was only Skull and he could jump a mile to the second before coming down. He caught the lady in this way: so when the lady was running away for her life, he hastily ran to her front and stopped her as a log of wood.

By and by, this lady followed the Skull to his house, and the house was a hole which was under the ground. When they reached there both of them entered the hole. But there were only Skulls living in that hole. At the same time that they entered the hole, he tied a single cowrie on the neck of this lady with a kind of rope, after that, he gave her a large frog on which she sat as a stool, then he gave a whistle to a Skull of this kind to keep watch on this lady whenever she wanted to run away. Because the Skull knew already that the lady would attempt to run away from the hole. Then he went to the back-yard to where his family were staying in the day time till night.

But one day, the lady attempted to escape from the hole, and at the same time that the Skull who was watching her whistle to the rest of the Skulls that were in the back-yard, the whole of them rushed out to the place where the lady sat on the bull-frog, so they caught her, but as all of them were rushing out, they were rolling on the ground as if a thousand petrol drums were pushing along a hard road. After she was caught, then they brought her back to sit on the same frog as usual. If the Skull who was watching her fell asleep, and if the lady wanted to escape, the cowrie that was tied on her neck would raise up the alarm with a terrible

205

noise, so that the Skull who was watching her would wake up at once and then the rest of the Skull's family would rush out from the back in thousands to the lady and ask her what she wanted to do with a curious and terrible voice.

But the lady could not talk at all, because as the cowrie had been tied on her neck, she became dumb at the same moment.

THE FATHER OF GODS SHOULD FIND OUT WHEREABOUTS THE DAUGHTER OF THE HEAD OF THE TOWN WAS

Now as the father of the lady first asked for my name and I told him that my name was "Father of gods who could do anything in this world," then he told me that if I could find out where his daughter was and bring her to him, then he would tell me where my palm-wine tapster was. But when he said so, I was jumping up with gladness that he should promise me that he would tell me where my tapster was. I agreed to what he said; the father and parent of this lady never knew whereabouts their daughter was, but they had information that the lady followed a complete gentleman in the market. As I was the "Father of gods who could do anything in this world," when it was at night I sacrificed to my juju with a goat.

And when it was early in the morning, I sent for forty kegs of palm-wine, after I had drunk it all, I started to investigate whereabouts was the lady. As it was the market-day, I started the investigation from the market. But as I was a juju-man, I knew all the kinds of people in that market.

When it was exactly 9 o'clock A.M., the very complete gentleman whom the lady followed came to the market again, and at the same time that I saw him, I knew that he was a curious and terrible creature.

THE LADY WAS NOT TO BE BLAMED FOR FOLLOWING THE SKULL AS A COMPLETE GENTLEMAN

I could not blame the lady for following the Skull as a complete gentleman to his house at all. Because if I were a lady, no doubt I would follow him to wherever he would go, and still as I was a man I would jealous him more than that, because if this gentleman went to the battle field, surely, enemy would not kill him or capture him and if bombers saw him in a town which was to be bombed, they would not throw bombs on his presence, and if they did throw it, the bomb itself would not explode until this gentleman would leave that town, because of his beauty. At the same time that I saw this gentleman in the market on that day, what I was doing was only to follow him about in the market. After I looked at him for so many hours, then I ran to a corner of the market and I cried for a few minutes because I thought within myself why was I not created with beauty as this gentleman, but when I remembered that he was only a Skull, then I thanked God that He had created me without beauty, so I went back to him in the market, but I was still attracted by his beauty. So when the market closed for that day, and when everybody was returning to his or her desti-

And when it was early in the morning, I sent for foarty kegs of palm-wine, after I had drunk it all, then I started to investigate where about was the lady. As it was the market day, I started the investigation from the market. But as I was a jujuman, I knew all the kinds of people in that market. When it was exactly 9 o'clock a.m., the very complete gentleman whom the lady followed came to the market again, and at the same time that I saw him, I knew that he was a curious and terrible creature.

"THE LADY WAS NOT TO BE BLAMED FOR FOLLOWING THE SKULL AS A COMPLETE GENTLEMAN."

I could not blame the lady for following the skull as a complete gentleman to his house. Because if I were a lady, no doubt I would follow him to where-ever he would go, and still as I was a man I would jealous him more than that, because if this gentleman to the battle field, surely, enemy would not kill him or capture him and if bombers see him in a town which was to be bombed, they would not throw bombs on his presence, and if they throw it, the bomb itself would not explode until this gentleman would leave that town, because of his beauty. At the same time that I saw this gentleman in the market on that day, what I was doing was only to follow him about in the market. After I looked at him for so many hours; then I ran to a corner of the market and I cried for a few minutes, because I thought within myself that I was not created with beauty as this gentleman, but when I remembered that he was only a —

A page from the author's MS. showing the publisher's 'corrections'

nation, this gentleman was returning to his own too and I
followed him to know where he was living.

INVESTIGATION TO THE SKULL'S FAMILY'S
HOUSE

When I travelled with him a distance of about twelve miles
away to that market, the gentleman left the really road on
which we were travelling and branched into an endless forest
and I was following him, but as I did not want him to see that
I was following him, then I used one of my juju which
changed me into a lizard and followed him. But after I had
travelled with him a distance of about twenty-five miles away
in this endless forest, he began to pull out all the parts of his
body and return them to the owners, and paid them.

After I had travelled with him for another fifty miles in
this forest, then he reached his house and entered it, but I
entered it also with him, as I was a lizard. The first thing
that he did when he entered the hole (house) he went
straight to the place where the lady was, and I saw the lady
sat on a bull-frog with a single cowrie tied on her neck and
a Skull who was watching her stood behind her. After he
(gentleman) had seen that the lady was there, he went to the
back-yard where all his family were working.

THE INVESTIGATOR'S WONDERFUL WORK IN
THE SKULL'S FAMILY'S HOUSE

When I saw this lady and when the Skull who brought her
to that hole or whom I followed from the market to that hole
went to the back-yard, then I changed myself to a man as

before, then I talked to the lady but she could not answer me at all, she only showed that she was in a serious condition. The Skull who was guarding her with a whistle fell asleep at that time.

To my surprise, when I helped the lady to stand up from the frog on which she sat, the cowrie that was tied on her neck made a curious noise at once, and when the Skull who was watching her heard the noise, he woke up and blew the whistle to the rest, then the whole of them rushed to the place and surrounded the lady and me, but at the same time that they saw me there, one of them ran to a pit which was not so far from that spot, the pit was filled with cowries. He picked one cowrie out of the pit, after that he was running towards me, and the whole crowd wanted to tie the cowrie on my neck too. But before they could do that, I had changed myself into air, they could not trace me out again, but I was looking at them. I believed that the cowries in that pit were their power and to reduce the power of any human being whenever tied on his or her neck and also to make a person dumb.

Over one hour after I had dissolved into air, these Skulls went back to the back-yard, but there remained the Skull who was watching her.

After they had returned to the back-yard, I changed to a man as usual, then I took the lady from the frog, but at the same time that I touched her, the cowrie which was tied on her neck began to shout; even if a person was four miles away he would not have to listen before hearing, but immediately the Skull who was watching her heard the noise and saw me when I took her from that frog, he blew the whistle to the rest of them who were in the back-yard.

Immediately the whole Skull family heard the whistle when blew to them, they were rushing out to the place and before they could reach there, I had left their hole for the forest, but before I could travel about one hundred yards in the forest, they had rushed out from their hole to inside the forest and I was still running away with the lady. As these Skulls were chasing me about in the forest, they were rolling on the ground like large stones and also humming with terrible noise, but when I saw that they had nearly caught me or if I continued to run away like that, no doubt, they would catch me sooner, then I changed the lady to a kitten and put her inside my pocket and changed myself to a very small bird which I could describe as a "sparrow" in English language.

After that I flew away, but as I was flying in the sky, the cowrie which was tied on that lady's neck was still making a noise and I tried all my best to stop the noise, but all were in vain. When I reached home with the lady, I changed her to a lady as she was before and also myself changed to man as well. When her father saw that I brought his daughter back home, he was exceedingly glad and said thus:—"You are the 'Father of gods' as you had told me before."

But as the lady was now at home, the cowrie on her neck did not stop making a terrible noise once, and she could not talk to anybody; she showed only that she was very glad she was at home. Now I had brought the lady but she could not talk, eat or loose away the cowrie on her neck, because the terrible noise of the cowrie did not allow anybody to rest or sleep at all.

THERE REMAIN GREATER TASKS AHEAD

Now I began to cut the rope of the cowrie from her neck and
to make her talk and eat, but all my efforts were in vain. At
last I tried my best to cut off the rope of the cowrie; it only
stopped the noise, but I was unable to loose it away from her
neck.

When her father saw all my trouble, he thanked me
greatly and repeated again that as I called myself "Father of
gods who could do anything in this world" I ought to do the
rest of the work. But when he said so, I was very ashamed
and thought within myself that if I return to the Skulls' hole
or house, they might kill me and the forest was very dangerous travel always, again I could not go directly to the Skulls
in their hole and ask them how to loose away the cowrie
which was tied on the lady's neck and to make her talk and
eat.

BACK TO THE SKULL'S FAMILY'S HOUSE

On the third day after I had brought the lady to her father's
house, I returned to the endless forest for further investigation. When there remained about one mile to reach the hole
of these Skulls, there I saw the very Skull who the lady had
followed from the market as a complete gentleman to the
hole of Skull's family's house, and at the same time that I
saw him like that, I changed into a lizard and climbed a tree
which was near him.

He stood before two plants, then he cut a single opposite
leaf from the opposite plant; he held the leaf with his right

hand and he was saying thus:—"As this lady was taken from me, if this opposite leaf is not given her to eat, she will not talk for ever," after that he threw the leaf down on the ground. Then he cut another single compound leaf from the compound plant which was in the same place with the opposite plant, he held the compound leaf with his left hand and said that if this single compound is not given to this lady, to eat, the cowrie on her neck could not be loosened away for ever and it would be making a terrible noise for ever.

After he said so, he threw the leaf down at the same spot, then he jumped away. So after he had jumped very far away (luckily, I was there when he was doing all these things, and I saw the place that he threw both leaves separately), then I changed myself to a man as before, I went to the place that he threw both leaves, then I picked them up and I went home at once.

But at the same time that I reached home, I cooked both leaves separately and gave her to eat; to my surprise the lady began to talk at once. After that, I gave her the compound leaf to eat for the second time and immediately she ate that too, the cowrie which was tied on her neck by the Skull, loosened away by itself, but it disappeared at the same time. So when the father and mother saw the wonderful work which I had done for them, they brought fifty kegs of palm-wine for me, they gave me the lady as wife and two rooms in that house in which to live with them. So, I saved the lady from the complete gentleman in the market who afterwards reduced to a "Skull" and the lady became my wife since that day. This was how I got a wife.

Now as I took the lady as my wife and after I had spent

the period of six months with the parents of my wife, then I remembered my palm-wine tapster who had died in my town long ago, then I asked the father of my wife to fulfil his promise or to tell me where my tapster was, but he told me to wait for some time. Because he knew that if he told me the place by that time, I would leave his town and take his daughter away from him and he did not like to part with his daughter.

I spent three years with him in that town, but during that time, I was tapping palm-wine for myself, of course I could not tap it to the quantity that I required to drink; my wife was also helping me to carry it from the farm to the town. When I completed three and a half years in that town, I noticed that the left hand thumb of my wife was swelling out as if it was a buoy, but it did not pain her. One day, she followed me to the farm in which I was tapping the palm-wine, and to my surprise when the thumb that swelled out touched a palm-tree thorn, the thumb bust out suddenly and there we saw a male child came out of it and at the same time that the child came out from the thumb, he began to talk to us as if he was ten years of age.

Within the hour that he came down from the thumb he grew up to the height of about three feet and some inches and his voice by that time was as plain as if somebody strikes an anvil with a steel hammer. Then the first thing that he did, he asked his mother:—"Do you know my name?" His mother said no, then he turned his face to me and asked me the same question and I said no; so, he said that his name was "ZURRJIR" which means a son who would change himself into another thing very soon. But when he told us his name, I was greatly terrified, because of his terrible

214

name, and all the while that he was talking to us, he was drinking the palm-wine which I had tapped already; before five minutes he had drunk up to three kegs out of four kegs. As I was thinking in my mind how we could leave the child in the farm and run to the town, because everybody had seen that the left hand thumb of my wife had only swelled out, but she did not conceive in the right part of her body as other women do. But immediately that I was thinking so, this child took the last keg of palm-wine which he drank through the left of his head and he was going to the town directly, but nobody showed him the road that led to the town. We stood in one place looking at him as he was going, then after a little time, we followed him, but we did not see him on the road before we reached the town. To our surprise the child entered the right house that we were living in. When he entered the house, he saluted everybody that he met at home as if he had known them before, at the same time, he asked for food and they gave him the food, he ate it; after, he entered the kitchen and ate all the food that he met there as well.

But when a man saw him eating the rest of the food in the kitchen which had been prepared for night, he told him to leave the kitchen; he did not leave but started to fight the man instead of that; this wonderful child flogged the man so that he could not see well before he left the kitchen and ran away, but the child was still in the kitchen.

When all the people in the house saw what the child had done to that man, then all of them started to fight him. As he was fighting with them he was smashing everything on the ground to pieces, even he smashed all the domestic animals to death, still all the people could not conquer him.

After a little we came from the farm to the house, but at the same time that he saw us, he left all the people with whom he was fighting and met us, so when we entered the house, he showed us to everybody in the house saying that these were his father and mother. But as he had eaten all the food which had been prepared against the night, then we began to cook other food, but when it was the time to put the food down from the fire, he put it down for himself and at the same time, he began to eat that again as it was very hot, before we could stop him, he had eaten all the food and we tried all our best to take it from him, but we could not do it at all.

This was a wonderful child, because if a hundred men were to fight with him, he would flog them until they would run away. When he sat on a chair, we could not push him away. He was as strong as iron, if he stood on a place nobody could push him off. Now he became our ruler in the house, because sometimes he would say that we should not eat till night and sometimes he would drive us away from the house at mid-night and sometimes he would tell us to lie down before him for more than two hours.

As this child was stronger than everybody in that town, he went around the town and he began to burn the houses of the heads of that town to ashes, but when the people in the town saw his havocs and bad character, they called me (his father) to discuss how we could exile him away from the town, then I told the people that I knew how I would exile him away from the town. So one night, when it was one o'clock in the mid-night, when I noticed that he slept inside the room I put oil around the house and roof, but as it was thatched with leaves and also it was in the dry season, I lighted the house with fire and closed the rest of the windows and doors which he did not close before he slept. Before he woke up, there was a great fire around the house and roof, smoke did not allow him to help himself, so he burnt together with the house to ashes.

When we saw that the child had burnt into ashes all the town's people were very glad and the town was in peace. When I saw that I had seen the end of the child, then I pressed my wife's father to tell me where my palm-wine tapster was and he told me.

ON THE WAY TO AN UNKNOWN PLACE

The same day that the father of my wife told me the place that my tapster was, I told my wife to pack all our belongings and she did so, then we woke up early in the morning and started to travel to an unknown place, but when we had travelled about two miles away to that town which we left, my wife said that she forgot her gold trinket inside the house which I had burnt into ashes, she said that she had forgotten to take it away before the house was burnt into ashes. She said that she would go back and take it, but I told her that it would burn into ashes together with the house. She said that it was a metal and it could not burn into ashes and she said that she was going back to take it, and I begged her not to go back, but she refused totally, so when I saw her going back to take it, then I followed her. When we reached there, she picked a stick and began to scratch the ashes with

217

it, and there I saw that the middle of the ashes rose up suddenly and at the same time there appeared a half-bodied baby, he was talking with a lower voice like a telephone.

At the same time that we saw the ashes rise up and change into half-bodied baby, and he was also talking with a lower voice, then we started to go. Then he was telling my wife to take him along with us, to wait and take him, but as we did not stop and take him with us, he then commanded that our eyes should be blinded and we became blinded at the same moment as he said it; still we did not come back and take him, but we were going on, when he saw that we did not come back and take him, he commanded again that we should stop breathing, truly speaking we could not breathe. When we could not breathe in or out, we came back and took him along with us. As we were going on the road, he told my wife to carry him by head, and as he was on my wife's head, he was whistling as if he was forty persons. When we reached a village we stopped and bought food from a food-seller to eat as we were very hungry before reaching there, but when we were about to eat the food, the half-bodied baby did not allow us to eat it, instead of that he took the food and swallowed it as a man swallows a pill, so when the food-seller saw him do so, she ran away and left her food there, but when our half-bodied baby saw that the food-seller had left her food, he crept to the food and swallowed it as well.

So this half-bodied baby did not allow us to eat the food, and we did not taste it at all. When the people of that village saw the half-bodied baby with us, they drove us away from the village. Then we started our journey again and when we had travelled about seven miles away from that village, there we reached another town; we stopped there also, and we bought other food there, but this half-bodied baby did not allow us to eat that again. But by that time we were annoyed and we wanted to eat it by force, but he commanded as before and at the same time we became as he commanded, then we left him to swallow it.

When the people of that town saw him there with us again, they drove us away with juju and they said that we were carrying a spirit about and they said that they did not want a spirit in their town. So if we entered any town or village to eat or sleep, they would drive us away at once and our news had been carried to all towns and villages. Now we could not travel the roads unless from bush to bush, because everybody had heard the information that a man and a woman were carrying a half-bodied baby or spirit about and they were looking for a place to put him and run away.

So by this time we were very hungry and then when we were travelling inside the bush, we tried all our efforts to put him down somewhere and run away, but he did not allow us to do that. After we had failed to put him down, we thought that he would sleep at night, but he did not sleep at night at all, and the worst part of it, he did not let my wife put him down once since she had put him on her head; we were longing to sleep heavily, but he did not allow us to do anything except carry him along. All the time that he was on my wife's head, his belly swelled out like a very large tube, because he had eaten too much food and yet he did not satisfy at any time for he could eat the whole food in this world without satisfaction. As we were travelling about in the bush on that night, my wife was feeling overloading of this baby and if we put him on a scale by that time, he would weigh at least 28 lbs; when I saw that my wife had tired of carrying him and she could not carry him any longer, then I took over to carry him along, but before I could carry him to a distance of about one quarter of a mile. I was unable to move again and I was sweating as if I bathe in water for overloading, yet this half-bodied baby did not allow us to put him down and rest.

Ah! how could we escape from this half-bodied baby? But God is so good and as we were carrying him to and fro in the bush on that night, we heard as if they were playing music somewhere in that bush and he told us to carry him to the place that we were hearing the music. Before an hour had passed we reached there.

THREE GOOD CREATURES TOOK OVER OUR TROUBLE—THEY WERE:—DRUM, SONG AND DANCE

When we carried him to the place, there we saw the creatures that we called "Drum, Song and Dance" personally and these three creatures were living creatures as ours. At the same time that we reached there the half-bodied baby came down from my head, then we thanked God. But as he came down from my head he joined the three creatures at once. When "Drum" started to beat himself it was just as if he was beaten by fifty men, when "Song" started to sing, it was just as if a hundred people were singing together and when "Dance" started to dance the half-bodied baby started too, my wife, myself and spirits etc., were dancing with "Dance" and nobody who heard or saw these three fellows would not follow them to wherever they were going. Then the whole of us were following the three fellows and dancing along with them. So we followed the three fellows and were dancing for a good five days without eating or stopping once, before we reached a place which was built in the form of a premises by these creatures with mud.

There were two soldiers stood at the front of the premises, but when we reached there with these three fellows, my wife and myself etc., stopped at the entrance of the premises, only the three fellows and our half-bodied baby entered the premises, after that, we saw them no more. N.B. We did not want to follow them up to that place, but we could not control ourselves as we were dancing along with them.

So nobody in this world could beat drum as Drum himself could beat, nobody could dance as Dance himself could dance and nobody could sing as Song himself could sing. We left these three wonderful creatures by two o'clock in the mid-night. Then after we had left these creatures and our half-bodied baby, we started a fresh journey, but we travelled for two days before we reached a town and stopped there and rested for two days. But we were penniless before reaching there, then I thought within myself how could we get money for our food etc. After a while I remembered my name which was "Father of gods who could do anything in this world." As there was a large river which crossed the main road to that town, then I told my wife to follow me to the river; when reaching there, I cut a tree and carved it into a paddle, then I gave it to my wife and I told her to enter the river with me; when we entered the river, I commanded one juju which was given me by a kind spirit who was a friend of mine and at once the juju changed me to a big canoe. Then my wife went inside the canoe with the paddle and paddling it, she used the canoe as "ferry" to carry passengers across the river, the fare for adults was 3d (three pence) and half fare for children. In the evening time, then I changed to a man as before and when we checked the money that my wife had collected for that day, it was £7: 5: 3d. After that we went back to the town, we bought all our needs.

Next morning we went there by 4 o'clock well before the people of that town woke up, so that they might not know the secret and when we reached there, I did as I did yesterday and my wife continued her work as usual, on that day we came back to home by 7 o'clock in the evening. So we stayed in that town for one month and doing the same work throughout that month, when we checked the money that we collected for that month, it was £56:11:9d.

Then we left that town with gladness, we started our journey again, but after we had travelled about eighty miles away to that town, then we began to meet gangs of the "highway-men" on the road, and they were troubling us too much. But when I thought over that the danger of the road might result to the loss of our money or both money and our lives, then we entered into bush, but to travel in this bush was very dangerous too, because of the wild animals, and the boa constrictors were uncountable as sand.

TO TRAVEL BY AIR

Then I told my wife to jump on my back with our loads, at the same time, I commanded my juju which was given me by "Water Spirit woman" in the "Bush of the Ghosts" (the full story of the "Spirit woman" appeared in the story book of the Wild Hunter in the Bush of the Ghosts). So I became a big bird like an aeroplane and flew away with my wife, I flew for 5 hours before I came down, after I had left the dangerous area, although it was 4 o'clock before I came down, then we began to trek the remaining journey by land or foot. By 8 o'clock P.M. of that day, then we reached the town in which the father of my wife told me that my palm-wine tapster was.

When reaching there, I asked from that town's people about my tapster who had died long ago in my town. But they told me that my tapster had left there over two years. Then I begged them if they could to tell me the town that he was at at present, and I was told that he was now at "Deads' town" and they told me that he was living with deads at the "Deads' town," they told me that the town was very far away and only deads were living there.

Now we could not return where we were coming from (my wife's father's town) we must go to the Deads' town. Then we left that town after the 3rd day that we arrived there; from that town to the Deads' town there was no road or path which to travel, because nobody was going there from that town at all.

NO ROAD—OUGHT TO TRAVEL FROM BUSH TO BUSH TO THE DEADS' TOWN

The very day that we left that town, we travelled up to forty miles inside the bush, and when it was 6.30 P.M. in the evening, we reached a very thick bush; this bush was very thick so that a snake could not pass through it without hurt.

So we stopped there, because we could not see well again, it was dark. We slept in that bush, but when it was about two o'clock in the night, there we saw a creature, either he was a spirit or other harmful creature, we could not say, he was coming towards us, he was white as if painted with white paint, he was white from foot to the topmost of his body, but he had no head or feet and hands like human-beings and he got one large eye on his topmost. He was long about ¼ of a mile and his diameter was about six feet, he resembled a white pillar. At the same time that I saw him coming towards us, I thought what I could do to stop him, then I remembered a charm which was given me by my father before he died.

The use of the charm was this:——If I meet a spirit or other harmful creature at night and if I used it, it would turn me into a great fire and smoke, so that the harmful creatures would be unable to reach the fire. Then I used the charm and it burnt the white creature, but before he could burn into ashes there we saw about ninety of the same kind as this long white creature, all of them were coming to us (fire) and when they reached the fire (us) the whole of them sur-rounded it and bent or curved towards the fire; after that the whole of them were crying:——"cold! cold! cold" etc., but as they surrounded the fire, they did not want to leave there, although they could not do anything to that fire (us). They were only warming themselves from the fire and they were exceedingly satisfied with the fire and to stay with it as long as it could remain there for them. Of course I thought that as we had turned into the fire, we would be safe, but not at all. When I thought over that how we would leave these white creatures, I remembered that if we began to move, perhaps these white creatures would go away, because since 1 o'clock A.M., of that night till 10 o'clock A.M. they were still warming themselves from the fire and did not attempt to go where they came from or to go and eat. Of course I could not say definitely whether they were eating creatures or not.

But do not think that as we had turned into the fire we should not feel hungry, for we were feeling hungry too much though we were fire, and if we turned to persons at once, these white creatures would get a chance to kill us or harm us.

Then we began to move, but as we were moving on, these white creatures were also moving with the fire until we left the thick bush, but when we had left there and when we reached a big field, then they went back to their thick bush. But although we did not know it these long white creatures were bound not to trespass on another's bush, and they did not enter into that field at all although they were satisfied with the fire, and the creatures of that field must not enter into their bush either. That was how we got away from the long white creatures.

As we had freed from the white creatures then we started our journey in that field. This field had no trees or palm-trees, only long wild grasses grew there, all resembled corn-plants, the edges of its leaves were as sharp as razor blades and hairy. Then we travelled in that field till 5 o'clock in the evening, after that, we began to look for a suitable place to sleep till morning.

But as we were looking for such place, there we saw a TERMITES' HOUSE which resembled an umbrella and it was 3 feet high and cream in colour. Then we put our loads under it; after that we rested there for a few minutes, then we thought of making fire there with which to cook our food as we were hungry. But as dried sticks were not near that place then we stood up and went further to gather the sticks for the fire, but as we went further there we met an image which knelt down. It was a female in form and it was also cream in colour. After we had collected the sticks, we came back to the termites' house, then we made the fire, cooked our food and ate it; when it was about 8 o'clock in the night, we slept at the foot of the termites' house, but we could not fall asleep, because of fear, and when it was about 11 o'clock of that night we began to hear as if we were in the middle of a market, then we listened to it very well and before we rose up our heads, we were in the centre of a market. Not knowing that it was the owner of the market, that we put our loads on, making fire and also slept under him, but we thought that it was only a termites' house, but no.

Then we started to pack our loads at once to leave the place, perhaps we might be safe, but as we were packing our loads, that field's creatures had surrounded us and caught us like a policeman, so we followed them, and also the termites' house (the owner of the market) under who we slept followed us too, as he was following us, he was jumping, because he had no foot, but a very small head like a one-month-old baby's head, and when we reached the place where the female image knelt down, she stood up and followed us too.

But after we had travelled about twenty minutes, we reached their king's palace, although he was not in when we reached there at that moment.

The Palm-Wine Drinkard

The palace was almost covered with refuse, it resembled an old ruined house, it was very rough. When these field creatures saw that the king was not at home, they waited for half an hour before he came, but when we (my wife and I) saw him, he himself was refuse, because he was almost covered with both dried and undried leaves and we could not see his feet and face etc. He entered the palace and at once came and sat down on the refuse. After that his people presented us to him and lodged complaint that we trespassed their town. When they had told him that, he asked them what were these two dulls, but his people said that they could not describe them at all, because they had not seen these kind of creatures before. As my wife and I did not talk a single word by that time, they thought that we were unable to talk, then their king gave one of them a sharp stick to stab us, perhaps we might talk or feel pain; he did as their king told him to do. So as he mercilessly stabbed us with that stick, we felt pain and talked out, but at the same time that the whole of them heard our voice, they laughed at us if bombs explode, and we knew "Laugh" personally on that night, because as every one of them stopped laughing at us, "Laugh" did not stop for two hours. As "Laugh" was laughing at us on that night, my wife and myself forgot our pains and laughed with him, because he was laughing with curious voices that we never heard before in our life. We did not know the time that we fell into his laugh, but we were only laughing at "Laugh's" laugh and nobody who heard him when laughing would not laugh, so if somebody continue to laugh with "Laugh" himself, he or she would die or faint at once for long laughing, because laugh was his profession and he was feeding on it. Then they began to beg "Laugh" to

227

stop, but he could not. Not knowing that these field creatures had never seen human-beings before, after a while, their king told them to take us to their "gods of war." But when I heard that from him, I was very glad, because I myself was "Father of gods." These field creatures pushed us to their "gods of war" as their king said, but they did not go near the "god" because nobody would and return alive. After they had pushed us to him and gone back to the market and as the "god" could talk and I myself was "Father of gods" also and I had known the secrets of all "gods," so I talked to this god with a kind of voice, then he did not harm us, instead he led us out of that field. As their king was talking, a hot steam was rushing out of his nose and mouth as a big boiler and he was breathing at five minutes interval. That was how we left the field creatures and their field.

THE "WRAITH-ISLAND"

Then we started our journey in another bush, of course, it was full of Islands and swamps and the creatures of the Islands were very kind, because as soon as we reached there, they received us with kindness and gave us a lovely house in their town to live in. The name of the Island was called "Wraith-Island," it was very high and it was entirely surrounded by water; all the people of the Island were very kind and they loved themselves, their work was only to plant their food, after that, they had no other work more than to play music and dance. They were the most beautiful creatures in the world of the curious creatures and also the most wonderful dancers and musicians, they were playing music

and dancing throughout the day and night. But as the
weather of the Island was suitable for us and when we saw
that we should not leave there at once, we were dancing
with them and doing as they were doing there. Whenever
these Island creatures dress, you would be thinking they
were human-beings and their children were performing
always the stage plays. As we were living with them I
became a farmer and planted many kinds of crops. But one
day, as the crops had ripened enough there, I saw a terrible
animal coming to the farm and eating the crops, but one
morning I met him there, so I started to drive him away
from the farm, of course I could not approach him as he was
as big as an elephant. His fingernails were long to about two
feet, his head was bigger than his body ten times. He had a
large mouth which was full of long teeth, these teeth were
about one foot long and as thick as a cow's horns, his body
was almost covered with black long hair like a horse's tail
hair. He was very dirty. There were five horns on his head
and curved and levelled to the head, his four feet were as big
as a log of wood. But as I could not go near him, I stoned
him at a long distance, but before the stone could reach him,
he had reached where I stood and got ready to fight me.

Then I thought over that how could I escape from this
fearful animal. Not knowing that he was the owner of the
land on which I planted the crops, by that critical time, he
was angry that I did not sacrifice to him before I planted
crops there, but when I understood what he wanted from
me, then I cut some of the crops and gave him, so when he
saw what I gave him, then he made a sign that I should
mount his back and I mounted his back, and by that time
I did not hear him any more, then he took me to his house

which was not so far from the farm. When we reached there, he bent down and I dismounted from his back, after that he entered his house and brought out four grains of corn, 4 grains of rice and 4 seeds of okra and gave them to me, then I went back to the farm and planted them all at the same time. But to my surprise, these grains and the seeds germinated at once, before 5 minutes they became full grown crops and before 10 minutes again, they had produced fruits and ripened at the same moment too, so I plucked them and went back to the town (the Wraith-Island).

But after the crops had produced the last fruits and when dried, I cut them and kept their seeds as a reference as we were travelling about in the bush.

NOT TOO SMALL TO BE CHOSEN

There were many wonderful creatures in the olden days. One day, the king of the "Wraith-Island" town chose all the people, spirits and terrible creatures of the Island to help him to clear his corn field which was about 2 miles square. Then one fine morning, we gathered together and went to the corn field, and cleared it away, after that, we returned to the king and told him that we had cleared his corn field, he thanked us, and gave us food and drinks.

But as a matter of fact none of the creatures is too small to choose for a help. We did not know that immediately we left the field, a tiny creature who was not chosen with us by the king went to the field and commanded all the weeds that we had cleared to grow up as if they were not cleared.

The Palm-Wine Drinkard

He was saying thus:—"THE KING OF THE 'WRAITH-
ISLAND' BEGGED ALL THE CREATURES OF THE 'WRAITH-ISLAND'
AND LEFT HIM OUT, SO THAT, ALL THE CLEARED-WEEDS RISE UP;
AND LET US GO AND DANCE TO A BAND AT THE 'WRAITH-
ISLAND'; IF BAND COULD NOT SOUND, WE SHOULD DANCE WITH
MELODIOUS MUSIC."

But at the same time that the tiny creature commanded
the weeds, all rose up as if the field was not cleared for two
years. Then early in the morning of the second day that we
had cleared it, the king went to the field to visit his corn, but
to his surprise, he met the field uncleared, then he returned
to the town and called the whole of us and asked that why
did we not clear his field? We replied that we had cleared
it yesterday, but the king said no, we did not clear it. Then
the whole of us went to the field to witness it, but we saw
the field as if it was not cleared as the king said. After that
we gathered together and went to clear it as before, then we
returned to the king again and told him that we had cleared
it. But when he went there, he found it uncleared as before
and came back to the town and told us again that we did not
clear his field, then the whole of us ran to the field and found
it uncleared. So we gathered together for the third time and
went to clear it, after we had cleared it, we told one of us to
hide himself inside a bush which was very close to the field,
but before 30 minutes that he was watching the field, he saw
a very tiny creature who was just a baby of one day of age
and he commanded the weeds to rise up as he was commanding before. Then that one of us who hid himself inside
the bush and was watching him tried all his efforts and
caught him, then he brought him to the king; when the king
saw the tiny creature, he called the whole of us to his palace.

231

After that, the king asked him who was commanding the cleared-weeds of his field to rise up after the field had been cleared: The tiny creature replied that he was commanding all the weeds to rise up, because the king chose all the creatures of the "Wraith-Island" town but left him out, although he was the smallest among all, but he had the power to command weeds etc. which had been cleared to grow up as if it was not cleared at all. But the king said that he had just forgotten to choose him with the rest and not because of his small appearance.

Then the king made excuses to him, after that he went away. This was a very wonderful tiny creature.

After we (my wife and I) had completed a period of 18 months in this "Wraith-Island," then I told them that we wished to continue our journey, because we were not reaching our destination at all. But as the creatures of this Island were very kind, they gave my wife many expensive articles as gifts then we packed all our loads and when it was early in the morning, the whole people of the "Wraith-Island" led us with a big canoe and they were singing the song of "good-bye" as they were paddling along on the river. When they accompanied us to their boundary, they stopped, but when we went down from their canoe, then they returned to their town with a lovely song and music and bade us good-bye. If it was in their power, they would have led us to our destination, but they were forbidden to touch another creature's land or bush.

While we had enjoyed everything in that "Wraith-Island," to our satisfaction, there were still many great tasks ahead. Then we started our journey in another bush, but remember that there was no road on which to travel in those bushes at all.

As we entered the bush, when we had travelled for about 2 miles inside the bush, then we began to notice that there were many trees without withered leaves, dried sticks and refuse on the ground of this bush as was usual in other bushes; as we were very hungry before reaching there, we put down our loads at the foot of a tree. Then we looked around the tree for pieces of dried wood with which to make a fire, but nothing was found there; to our surprise, there was a sweet smelling in every part of the bush, the smelling was just as if they were baking cakes, bread and roasting of fowls or meat; God was so good, we began to snuff the sweet smelling and we were very satisfied with it and we did not feel hungry again. That bush was very "greedy," so that within an hour from when we sat at the foot of the tree, the ground on which we sat began to warm and we could not sit on it any longer, then we took our loads and went further.

As we were going on in this bush, we saw a pond and we branched there, then we started to drink the water from it, but as the water dried away at our presence and also as we were thirsty all the time, and there we saw that there was not a single living creature. But when we saw that the ground of this bush was very hot for us to stand, sit or to sleep on till morning and again the bush did not like anybody to remain there any longer than necessary, then we left there and went further, but as we were going on, we saw again many palm-trees without leaves, but only small birds represented the leaves, all these palm-trees were in a row. The first one that we reached was very tall and as we appeared to him, he laughed, then the second to him asked what was making him laugh; he replied that he saw two living creatures in their bush today, but as soon as we got to the second he also laughed at us too so loudly that as if a person was five miles away would hear, then the whole of them were laughing at us together and the whole of that bush was just as if it was full of a big market's noises as they were in the same row. But when I rose up my head and looked at the top of them I noticed that they had heads, and the heads were artificial heads, but they were talking as human-beings, although they were talking with curious language, and the whole of them were smoking very big and long smoking pipes as they were looking at us, of course, we could not say where they got the pipes. We were so very curious to them as they had never seen human-beings before.

As we were thinking to sleep there, we were unable to sleep or stay for their noise and laughing. After we had left the "Greedy-Bush," then we entered into a forest at about 1.30 in the mid-night, then we slept under a tree till morning and nothing happened to us throughout that night, but we had not eaten anything since the day that we had left the "Wraith-Island," the most beautiful Island in the world of the curious creatures. When it was dawn we woke up under the tree and made a fire with which we cooked our food and ate it there, but before we finished with the food, we saw that animals of that forest were running to and fro, we saw a lot of birds were chasing the animals up and down, these birds were eating the flesh of the animals; the birds were about 2 feet long and their beaks were also one foot and very sharp as a sword.

The Palm-Wine Drinkard

When these birds started to eat the flesh of those animals, within a second there we saw about 50 holes on the bodies of those animals and within a second the animals fell down and died, but when they began to eat the dead bodies it did not last them more than 2 minutes before they finished them (bodies) and as soon as they had eaten that, they would start to chase others about. But when these birds saw us where we sat down they were looking at us fiercely and also with astonishment, but when I thought that these might set us as they were eating the animals, then I gathered dried leaves and set fire to them, after that I put on it juju-power which was given me by my friend who was the two-headed creature in the "Bush of the Ghosts, 2nd Country of the Ghosts." The smelling powder drove all these birds away for a few minutes. So we could travel in that forest by day as far as we could. But when it was night, we sat down under a tree and laid down our loads; we were sitting down and sleeping under trees whenever it was night as a shelter. As we sat down under this tree and were thinking about that night's danger, there we saw a "Spirit of Prey," he was big as a hippopotamus, but he was walking upright as a human-being; his both legs had two feet and tripled his body, his head was just like a lion's head and every part of his body was covered with hard scales, each of these scales was the same in size as a shovel or hoe, and all curved towards his body. If this "Spirit of Prey" wanted to catch his prey, he would simply be looking at it and stand in one place, he was not chasing his prey about, and when he focused the prey well, then he would close his large eyes, but before he would open his eyes, his prey would be already dead and drag itself to him at the place that he stood. When this "Spirit of Prey"

235

came nearer to the place where we slept on that night, he stood at about 80 yards away from us, and looked at us with his eyes which brought out a flood-light like mercury in colour.

As that light was shining on us, we at once began to feel heat as if we had bathed with water, even my wife fainted of this heat. But I was praying to God by that time not to let this "Spirit of Prey" close his eyes, because if he closed them, no more, we had perished there. But God is so good he did not remember to close his eyes by that time, and I myself was feeling the heat of his eyes too much and also I nearly fainted with suffocation. Then I saw a buffalo which was passing that way at that time, then this "Spirit of Prey" closed his eyes as usual and the buffalo died and dragged itself to him, after that he began to eat it. So by that time I got a chance to escape from him, but when I remembered that my wife had fainted then I looked around the place where we sat and saw a tree with many branches, then I climbed it with my wife and left our loads at the foot of that tree. To my surprise, he had eaten off the dead body of the buffalo within four minutes and at once he pointed the flood-light of his eyes towards the place where we sat before we climbed the tree; he found nothing there but our loads. So when he directed the flood-light of his eyes to the loads, the loads dragged themselves to him but when he loosened the loads, he found nothing edible there. After that, he waited for us till the day was nearly breaking and when he saw that he could not get us any more, then he went away.

As I was treating my wife throughout that night, she was very well before early in the morning. Then we got down from the tree and packed our loads and we started our journey at once. Before 5 P.M. we had left that bush behind. That was how we were saved from the "Spirit of Prey" etc.

We started our journey in another bush with new creatures, this bush was smaller than that one which we had passed behind and it was also a various bush, because there we met many houses which had been ruined for hundreds of years and all the properties of those who had left there remained as if they were using them every day; there we saw an image which sat down on a flat stone, it had two long breasts with deep eyes, it was very ugly and terrible to see. After that we went further in this ruined town and saw another image with a full basket of colas on its front, then I took out one of the colas, but to our surprise, at the same time that I took it, we heard a voice of somebody suddenly, which said:—DON'T TAKE IT! LEAVE IT THERE! but I did not listen to the voice that we heard. Immediately I had taken the cola, we kept going, and again to our surprise, there we saw a man who was walking towards his back or backwards, his both eyes were on his knees, his both arms were at his both thighs, these both arms were longer than his feet and both could reach the topmost of any tree; and he held a long whip too. He was chasing us as we were going on hastily with that whip, so by that time, we started to run for our life, but he was chasing us to and fro in that bush for two hours; he wanted to flog us with that whip. But as we were running away from this creature, we entered into a wide road unexpectedly, as we entered the road, he got back from us at once, although we could not say, whether he was bound to trek on that road.

When we reached this road, we waited for thirty minutes; perhaps we might see somebody pass, because we did not

237

know to which side of the two to travel, again the road might not be there at all. But though we waited for 30 minutes there, nobody passed, even a fly did not fly on it.

As the road was very clean, we noticed that a foot mark could not be traced, then we believed that it was the road which led to the—"UNRETURNABLE-HEAVEN'S TOWN" the town in which human-beings or other creatures were bound to enter; if anybody entered it, no doubt he or she would not return again, because the inhabitants of the town were very bad, cruel and merciless.

ON OUR WAY TO THE UNRETURNABLE-HEAVEN'S TOWN

Now we followed this road from the north side and we were very glad to be travelling on it, but still no trace of foot mark or of anybody met on the way. As we travelled along it from two o'clock till seven o'clock in the evening without reaching a town or the end, then we stopped at the roadside and made a fire there; we cooked our food and ate it there and slept there as well, but nothing happened to us throughout the night. When it was dawn we woke up and cooked our food and ate it.

After that we started our journey, but although we had travelled from that morning till 4 o'clock in the evening, yet we did not see or meet anybody on this road, then we were quite sure that it was "Unreturnable-Heaven's town" road, so we did not go further; we stopped and slept there till the morning. Very early in the morning, we woke and prepared our food and ate it, after that, we thought to go on a little bit before we should leave the road.

But as we were going on and when it was time that we wanted to branch to our left, to continue the journey inside another bush as usual, we were unable to branch or to stop, or to go back, we were only moving on the road towards the town. We tried all our best to stop ourselves but all were in vain.

How could we stop now was the question that we asked ourselves, because we were approaching the town. Then I remembered one of my juju which had escaped me and I performed it to stop us, but instead of that, we started to move faster than before. When there remained one quarter of a mile to reach the town, we came to a large gate which crossed the road, it was closed then. When we reached the gate, then we could stop, but we could not move to front or back. We stood before this gate for about 3 hours before it opened itself, then we moved to the town unexpectedly and we did not know who was pushing us. When we entered this town we saw creatures that we had never seen in our life and I could not describe the whole of them here, but however, I should tell some of their stories which went thus:—This town was very big and full of unknown creatures, both adults and children were very cruel to human-beings, and yet they were looking for ways of making their cruelties even worse; as soon as we entered their town, six of them held us firmly and the rest were beating us and also their children were stoning us repeatedly.

These unknown creatures were doing everything incorrectly, because there we saw that if one of them wanted to climb a tree, he would climb the ladder first before leaning it against that tree; and there was a flat land near their town but they built their houses on the side of a steep hill, so all the houses bent downwards as if they were going to fall, and their children were always rolling down from these houses, but their parents did not care about that; the whole of them did not wash their bodies at all, but washed their domestic animals; they wrapped themselves with a kind of leaves as their clothes, but had costly clothes for their domestic animals, and cut their domestic animals' finger nails, but kept their own uncut for one hundred years; even there we saw many of them sleeping on the roofs of their houses and they said that they could not use the houses that they built with their hands except to sleep on them.

Their town was surrounded with a thick and tall wall. If any earthly person mistakenly entered their town, they would catch him or her and begin to cut the flesh of his or her body into pieces while still alive, sometimes they would stab a person's eyes with a pointed knife and leave it there until that person would die of much pain. As six of them held us firmly, they were taking us to their king, but as we were taken along, the rest and their children were beating and stoning us. But as we wanted to enter the palace of their king, there we met uncountable of them at the gate of their king's palace and waiting for to beat. When we entered the palace, they handed us to the king's attendants. After the attendants took us to the king, but as we were inside the palace, thousands of them were waiting for us at the gate of the palace, some of them held clubs, knives, cutlasses and other fighting weapons and all their children held stones.

The questions that their king asked us went thus:—From

where were you coming? I replied that we were coming from the earth. He asked again how did we manage to reach their town? I replied that it was their road brought us to the town and we did not want to come there at all. After that he asked us where were we going to? Then I replied that we were going to my palm-wine tapster's town who had died in my town sometime ago. As I had said already that these unknown creatures were very cruel to anybody that mistakenly entered their town, as I answered all the questions, he repeated the name of their town for us again—"Unreturnable-Heaven's town." He said:—a town in which are only enemies of God living, only cruel, greedy and merciless creatures. After he said so, he commanded his attendants to clear all the hair from our heads, but when the attendants and the people at the gate heard that from their king, they jumped up with gladness and shouted. God is so good, that the attendants did not take us to the outside of the palace before they started to shave our heads as the king ordered them, otherwise we would be torn into pieces by the people waiting for us at the gate of the palace.

Then the king gave them flat stones to use as razor blades, and as the attendants were clearing the hair with the flat stones, the flat stones were unable to clear the hair as razor blades would and only hurt every part of our heads After they had tried all their efforts and failed, then the king gave them pieces of broken bottle to use, when they got that, it cleared some of the hair by force, and blood did not allow them to see the rest of our hair again. But before they started to shave off the hair, they had tied us with strong ropes to one of the pillars of that palace. After they had cleared some of the hair, they left us there loosened and went to grind pepper, after a while, they brought the pepper and rubbed our heads with it, then they lighted a thick rag with fire and tied it on the centre of our heads so that it nearly touched our heads. By that time, we did not know whether we were still alive or dead, although we could not defend our heads, because both our hands and bodies were tied to that pillar. When it was about half an hour since they had hung the fire near our heads, they took it away and started to scrape our heads again with a big snail's shell, so by that time, every part of the heads was bleeding; but before that time all the people that were waiting for us at the gate had returned to their houses, tired of long waiting.

After that, they took us to a wide field which was in the full heat of the sun, there were no trees or shadow near there and it was cleared as a football field; it was near the town. Then they dug two pits or holes side by side, in size of which would reach the jaw of a person, in the centre of the field. After that they put me into one and my wife into the second and replaced the earth that they had dug out and pressed it hard in such a way that we could hardly breathe. Then they put food near our mouths, but we were unable to touch or eat it; they knew that we were very hungry by that time. And after that, the whole of them cut whips and began to flog our heads, but we had no hands to defend our heads. At last they brought an eagle before us to take out our eyes with its beak, but the eagle was simply looking at our eyes, it did no harm to us. Then these people went back to their houses and left the eagle there with us. But as I had tamed such a bird in my town before I left there, so this one did not harm us at all and we remained in these holes from three o'clock P.M. till morning and at about 9 o'clock of that morning the sun came and shone severely on us; when it was 10 o'clock, these people came again and made a big fire around us and flogged us for some minutes, then they went away. But when the fire was about to quench, their children came with whips and stones then they began to whip and stone our heads; when they left that, they began to climb on our heads and jump from one to the second; after that they started to spit, make urine and pass excreta on our heads; but when that eagle saw that they wanted to nail our heads, then it drove all of them away from the field with its beak. But before that people (adults) left, they scheduled the time that they would come and pay us the last visit for 5 o'clock in the evening of the second day that we were in those holes. God is so good, when it was 3 o'clock P.M., a heavy rain came and it rained till a late hour in the night and it disappointed them from coming to pay the last visit.

As it rained heavily, when it was one o'clock in the night, the holes became soft, so when that eagle saw us trying to get out of the holes, it came nearer and began to scratch the hole in which I was, but as the holes were very deep, it could not scratch it out as quickly as it wanted to. But when I shook my body to left and right, then I got out and ran to my wife and pulled her out of her own too. Then we hastily left that field and went to the main gate of the town, but unluckily, we found it closed and the town was entirely surrounded by a thick and tall wall, so we hid ourselves under a bush which had not been cleared for long time and was near the wall. When the day broke the people came to the field and found nothing there; after that they began to search for us and when they reached the bush in which we hid ourselves, they were smashing it together with us, so when they could not trace us out they thought that we had left their town.

As the sun of that town was very hot, every place dried early; when it was about two o'clock in the mid-night, and when the whole of them slept, then we went into the town cautiously and took some fire from their fire which was not yet quenched. All their houses were thatched with grasses and also it was in the dry season, as again the houses touched each other, then we lighted some of the houses with the fire; it caught fire at once and before they could wake up, all the houses had burnt into ashes and about ninety per cent of them also burnt with the houses and none of their children were saved. Then the rest of them that were saved, stole away that night.

When it was dawn, then we went to the town and found nobody there, so we took one of their sheep and killed it, then roasted it, after that, we ate as much of it as we could and packed the rest and took one of their axes and left the town empty, so when we reached the thick wall, I cut a part of it like a window and passed out through that place.

That was how we were saved from the Unknown creatures of the "Unreturnable-Heaven's town." After we had left that town very far away and believed that we were freed from the unknown creatures, then we stopped and built a small temporary house inside the bush in which we were travelling along, it was built in form of an upstairs and thatched with grasses, then I surrounded it with sticks as fence, so that it might keep us from the animals etc. Then I began to treat my wife there. In the daytime, I would go around the bush, I should kill bush animals, after that I should pick edible fruits and we were feeding on them as food. When we completed the period of three months there for treatment, my wife was very well, but as I was roaming about in that bush in search of animals, there I discovered an old cutlass which had had its wooden handle eaten off by insects, then I took it and coiled it round with the string of a palm-tree, then I sharpened it on a hard ground, because there was no stone, and cut a strong and slender stick and then bent it in form of a bow and sharpened many small sticks as arrows, so I was defending ourselves with it. But after we had completed the period of five months and some days in that house, we thought that to go back to the town of my wife's father was dangerous, because of various punishments, and we could not trace out the right way on which we travelled from that place again. To go back was harder and to go further was the hardest, so at last we made up our mind and started to go forward. In case of emergency, I took the bow and arrows with the cutlass with us, but we had no other load more than that, because our loads had been taken from us in the town of "Unreturnable-Heaven's," and of course we had burnt our loads together with their houses. Then we started our journey very early in the morning, but it was a very dark day which seemed as if rain was coming heavily. After we had travelled about seven miles from that house which we left, then we stopped and ate some of the roasted meat which we took along with us. After that we started to travel again, but we did not travel more than a mile in that bush before we reached a large river which crossed our way to pass; when we reached there, we could not enter it, because it was very deep as we were looking at it and noticing that there was no canoe or other thing with which to cross it. When we had stopped there for a few

minutes, we travelled to our right along the bank of this
river as perhaps we might reach the end of it, but we
travelled more than four miles without seeing the end at all.
Then we turned back and travelled to our left again. When
we had travelled about six miles away without seeing the
end, then we stopped to think what we could do to cross the
river. But at that moment we thought to go further along
the bank perhaps we could reach the end or a safe place to
rest or sleep at night. As we were going further, we did not
travel more than one third of a mile on this river-bank,
before we saw a big tree which was about one thousand and
fifty feet in length and about two hundred feet in diameter.
This tree was almost white as if it was painted every day
with white paint with all its leaves and also branches. As we
were about forty yards away from it, there we noticed that
somebody peeped out and was focusing us as if a photographer was focusing somebody. So, at the same time we saw
him focusing us like that, we started to run to our left, but
he turned to that place too, and we turned to our right again,
and he did so, and still focusing us like that and we did not
see who was focusing us, but only that tree which was
turning as we were doing. After we had seen this terrible
tree which was focusing us, then we said that we should not
wait for this again, then we were running away for our life
at once. But immediately we were running away from this
tree, we heard a terrible voice suddenly as if many persons
talked into a big tank, then we looked at our back and there
we saw two large hands which came out from the tree and
made a sign of "Stop," but directly we saw him saying so,
we did not stop at all, after that he said again—"Stop-there
and come-here" but still, we did not go to him as he said.

He told us again with another curious and larger voice to stop, but that time we stopped and looked at our back.

But as we looked at our back, we were looking at the large hands with fear, so when the hands gave us sign to come to him, now my wife and myself betraited ourselves, because when the hands told both of us to come to him, my wife pointed me to the hands and I myself pointed her to the hands too; after that, my wife forced me to go first and I pushed her to go first. As we were doing that, the hands told us again that both of us were wanted inside the tree, so when we thought that we had never seen a tree with hands and talking in our life, or since we have been travelling in the bushes, then we started to run away as before, but to our surprise, when the hands saw that we took to our heels again, they stretched out from the tree without end and then picked both of us off the ground as we were running away. After that they were drawing back to the inside of the tree, but when we nearly touched the tree, there we saw that a large door opened and the hands drew us through that door to the inside of the tree.

Now by that time and before we entered inside the white tree, we had "sold our death" to somebody at the door for the sum of £70: 18: 6d and "lent our fear" to somebody at the door as well on interest of £3: 10: 0d per month, so we did not care about death and we did not fear again. When we entered inside the white tree, there we found ourselves inside a big house which was in the centre of a big and beautiful town, then the hands directed us to an old woman, and after the hands disappeared. So we met the old woman sat on a chair in a big parlour which was decorated with costly things, then she told us to sit down before her and we

247

did so. Then she asked us did we know her name; we said no; then she said that her name was called "FAITHFUL-MOTHER" and she told us that she was only helping those who were in difficulties and enduring punishments but not killing anybody.

After that, she asked us did we know the name of the big hands who brought us to her; we said no. Then she told us that the big hands' name was called "FAITHFUL-HANDS," she said that the work of Faithful-hands was to watch out for those who were passing or going about in their bush with difficulties etc. and bring them to her.

THE WORK OF THE FAITHFUL-MOTHER IN THE WHITE TREE

After she had related her story, then she told one of her servants to give us food and drinks and at the same time the servant served us with the food and drinks, but after we had eaten and drank to our satisfaction, then the Faithful-Mother told us to follow her and we did so. She took us to the largest dancing hall which was in the centre of that house, and there we saw that over 300 people were dancing all together. The hall was decorated with about one million pounds (£) and there were many images and our own too were in the centre of the hall. But our own images that we saw there resembled us too much and were also white colour, but we were very surprised to meet our images there, perhaps somebody who was focusing us as a photographer at the first time before the hands drew us inside the white tree had made them, we could not say. So we asked from Faithful-Mother what she was doing with all of the images. She replied that they were for remembrance and to know those she was helping from their difficulties and punishments. This beautiful hall was full of all kinds of food and drinks, over twenty stages were in that hall with uncountable orchestras, musicians, dancers and tappers. The orchestras were always busy. The children of seven to eight years etc. of age were always dancing, tapping on the stage with melodious songs and they were also singing with warm tones with non-stop dance till morning. There we saw that all the lights in this hall were in technicolours and they were changing colours at five minutes intervals. After that she took us to the dining hall and then to the kitchen in which we met about three hundred and forty cooks who were always busy as bees and all the rooms in this house were in a row. Then she took us to her hospital where we met again many patients on sick beds and she handed us to one of the patentees to treat our heads without hair which the people of the "Unreturnable-Heaven's town" had cleared with broken bottle by force.

We remained in that hospital for a week under treatment before our heads brought out full-grown hair, then we went back to the the Faithful-Mother and she gave us a room.

OUR LIFE WITH THE FAITHFUL-MOTHER IN THE WHITE TREE

Now we were living with the Faithful-Mother and she was taking care of us with her faithfulness, but within a week that we were living with this mother, we had forgotten all our past torments and she told us to go to the hall at any time we liked. So early in the morning, we should go to the hall and begin to eat and drink, because we were not buying anything that we wanted, so that I began to lavish all the drinks as I had been a great palm-wine drinkard in my town before I left. And within one month my wife and I became good dancers. This was rather queer. One night, when we were short of drinks at about two o'clock in the mid-night, then the chief waiter reported to the Faithful-Mother that we were short of drinks and there was none in the store, then she gave the chief waiter a small bottle which was exactly the size of injection's bottle and it contained only a little quantity of wine. After the chief waiter brought it to the hall we began to drink it, but for three days and nights, the whole of us could not drink the wine which the bottle contained to one-fifth. So after about three months that we were inside this white tree, we became the inhabitants of the house and we were feeding on anything that we liked free of charge. There was a special room in this house to play gamble and I joined the gang, but I was not perfect enough, so that all the money for which I sold our "death" was taken away from me by the expert gamblers, but I had forgotten that one day, we should leave there and need money to spend. Of course the borrower of our "fear" was paying us regularly every month. Now we disliked to continue our journey to the town that we were going to before we entered inside the white tree, as a matter of fact we did not like to leave there ever.

But after we had completed the period of one year and two weeks with Faithful-Mother, one night she called my wife and me and told us that it was time for us to leave there and continue our journey as usual. When she said this we begged her not to let us leave there ever, then she replied that she had no right to delay anybody more than a year and some days, she said again that if that had been in her power, she would grant our request. After that, she told us to go and pack all our loads and be ready to leave there tomorrow morning. Then we went back to our room, and began to think that we were going to start our punishments again. We did not go to the hall that night and we did not sleep till the daybreak, so early in the morning we thought within ourselves to tell her to escort us to our destination. Then we went to her and told her we were ready to leave and we wanted her to lead us to our destination because of fearful creatures in the bush. But she told us that she could not do such request, because she must not go beyond their boundary. So she gave me a gun and ammunitions and a cutlass, then she gave my wife many costly clothes etc. as gifts and gave us plenty of roasted meat with drinks and cigarettes. After that she accompanied us, but what made us very surprised was that we saw the tree opened as a large door, and we simply found ourselves inside the bush unexpectedly, and the door closed at once and the tree seemed as an ordinary tree which could not open like that. But at the same time that we found ourselves at the foot of this white tree inside the bush, both of us (my wife and I) said suddenly "We are in the bush again." Because it was just as if a person slept in his or her room, but when he woke up, he found himself or herself inside a big bush.

Then we took our "fear" back from the borrower and he paid us the last interest on it. Then we found the one who had bought our "death" and told him to bring it, but he told us that he could not return it again, because he bought it from us and had paid for it already, so we left our "death" for the buyer, so we took only our "fear." So when the Faithful-Mother led us to the river which we could not cross before we saw the white tree and entered it, we stopped and looked at her. After a while, she picked up a small stick like a match stick on the ground and she threw it on that river, but at the same moment, there we found a narrow bridge which crossed the river to the other edge. Then she told us to cross it to the other edge or the second side, but she stood in the same place, at the same time that we reached the end of the other edge, she stretched out her hand and touched the bridge, but it was only that stick we saw in her hand. After that she was singing and waving her hand to us and we were doing the same thing to her as well, then she disappeared at once. That was how we left the Faithful-Mother in the white tree who was faithful to every creature.

So we took our "fear" back and started our journey as usual, but before an hour passed since we had left the Faithful-Mother, a heavy rain came and we were beaten by the rain for two hours before it stopped, as there was no shelter in this bush for rain or anything. My wife could not travel as quickly as we wished to, so we stopped and ate the roasted meat which the Faithful-Mother gave us, and we rested there for two hours, then we started to travel again. But as we were travelling along in this bush, we met a young lady who was coming towards us, but as we saw her, we bent to another way, but she bent to the place too, then we stopped for her to come and do anything that she wanted to do, because we had sold our "death" and we could not die again, but we feared her because we did not sell our "fear."

252

When this lady approached us, we noticed that she was dressed in a long fancy gown, and there were many gold-beads around her neck and she wore high-heel shoes which resembled aluminium in colour, she was as tall as a stick of about ten feet long, she was of deep red complexion. After she had approached us, she stopped and asked where we were going to. We replied that we were going to "Deads' Town," and she asked again from where were we coming. We replied that we were coming from the Faithful-Mother in the white tree. After we had told her that, then she told us to follow her, but when she said so, we feared her and my wife said—"This is not a human-being and she is not a spirit, but what is she?" Then we were following her as she told us. After we had travelled with her to a distance of about 6 miles in this bush, then we entered inside a "Red-Bush" and the bush was in deep red together with all the trees, ground and all the living creatures therein. Immediately we entered this "Red-Bush" my wife and myself turned deep-red as that bush, but at the same time that we entered the "Red-Bush," these words came out from my wife's mouth—"This is only fear for the heart but not dangerous to the heart."

WE AND THE RED-PEOPLE IN THE RED-TOWN

After we had travelled about 12 miles away in the "Red-Bush" with the Red-lady, we entered a Red-town and there we saw that both people and their domestic animals were deep-red in colour. So we entered a house which was the largest in that area, but as we were feeling hungry before reaching there, we asked the lady to give us food and water. After a while she brought both for us, but to our surprise, both food and water were as red as red paint, but both tasted as ordinary food and water so we ate the food and drank the water also. After she had brought the food for us, she left us there and went away, but as we sat down there, these Red-people were coming and looking at us with astonishment. After a few minutes the lady came back and told us to follow her and we did so. Then she took us around the town and showed us everything, after that she took us to their king who was also red as blood. The king saluted us well and told us to sit down before him. Then he asked us where were we coming from? We replied that we were coming from the Faithful-Mother who was in charge of the white tree. When he heard so from us, he said that the Faithful-Mother was his sister, then we told him how she helped us from our difficulties etc. After that he asked us what was the name of our town. We told him the name. Then he asked whether we were still alive or dead before coming there. We told him that we were still alive and we were not deads.

After that he told the Red-lady that brought us to him to put us in one of the rooms in his palace, but the room was very far from the other rooms and nobody was living near there. So we entered the room and began to think—What was his aim, the Red-king of the Red-people in the Red-town, was the question we asked ourselves, and we could not sleep till morning, because of this question.

When it was early in the morning, we went to the Red-king and sat down before him and waited for what he would say. But when it was about 8 o'clock, the Red-lady who brought us to the Red-king came and sat down behind us.

After a while the Red-king started the story of the Red-town, Red-people, and the Red-Bush thus:—He said—"The whole of us in this Red-town were once human-beings; in the olden days when the eyes of all the human-beings were on our knees, when we were bending down from the sky because of its gravitiness and when we were walking backwards and not forwards as nowadays." He said also "One day, when I was still among the human-beings I set one trap in a bush which was very far away from any river, even a pond did not be near there, then I set one fish-net inside a river which was very far away from any bush, even a piece of land did not be near there. But when it was next morning, I went first to the river in which I set the fish-net for fish, but to my surprise, the net had caught a red-bird instead of a fish and the red-bird was still alive as it was in a river. Then I took out the net together with the red-bird and put it down on the bank of the river. Next I went to the bush in which I had set the trap for bush animals and again the trap had also caught a big red-fish and it was still alive. After that, I took both the net and the trap with red-bird and red-fish to my town. But when my parents saw the red-fish that the trap caught instead of a bush animal and again that the fish-net had caught a red-bird instead of a fish, and both were still alive, they told me to return them to the place that I brought them from, and I took both of them and returned to put them in the place where I had caught them.

"But when I was going along the way, I stopped mid-way under the shade of a tree and made a fire there, then I put these two red creatures inside the fire. My aim was to burn them into ashes and return to my town from there. But what surprised me most was that, when I was going to put these

red creatures in the fire, they were talking like human-
beings, saying that I must not put them in the fire, because
red creatures were not to go near fire at all, but when I heard
that from them, I was greatly terrified. Of course, I did not
listen to them, I was only taking both of them from the net
and trap to the fire, but as I was taking them out of the net
and trap, they were still boasting that I could not put them
in that fire at all. Although when I heard that from them,
I was greatly annoyed and put them in that fire by force. As
these red creatures were inside that fire, they were saying
that I should take them out of the fire at once, but I told
them that that could not be done at all. After a little time,
they burnt into halves, but they were still talking. Then I
gathered more dried sticks and put them inside the fire, but
when the fire rose up, I was suddenly covered by the smoke
which came out from the fire, and I could hardly breathe.
Before I could find my way out from the smoke I had turned
red, and when I saw that I had become red, then I ran to my
town and entered our house, but the smoke was following
me as I was running to our house, and entered the house
with me. When my parents saw that I had turned into red,
they wanted to wash me, perhaps the red would be washed
away, but as soon as the smoke entered with me the whole
people became red also, then we went before the king who
was on the throne to show him what had happened, but the
smoke did not allow the king to say anything, before it
scattered all over the town and all the people, domestic
animals, town, river and bush became red at the same time.

"But when everyone of us had failed to wash his or her
red away, then on the 7th day after we had turned into the
red the whole of us died with our domestic animals, and we

left that town and settled down here, but we were still red as before we died and also our domestic animals, rivers, town and bush or anything we met here became red, so that since that time we were called Red-people and our town was called Red-town etc. But some days after we had settled down here, the red-fish and the red-bird came and lived inside a big hole which was very near this town. Since both red creatures came here they have been coming out from the hole every year for human sacrifice and we are sacrificing one of us to them yearly to save the rest of us. So we are very glad that both of you came to the Red-town just now because there remain only three days before these two creatures come out for their sacrifice of this year and I should be very glad too if one of you would volunteer his or her life for these two creatures."

After the Red-king had related the story for us and in his conclusion had said that one of us should volunteer his or her life for the two creatures, willingly or not, I asked my wife what could we do now? Because I do not want to leave her or she to leave me here alone and none of these Red-people wanted to volunteer his or her life for these creatures and again the king wanted to hear from us as soon as possible.

But my wife said these words—"This would be a brief loss of woman, but a shorter separation of a man from lover." But I did not understand the meaning of her words, because she was talking with parables or as a foreteller. After a little time I went to the Red-king and told him that I should volunteer my life for the two red creatures. And when the Red-king and Red-people heard that from me, they were exceedingly glad. The reason why I volunteered my life was that when I remembered that we had sold away our "death" to somebody, I knew these two creatures would be unable to kill me at all. I did not know that these Red-people would perform their native ceremony for me or anybody who volunteers his or her life to the two creatures before the very day that the two creatures would come out from their hole.

Now the Red-people removed all the hair of my head and painted the half part of it with a kind of red paint and the other part with white native paint, after that, the whole of them gathered together and put me on their front with their drummers and singers. They told me to dance as the drummers were beating their drums around the town. My wife was also following us, but she did not show that she would lose me soon at all. But when it was 5 o'clock early in the morning that the two red creatures would come out, I took my gun, ammunitions and cutlass which the Faithful-Mother gave me before we left her, then I loaded the gun with the most powerful ammunitions and put it on my shoulder and sharpened the cutlass and held it firmly with my right hand. When it was 7 o'clock of that morning, the Red-king and all the Red-people took me to the place where the hole was, and put me there for the red creatures, then the whole of them went back to the town. The place was not more than half a mile from the town.

They left me there alone and ran back to the town, because if the two red creatures should see more than one person whom they give them as sacrifice, they would kill them as well. But my wife did not return to the town with them, she hid herself near the place I was but I did not know at all. When it was half an hour that I stood before the hole, I began to hear that something was making a noise as if it was a thousand persons in that hole, every part of that place was shaking, by that time I took only my gun from my shoulder and held it firmly, then I sighted the hole. But when these two red creatures were coming out from the hole, they did not walk side by side but following each other and when the one at the front appeared and was coming towards me, it was red-fish in form. As a matter of fact, when I saw this red-fish, I was greatly terrified and I was soon faint, but I remembered that we had sold our "death" and I could not die again, so I did not care about it again, but I feared it greatly because we did not sell our "fear." At the same time that the red-fish appeared out, its head was just like a tortoise's head, but it was as big as an elephant's head and it had over 30 horns and large eyes which surrounded the head. All these horns were spread out as an umbrella. It could not walk but was only gliding on the ground like a snake and its body was just like a bat's body and covered with long red hair like strings. It could only fly to a short distance, and if it shouted a person who was four miles away would hear. All the eyes which surrounded its head were closing and opening at the same time as if a man was pressing a switch on and off.

At the same time that this red-fish saw me stood before their hole, it was laughing and coming towards me like a human-being, but I said within myself that this was a really human-being. Then I got ready as it was coming laughing towards me, but when it still had about twenty feet to reach where I stood, then I fired at it on the centre of its head and before the smoke of the gun scattered away, I had loaded again and shot it once more, so it died at that same spot. But when my wife saw the red-fish when coming out from the hole, from the place where she hid herself, she ran back to the town. As the red-fish was coming out from the hole, I knew that I should kill it, but I had no juju any more, all had become powerless from long using.

After that I loaded the gun for the second red creature (red-bird) and within 5 minutes it appeared out again, then I got ready for it. I saw that it was a red-bird, but its head could weigh one ton or more and it had six long teeth of about half a foot long and very thick, which appeared out with its beak. Its head was almost covered with all kinds of insects so that I could hardly describe it here fully. So immediately this bird saw me, it opened its mouth and was coming to swallow me, but I had got ready then, and when it had nearly reached the place that I stood, it stopped and swallowed the red-fish which I had killed already the first time. After that it was coming directly and I fired at it, then I loaded the gun for the second time and shot it to death.

When I saw that I had killed these two red creatures, then I remembered what my wife had said immediately we met the Red-lady who took us to the Red-king. My wife said thus:—It would be a "fear" of heart, but it would not be dangerous to the heart."

Now I went to the Red-king of the Red-town and told him that I had killed both red creatures, and as soon as he heard so from me, he got up from his chair and followed me to the place where I killed the two red creatures. But when the Red-king saw the two red creatures already dead, he said—"Here is another fearful and harmful creature who could ruin my town in future." (He called me a fearful and harmful creature.) At the same time that he said this, he left me there and went back to the town, then he called all the people of his town together and told them what he had seen. As these Red-people could change themselves to anything that they liked, before I could reach the town, the whole of them had changed into a great fire which burnt their houses and all their properties. By the time that the houses were burning, I could not enter the town, because of the thick smoke of the fire, but after a little time the fire and smoke disappeared and I thought that the whole of them together with my wife had burnt into ashes. But as I stood in one place looking at the empty town, there I saw that two red trees appeared again at the centre of the town. One of the trees was shorter than the second and also slender and it was at the front of the bigger one. That bigger one which was at the back had many leaves and branches. When I saw that these two red trees appeared in the centre of the town I was going to them, but both were moving towards the west of the town before I reached there, and all the leaves on these trees were singing as human-beings as they were moving on and within five minutes, I could not see them any more, and all the while I did not know that it was the whole Red-people who had changed themselves into that two red trees. As my wife had disappeared with these Red-people, I began to seek her about both night and day, but one day, I heard information that she was among the Red-people who had changed themselves into two red trees before they left the Red-town. Then I started to the place where I heard that they had settled down, but the new town that they had just settled down in was about eighty miles away from the Red-town which they left ruined. After I had travelled for two days, then I reached there, but they had left there when they heard information that I was coming there too, and I did not know that these Red-people were thinking while running away from me that I should kill them as I had killed the two red creatures. So they left that place again and were looking for a suitable place to settle down, but they never got to such a place before I met them, although I was thinking that I would meet them in the form of persons, but they were the two red trees.

As I met them in the midway, my wife had seen me and was calling me, but I did not see her at all, and as I was still following these two red trees to wherever they could get a suitable place to settle down for a week. Then they got a suitable place and they stopped, but I was very far away by that time. And when I came up with them I saw that every part was full of houses, people and their domestic animals etc., exactly as when they were in the town which they had burnt into ashes before they left there. But when I entered the new town, I went directly to the Red-king of this new town (the same king) and told him that I wanted my wife, but when he heard so, he called her for me at once and she saw me, she repeated her words again which she had said before—"This would be a brief loss of woman and a shorter separation from lover," and she said that this was the meaning of the words. Then I believed her. But when the Red-people had settled down in a new town, they were no longer red, because I had killed the two red creatures which had changed them like that.

My wife had said of the woman we met: "She was not a human-being and she was not a spirit, but what was she?" She was the Red-smaller-tree who was at the front of the bigger Red-tree, and the bigger Red-tree was the Red-king of the Red-people of Red-town and the Red-bush.

The Palm-Wine Drinkard

Now my wife and I became friends with these people and we were living with them in that new town. After some days, the lady who brought us to the former town (Red-town) gave us a big house in which we were living comfortably. "She was not a human-being and she was not a spirit but what was she?" She was also the "Dance" (the lady that brought us to the Red-town) and you will remember when I mentioned the tree fellows, namely:—"DRUM, SONG AND DANCE." So when this lady (Dance) saw that I helped them greatly and they were also in a comfortable place and were no longer red, she sent for the other two fellows (Drum and Song) to come to their new town for a special occasion. But how could we enjoy these three fellows? Because nobody could beat drum as "Drum" could beat himself, nobody could sing as "Song" could sing himself, and nobody could dance as "Dance" could dance herself in this world. Who would challenge them? Nobody at all. But when the day that they appointed for this special occasion was reached, these fellows came and when "Drum" started to beat himself, all the people who had been dead for hundreds of years, rose up and came to witness "Drum" when beating; and when "Song" began to sing all domestic animals of that new town, bush animals with snakes etc, came out to see "Song" personally, but when "Dance" (that lady) started to dance the whole bush creatures, spirits, mountain creatures and also all the river creatures came to the town to see who was dancing. When these three fellows started at the same time, the whole people of the new town, the whole people that rose up from the grave, animals, snakes, spirits and other nameless creatures, were dancing together with these three fellows and it was that day that I saw that snakes were dancing

263

more than human-beings or other creatures. When the whole people of that town and bush creatures started dancing together none of them could stop for two days. But at last "Drum" was beating himself till he reached heaven before he knew that he was out of the world and since that day he could not come to the world again. Then "Song" sang until he entered into a large river unexpectedly and we could not see him any more and "Dance" was dancing till she became a mountain and did not appear to anybody since that day, so all the deads rose up from the grave returned to the grave and since that day they could not rise up again, then all the rest of the creatures went back to the bush etc. but since that day they could not come to the town and dance with anybody or with human-beings.

So when these three fellows (Drum, Song and Dance) disappeared, the people of the new town went back to their houses. Since that day nobody could see the three fellows personally, but we are only hearing their names about in the world and nobody could do in these days what they did. After I had spent a year with my wife in this new town, I became a rich man. Then I hired many labourers to clear bush for me and it was cleared up to three miles square by these farm-labourers, then I planted the seeds and grains which were given me in the "Wraith-Island" by a certain animal (as he was called) the owner of the land on which I planted my crops, before he gave me the seeds and grains which germinated the same day as I planted them. As the seeds and grains grew up and yielded fruits the same day, so it made me richer than the rest of the people in that town.

The Palm-Wine Drinkard
THE INVISIBLE-PAWN

One night, at about ten o'clock, I saw a certain man who
came to my house. He told me that he was always hearing
the word—"POOR," but he did not know it and he wanted
to know it. He said that he wanted to borrow some amount
and he would be working for me in return as a "pawn" or
as permanent hired labourer.

But when he said this, I asked how much did he want to
borrow? He said that he wanted to borrow two thousand
cowries (COWRIES), which was equivalent to six-pence
(6d) in British money. Then I asked from my wife whether
I should lend him the amount, but my wife said that the
man would be a—"WONDERFUL HARD WORKER, BUT
HE WOULD BE A WONDERFUL ROBBER IN FU-
TURE."—Of course, I did not understand what my wife
meant by that, but I simply gave the man the six-pence that
he demanded. When he wanted to go, I asked for his name,
then he told me that his name was "GIVE AND TAKE,"
after that I asked him where he was living, and he replied
that he was inside a bush which nobody could trace. When
he said so, I asked him again, how could the other labourers
reach him whenever they were going to the farm, then he
replied that if the rest of the labourers were going to the
farm very early in the morning, they should call his name
out as they reached a junction of roads on the way to the
farm. Then he went away. But when my labourers were
going to the farm early in the morning, when they reached
the junction and called his name out as he said (with loud
voice), he answered with song. After that he asked them

what kind of work they were going to do that day. Then they told him that it was only to till the ground, after that, he told them to go and till their own ground, but he would go and till his own at night, because small children must not see him and it was forbidden for adults to look at him. Then the rest of the labourers went to the farm and tilled their portion. When it was early on the following morning, the rest of the labourers went to the farm as usual, but they saw the whole farm and bushes around there cleared as from a mile to fifty by this Invisible-Pawn and he had cleared all the farms which belonged to my neighbours too. So when the other labourers were going to the farm early in the morning as usual, I told them that they should tell "Invisible-Pawn" that today's work was to cut fire wood from the farm to my house. When the rest of the labourers reached there they called him and told him that today's work was to cut fire wood from the farm to the house. Then he told them to go and cut their own, and he would cut and bring his own to the house at night. As the rest of the labourers were calling him at the junction, he was not visible to them at all. But to my surprise, when everybody woke up early in the morning, we could not come out from our houses, because this man (Invisible-Pawn) had brought both fire wood and logs of wood together with palm-trees and other trees to the town, and all the town was almost covered with this wood, so that nobody could move about in the town and we did not know the time he brought them. Then all of the town's people began to clear the woods with axes etc., but it took a week before we could clear away the wood from the town. As I wanted to see him (Invisible-Pawn or Give and Take) and how he was working I told the rest farm labourers to tell

The Palm-Wine Drinkard

"Give and Take" that today's work was to be barber for my children at home, but he told his colleagues that they should go and barb their own, he would come and barb his own at night, so the rest of the labourers went away. When it was night, I told the rest of the labourers to keep watch on him and see how he would barb heads for my children, but to my surprise, it was not yet 8 o'clock in the night before everybody slept in that town, even no domestic animal was awake. After that the "Invisible-Pawn" came and barbed for all of the people in that town, adults or females with domestic animals, he took everybody to the outside before he shaved their heads, then he painted the heads with white paint, then he went back to his bush and nobody woke up till he had completed that evil work. When it was early in the morning, everybody met himself or herself outside, and when we touched our heads, they were shaven and painted with white paint. But at the same time that this new town's people woke up and saw that all the hair on the heads of their domestic animals had been cleared as well, then they rose up in alarm that they had fallen into another terrible creature's hand again. But I checked them and explained how the matter went, so by that time, they wanted me to leave their town, but I thought that I should do something to please these people, so that they would not drive me away from the town. One day, when the labourers were going to the farm, I told them to tell "Invisible-Pawn" that today's work was to go and kill bush animals and bring them to my house. When he heard so, he told them as usual. But when the day broke, the town was full of bush animals, so that all the people in the town were now pleased and did not want me to leave there again.

267

The Palm-Wine Drinkard

After that, one day, I sat down and I began to think over how this man was working like this and he did not ask for food etc., so when the corn was ripe then I told the labourers to tell him that if he went to the farm, he should take some yams, corn etc. So they told him this when they reached the usual junction.

I did not know that this "Invisible-Pawn" or "Give and Take" was the head of all the Bush-creatures and he was the most powerful in the world of the Bush-creatures, all of these Bush-creatures were under him and working for him every night. So after he had finished that night's work in my farm together with his followers, then the whole of them took all the yams and corn etc. of my farm and took all the yams and corn etc. from my neighbour's also. I did not know that he had followers at all who were working for him and instead of him alone taking some yams and corn, so all of them took the whole lot away at night.

Then I remembered what my wife foresaid that—"This man would be a wonderful hard worker, but he would be a wonderful robber in future." So the following morning when the labourers had told him to take some yams and corn from the farm, everybody went to his farm, but unfortunately they found their farms without crops that they had planted there, for all the farms had been cleared by these bush-creatures as flat as a football field.

But when all the farmers or my neighbours saw what "Give and Take" had done, they grew annoyed with me, because they could not plant other crops throughout that year again and had nothing for themselves and their children to eat at all and all of my own crops were taken away too, but I could not tell my neighbours. When these people

saw what "Invisible-Pawn" or "Give and Take" with his
followers had done for them, then they united together to
raise up an Army against me, so that I might leave their
town and also to revenge for the great loss which "Give and
Take" had given them through me. Then these people gathered together and formed a great army. Then I asked my
wife what should be the end of us in this town? But my wife
said that it would be the loss of lives of the natives, but it
would save the two non-natives. By that time, I was hiding
my wife and myself in that town, because all the natives of
the town were hunting for us up and down, of course they
did not want to fire guns inside their town, because of their
children and wives and we (my wife and I) did not leave
their town because they could not fire their guns inside the
town. But as I was thinking how my wife and myself could
be safe from these people, so my wife remembered me to call
for the help of the "Invisible-Pawn" (Give and Take), perhaps he might render his help. When my wife advised me
like that, then I sent for one of my labourers to go and tell
the "Invisible-Pawn" that the people of new town would
raise up an Army against me in two days to come, so that I
begged him to come and help me early in the morning of
that day.

THE INVISIBLE-PAWN ON THE FRONT

But as the "Invisible-Pawn" could not do anything in the
day time, he came with his followers or helpers to this town
at about two o'clock in the mid-night, then the whole of
them started to fight these people and killed the whole of

them and left my wife and me there alone. As my wife had said before, all the lives of the natives were lost and the life of the non-natives saved. After that the "Invisible-Pawn" and his followers went back to their bush before dawn. But when I saw that we alone (my wife and me) could not live in that town, then we packed our loads and my gun with my cutlass and left the town as soon as all of the natives of the town had perished.

That was how our life went in the Red-town with the Red-people and the Red-king and how we saw the end of them in their new town.

So we started our journey to unknown Deads' Town, where my palm-wine tapster who had died in my town long ago was and we were travelling inside bush to bush as before, but the bush in which we were travelling by that time was not so thick and was not so fearful too. But as we were going on, my wife told me that we should not stop in there two days and nights before we should reach the place that we met the Red-lady that we followed to the Red-town and before we could reach that place, we should travel about fifty-five miles. But when we had travelled both day and night for two days, we reached there and stopped and rested there for two days. After that we started our journey to an unknown town directly, and after we had travelled ninety miles to that place, there we met a man who sat down and had a full-bag of load on his front. We asked him where was Deads' Town, and he told us that he knew, and it was the very town that he was going to at present. When he told us so, then we told him that we should follow him to the town, but when he heard so from us, he begged us to help him to carry his load which was on his front. Of course, we did not know what was inside the bag, but the bag was full, and he told us that we should not put the load down from head until we should reach the said town. Again he did not allow us to test the weight of it, whether it was heavier than what we could carry. Then my wife asked him how could a man buy a pig in a bag? But the man replied that there was no need of testing the load, he said that once we put it on our head either it was heavier than what we could carry or not, anyhow we should carry it to the town. So we stood before that man and his load. But when I thought over that if I put it on my head and could not carry it, then I should put it down at once, and if that man would force me not to put it down, I had gun and cutlass here, I should shoot him immediately.

Then I told the man to put it on my head, but he said that two hands must not touch the load. When he said so, I asked him what kind of load was this? He replied that it was the load which two persons must not know the content of. So, I put hope on my gun and I trusted my cutlass as God, then I told my wife to put the load on my head and she helped me. When I put it on my head it was just like a dead body of a man, it was very heavy, but I could carry it easily. So the man was on our front and we followed him.

But after we had travelled about 36 miles, we entered into a town and we did not know that he was telling us a lie in saying that he was going to Deads' Town and we did not know that the load was the dead body of the prince of the town that we entered. That man had mistakenly killed him in the farm and was looking for somebody who would represent him as the killer of the prince.

WE AND THE WISE KING IN THE WRONG TOWN
WITH THE PRINCE KILLER

Because he (the killer of the Prince) knew that if the king realised who killed his son he (king) would kill the man instead, so this man did not want to prove out that he was the killer of the prince. So when we reached the town with him (not Deads' Town), he told us to wait for him in a corner and he went to the king and reported to him (king) that somebody had killed his son in the bush and he had brought them to the town. Then the king sent about thirty of his attendants with the man who killed the prince to come and escort us to him with the load. When we reached the palace, they loosened the bag and saw it was the dead body of the king's son (prince), but when the king saw that it was his son, then he told his attendants to put us inside a dark room.

Early in the morning, the king told the attendants to wash and dress us with the finest clothes and put us on horse and they (attendants) must take us around the town for seven days which meant to enjoy our last life in the world for that 7 days, after that he (king) should kill us as we killed his son.

But these attendants and the right man who killed the prince in the bush did not know the king's aim at all. When it was early in the morning, the attendants washed us and dressed us with costly clothes and dressed the horse as well. Then we mounted the horse. After that they were following us about in the town, they were beating drums, dancing and singing the song of mourning for six days, but when it was early on the 7th day's morning that we should be killed and they (attendants) were taking us around the town for the last time, we reached the centre of the town, and there we saw the right man who killed the prince and told us to carry him (prince) to that town. He pushed us away from the horse's back and mounted the horse for himself, and he told the attendants that he was the right man who killed the king's son in the bush, he said that he was thinking that the king would kill him as a revenge and that was the reason why he told the king that it was us who killed the prince in the bush. This man thought now that the king was pleased that some-body killed his son in the farm and that was the reason why the king told the attendants to dress us and take us on a riding horse about in the town, and he told the attendants again to take him to the king and repeat the same words in his presence.

So he was taken to the king and he repeated that he was the right man who killed his son in the bush. At the same time that the king heard so from him, he told the attendants to dress him as they had dressed us, then the man mounted the horse, and riding it about in the town as we had done, as he was on the horse's back, he was jumping up and laughing with gladness. When it was 5 o'clock in the eve-ning, he was taken to their bush reserved for such occasion and he was killed there and they presented his dead body to their gods in that reserve-bush.

After we had spent 15 days in that town, then we told the king that we wanted to continue our journey to the Deads' Town, and he gave us presents and told us the shortest way to the Deads' Town. A full loaded bag would cause seven days' dance, but there would be a "WISE-KING" in the town, as my wife had foresaid. This was the end of the story of the bag which I carried from the bush to the "wrong town."

Then we continued our journey as usual to the Deads' Town and when we had travelled for 10 days we were looking at the Deads' Town about 40 miles away and we were not delayed by anything on the way again. But as we were looking at the town from a long distance, we thought that we could reach there the same day, but not at all, we travelled for 6 more days, because as we nearly reached there, it would still seem to be very far away to us or as if it was running away from us. We did not know that anybody who had not died could not enter into that town by day time, but when my wife knew the secret, then she told me that we should stop and rest till night. When it was night, then she told me to get up and start our journey again. But soon after we started to go, we found that we need not travel more than one hour before we reached there. Of course we did not enter into it until the dawn, because it was an unknown town to us.

I AND MY PALM-WINE TAPSTER IN THE DEADS' TOWN

When it was 8 o'clock in the morning, then we entered the town and asked for my palm-wine tapster whom I was looking for from my town when he died, but the deads asked for his name and I told him that he was called "BAITY" before he died, but now I could not definitely know his present name as he had died.

When I told them his name and said that he had died in

my town, they did not say anything but stayed looking at us.
When it was about five minutes that they were looking at
us like that, one of them asked us from where did we come?
I replied that we were coming from my town, then he said
where. I told him that it was very far away to this town and
he asked again were the people in that town alives or deads?
I replied that the whole of us in that town had never died.
When he heard that from me, he told us to go back to my
town where there were only alives living, he said that it was
forbidden for alives to come to the Deads' Town.

As that dead man told us to go back, I began to beg him
to allow us to see my palm-wine tapster. So he agreed and
showed us a house which was not so far from the place
where we stood, he told us to go there and ask for him, but
as we turned our back to him (dead man) and were going
to the house that he showed us, the whole of them that stood
on that place grew annoyed at the same time to see us
walking forward or with our face, because they were not
walking forward there at all, but this we did not know.

As soon as the dead man who was asking us questions saw
us moving he ran to us and said that he had told us to go
back to my town because alives could not come and visit any
dead man in the Deads' Town, so he told us to walk backward or with our back and we did so. But as we were
walking backward as they themselves were walking there, I
stumbled over suddenly and as I was trying not to fall into
a deep pit which was near there, I mistakenly turned my
face towards the house that he showed us. But when he saw
me again like that, he came to us as before and said that he
would not allow us to go to the house any more, because
people were not walking forward in that town. Then I

275

begged him again and explained to him that we came to see him (palm-wine tapster) from a very far town. But I stumbled on a sharp stone in that pit, some part of me was scratched and bleeding, then we stopped to rub off the blood as it was bleeding too much. When this dead man saw that we stopped, he came nearer and asked what stopped us, then I pointed my finger to the bleeding part of my body, but when he saw the blood, he was greatly annoyed and dragged us out of the town by force. As he was dragging us out of the town, we wanted to beg him, but he said, no more excuse. We did not know that all the deads did not like to see blood at all, and it was that day I knew. He dragged us out of their town and told us to stay there and we did as he said. Then he went back to the house of my tapster and told him that two alives were waiting for him. After a few minutes, my palm-wine tapster came, but immediately he saw us, he thought that I had died before coming there, so he gave the sign of deads to us, but we were unable to reply to him, because we never died, and at the same time that he reached us, he knew that we could not live with them in the town as we could not reply to his signal, then before we started any conversation, he built a small house there for us. After that we put our loads inside the house, but to my surprise, this my tapster was also walking backward and he was not walking like that before he died in my town. After he had built the house, he went back to the town and brought food and ten kegs of palm-wine for us. As we were very hungry before reaching there, we ate the food to excess and when I tasted the palm-wine, I could not take my mouth away until I drank the whole ten kegs. After that we started conversation which went thus—I told him that after he had died, I wanted to die with him and follow him to this Deads' Town because of the palm-wine that he was tapping for me and nobody could tap it for me like him, but I could not die. So one day, I called two of my friends and went to the farm, then we began to tap for ourselves, but it did not taste like the wine he was tapping before he died. But when all my friends saw that if they come to my house there was no more palm-wine to drink again, then they were leaving me one by one until all of them went away, even if I should see one of them at outside and call him, he would only say that he would come, but I would not see him come.

Though my father's house was full of people before, nobody at present was coming there. So one day, I thought what I could do, then I thought within myself that I should find him (palm-wine tapster) wherever he might be and tell him to follow me to my father's town and begin to tap palm-wine for me as usual. So I started my journey early in the morning, and at every town or village that I reached I asked them whether they had seen him or knew where he was, but some would say unless I should help them to do something, they would not tell. Then I showed the tapster my wife and told of how, when I went to a certain town and her father who was the head of that town received me as his guest, my wife was taken to a far forest by a gentleman who afterwards was reduced to a "Skull" and how I went there and brought her to her father, so after he had seen the wonderful work which I did for him, then he gave her to me as a wife and after I had spent about one and half or more years with them there, then I took her and sought him about. And how before reaching here, we met much difficulty in the bush, because there was no road to this Deads'

The Palm-Wine Drinkard

Town and we were travelling from bush to bush every day and night, even many times, we were travelling from branches to branches of trees for many days before touching ground and it was ten years since I had left my town. Now I was exceedingly glad to meet him here and I should be most grateful if he would follow me back to my town.

So after I had related how the story went to him, he did not talk a single word, but he went back to the town, and after a while, he brought about twenty kegs of palm-wine for me, then I started to drink it. After that he started his own story:—He said that after he had died in my town, he went to a certain place, which anybody who just died must go to first, because a person who just died could not come here (Deads' Town) directly. He said that when he reached there, he spent two years in training and after he had qualified as a full dead man, then he came to this Deads' Town and was living with deads and he said that he could not say what happened to him before he died in my town. But when he said so, I told him that he fell down from a palm-tree on a Sunday evening when he was tapping palm-wine and we buried him at the foot of the very palm-tree on which he fell.

Then he said that if that should be the case, he over-drank on that day.

After that, he said that he came back to my house on the very night that he fell and died at the farm and looked at everyone of us, but we did not see him, and he was talking to us, but we did not answer, then he went away. He told us that both white and black deads were living in the Deads' Town, not a single alive was there at all. Because everything that they were doing there was incorrect to alives and every-

278

thing that all alives were doing was incorrect to deads too.

He said that did I not see that both dead persons and their domestic animals of this town were walking backwards? Then I answered "Yes." Then he told me that he could not follow me back to my town again, because a dead man could not live with alives and their characteristics would not be the same and said that he would give me anything that I liked in the Deads' Town. When he said so, I thought over what had happened to us in the bush, then I was very sorry for my wife and myself and I was then unable to drink the palm-wine which he gave me at that moment. Even I myself knew already that deads could not live with alives, because I had watched their doings and they did not correspond with ours at all. When it was five o'clock in the evening, he went to his house and brought food for us again and he went back after three hours. But when he came back early in the morning, he brought another 50 kegs of palm-wine which I drank first of all that morning. But when I thought that he would not follow us to my town, and again, my wife was pressing me too much to leave there very early, when he came, I told him that we should leave here tomorrow morning, then he gave me an "EGG." He told me to keep it as safely as gold and said that if I reached my town, I should keep it inside my box and said that the use of the egg was to give me anything that I wanted in this world and if I wanted to use it, I must put it in a big bowl of water, then I would mention the name of anything that I wanted. After he gave me the egg we left there on the third day after we arrived there and he showed us another shorter road and it was a really road, not a bush as before.

Now we started our journey from the Deads' Town directly to my home town which I had left for many years. As we were going on this road, we met over a thousand deads who were just going to the Deads' Town and if they saw us coming towards them on that road, they would branch into the bush and come back to the road at our back. Whenever they saw us, they would be making bad noise which showed us that they hated us and also were very annoyed to see alives. These deads were not talking to one another at all, even they were not talking plain words except murmuring. They always seemed as if they were mourning, their eyes would be very wild and brown and everyone of them wore white clothes without a single stain.

NONE OF THE DEADS TOO YOUNG TO ASSAULT. DEAD BABIES ON THE ROAD-MARCH TO THE DEADS' TOWN

We met about 400 dead babies on that road who were singing the song of mourning and marching to Deads' Town at about two o'clock in the mid-night and marching towards the town like soldiers, but these dead babies did not branch into the bush as the adult-deads were doing if they met us, all of them held sticks in their hands. But when we saw that these dead babies did not care to branch for us then we stopped at the side for them to pass peacefully, but instead of that, they started to beat us with the sticks in their hands, then we began to run away inside the bush from these babies, although we did not care about any risk of that bush which might happen to us at night, because these dead babies were the most fearful creatures for us. But as we were running inside the bush very far off that road, they were still chasing us until we met a very huge man who had hung a very large bag on his shoulder and at the same time that he met us, he caught us (my wife and myself) inside the bag as a fisherman catches fishes inside his net. But when he caught us inside his bag, then all of the dead babies went back to the road and went away. As that man caught us with that bag, we met inside it many other creatures there which I could not describe here yet, so he was taking us far away into the bush. We tried with all our power to come out of the bag, but we could not do it, because it was woven with strong and thick ropes, its size was about 150 feet diameter and it could contain 45 persons. He put the bag on his shoulder as he was going and we did not know where he was taking us to by that night and again we did not know who was taking us away, whether he was a human-being or spirit or if he was going to kill us, we never knew yet at all.

AFRAID OF TOUCHING TERRIBLE CREATURES IN BAG

We were afraid of touching the other creatures that we met inside that bag, because every part of their bodies was as cold as ice and hairy and sharp as sand-paper. The air of their noses and mouths was hot as steam, none of them talked inside the bag. But as that man was carrying us away inside the bush with the bag on his shoulder the bag was always striking trees and ground but he did not care or stop, and he himself did not talk too. As he was carrying us far away into that bush, he met a creature of his kind, then he stopped and they began to throw the bag to and fro and they would take it up again and continue. After a while they stopped that, then he kept going as before, but he travelled as far as 30 miles from that road before daybreak.

HARD TO SALUTE EACH OTHER, HARDER TO DESCRIBE EACH OTHER, AND HARDEST TO LOOK AT EACH OTHER AT DESTINATION

Hard to salute each other, harder to describe each other, and hardest to look at each other at our destination. When it was 8 o'clock in the morning, this huge creature stopped when he reached his destination, and turned upside-down the bag and the whole of us in the bag came down unexpectedly. It was in that place that we saw that there were 9 terrible creatures in that bag before he caught us. Then we saw each other when we came down, but the nine terrible creatures were the hardest creatures for us to look at, then we saw the huge creature who was carrying us about in the bush throughout that night, he was just like a giant, very huge and tall, his head resembled a big pot of about ten feet in diameter, there were two large eyes on his forehead which were as big as bowls and his eyes would be turning whenever he was looking at somebody. He could see a pin at a distance of about three miles. His both feet were very long and thick as a pillar of a house, but no shoes could size his feet in this world. The description of the 9 terrible creatures in the bag is as follows. These 9 terrible creatures were short or 3 feet high, their skin as sharp as sand-paper with small short horns on their palms, very hot steam was rushing out of their noses and mouths whenever breathing, their bodies were as cold as ice and we did not understand their language, because it was sounding as a church bell. Their hands were thick about 5 inches and very short, with fingers, and also their feet were just like blocks. They had no shape at all like human-beings or like other bush-creatures that we met in the past, their heads were covered with a kind of hair like sponge. Though they were very smart while walking, of course their feet would be sounding on either hard or soft ground as if somebody was walking over or knocking a covered deep hole. But immediately we came down with them from the bag and when my wife and I myself saw these terrible creatures, we closed our eyes, because of their terrible and fearful appearance. After a while, the huge creature carried us to another place, opened a rise-up hill which was in that place, he told the whole of us to enter it, then he followed us and closed the hole back, we not knowing that he would not kill us but he had only captured us as slaves. When we entered the hole, there we met other more fearful creatures who I could not describe here. So when it was early in the morning, he took us out of the hole and showed us his farm to clear as the other more fearful creatures we met in the hole were doing. As I was working with these nine creatures in the farm, one day, one of them abused me with their language which I did not understand, then we started to fight, but when the rest saw that I wanted to kill him, then the whole of them started to fight me one by one. I killed the first one who faced me, then the second came and I killed him too, so I killed all of them one by one until the last one came who was their champion. When I started to fight him, he began to scrape my body with his sand-paper body and also with small thorns on his palms, so that every part of my body was bleeding. But I tried with all my power to knock him down and I was unable to as I could not grip him firmly with my hands, so he knocked me down and I fainted. Of course, I could not die because we had sold our death away. I did not know that my wife hid herself behind a big tree which was near the farm and that she was looking at us as we were fighting.

As there remained only the champion of the nine terrible creatures, when he saw that I had fainted, he went to a kind of plant and cut 8 leaves on it. But my wife was looking at him by that time. Then he came back to his people. After that, he squeezed the leaves with both his palms until water came out, then he began to put the water into the eyes of his people one by one and the whole of them woke up at once and all of them went to our boss (the huge creature who brought us to that place) to report what had happened in the farm to him. But at the same time that they left the farm, my wife went to that plant and cut one leaf and did as the champion did to his people, and when she pressed the water in that leaf to my eyes, then I woke up at once. As she had managed to take our loads before she left that hole and followed us to the farm, we escaped from that farm and before the nine terrible creatures reached the hole of our boss, we had gone far away. That was how we were saved from the huge creature who caught us in his bag.

As we had escaped, we were travelling both day and night so that the huge creature might not re-capture us again. When we travelled for two and half days, we reached the Deads' road from which dead babies drove us, and when we reached there, we could not travel on it because of fearful dead babies, etc. which were still on it.

TO TRAVEL IN THE BUSH WAS MORE DANGEROUS AND TO TRAVEL ON THE DEADS' ROAD WAS THE MOST DANGEROUS

Then we began to travel inside the bush, but closely to the road, so that we might not be lost in the bush again.

When we had travelled for two weeks, I began to see the leaves which were suitable for the preparation of my juju, then we stopped and prepared four kinds which could save us whenever and wherever we met any dangerous creature.

As I had prepared the juju, we did not fear anything which might happen to us inside the bush and we were travelling both day and night as we liked. So one night, we met a "hungry-creature" who was always crying "hungry" and as soon as that he saw us, he was coming to us directly. When he was about five feet away from us, we stopped and looked at him, because I had got some juju in hand already and because I remembered that we had sold our death before entering inside the white tree of the Faithful-Mother, and so I did not care about approaching him. But as he was coming towards us, he was asking us repeatedly whether we had anything for him to eat and by that time we had only bananas which were not ripe. We gave him the bananas but he swallowed all at the same moment and began to ask for another thing to eat again and he did not stop crying "hungry-hungry-hungry" once, but when we could not bear his crying, then we loosened our loads. Perhaps we could get another edible thing there to give him, but we found only a split bean and before we gave it to him, he had taken it from us and swallowed it without hesitation and began to cry "hungry-hungry-hungry" as usual. We did not know that this "hungry-creature" could not satisfy with any food in this world, and he might eat the whole food in this world, but he would be still feeling hungry as if he had not tasted anything for a year. But as we were searching our loads, as perhaps we could get something for him again, the egg which my tapster gave me in the Deads' Town fell down from my wife. The hungry-creature saw it, and he wanted to take it and swallow but my wife was very clever to pick it up before him.

When he saw that he could not pick it up before my wife, then he began to fight her and he said that he wanted to swallow her. As this hungry-creature was fighting with my wife, he did not stop to cry "hungry" once. But when I thought within myself that he might harm us, then I performed one of my jujus and it changed my wife and our loads to a wooden-doll and I put it in my pocket. But when the hungry-creature saw my wife no more, he told me to bring out the wooden-doll for identification, so I brought it and he was asking me with doubtful mind, was this not my wife and loads? Then I replied that it was not my wife etc., but it only resembled her, so he gave the wooden-doll back to me, then I returned it to my pocket as before and I kept going. But he was following me as I was going on, and still crying "hungry." Of course, I did not listen to him. When he had travelled with me to a distance of about a mile, he asked me again to bring out the wooden-doll for more identification and I brought it out to him, then he looked at it for more than ten minutes and asked me again was this not my wife? I replied that it was not my wife etc. but it only resembled her, then he gave it to me back and I was going as usual, but he was still following me and crying "hungry" as well. When he had travelled with me again to about two miles, he asked for it for the third time and I gave it to him, but as he held it he looked at it more than an hour and said that this was my wife and he swallowed it unexpectedly. As he swallowed the wooden-doll, it meant he swallowed my wife, gun, cutlass, egg and load and nothing remained with me again, except my juju.

So immediately he had swallowed the wooden-doll, he was going far away from me and crying "hungry" as well. Now the wife was lost and how to get her back from the hungry-creature's stomach? For the safety of an egg the wife was in hungry-creature's stomach. As I stood in that place and was looking at him as he was going far away, I saw him go so far from me that I could hardly see him, then I thought that my wife, who had been following me about in the bush to Deads' Town had not shrunk from any suffering, so I said that, she should not leave me like this and I would not leave her for the hungry-creature to carry away. So I followed, and when I met him I told him to vomit out the wooden-doll which he had swallowed, but he refused to vomit it out totally.

The Palm-Wine Drinkard
BOTH WIFE AND HUSBAND IN THE
HUNGRY-CREATURE'S STOMACH

I said that, rather than leave my wife with him, I would die with him, so I began to fight him, but as he was not a human-being, he swallowed me too and he was still crying "hungry" and going away with us. As I was in his stomach, I commanded my juju which changed the wooden-doll back to my wife, gun, egg, cutlass and loads at once. Then I loaded the gun and fired into his stomach, but he walked for a few yards before he fell down, and I loaded the gun for the second time and shot him again. After that I began to cut his stomach with the cutlass, then we got out from his stomach with our loads etc. That was how we were freed from the hungry-creature, but I could not describe him fully here, because it was about 4 o'clock A.M. and that time was very dark too. So we left him safely and thanked God for that.

We started our journey again to my home town after we left the hungry-creature, but as he had carried us far into the bush, we could not trace out our way to the deads' road again, so we were travelling in the middle of the bush. But when we had travelled for 9 days, we entered a town in which we met mixed people, and before we reached the "mixed town" my wife was seriously ill, then we went to a man who resembled a human-being, and he received us as strangers into his house, then I began to treat my wife there. They had one native court in this "mixed town" and I was always attending the court to listen to many cases. But to my surprise, one day I was told to judge a case which was brought to the court by a man who had lent his friend a pound (£).

The Palm-Wine Drinkard

The story went thus:—There were two friends, one of these two friends was money borrower, he had no other work than to borrow and he was feeding on any money that he was borrowing. One day, he borrowed £1 from his friend. After a year his friend who lent him the money, asked him to refund the £1 to him, but the borrower said that he would not pay the £1 and said that he had never paid any debit since he was borrowing money and since he was born. When his friend who lent him the £1 heard so from him, he said nothing, but went back to his house quietly. One day, the lender heard information that there was a debit-collector who was bold enough to collect debits from anybody whatsoever. Then he (lender) went to the debit-collector and told him that somebody owed him £1 since a year, but he refused to pay it back; after the debit-collector heard so, then both of them went to the house of the borrower. When he had showed the house of the borrower to the collector, he went back to his home.

When the debit-collector asked for the £1 which he (borrower) had borrowed from his friend since a year, the debitor (borrower) replied that he never paid any of his debits since he was born, then the debit-collector said that *he* never failed to collect debits from any debitor since *he* had begun the work. The collector said furthermore that to collect debits about was his profession and he was living on it. But after the debitor heard so from the collector, he also said that his profession was to owe debits and he was living only on debits. In conclusion, both of them started to fight but, as they were fighting fiercely, a man who was passing that way at that time saw them and he came nearer; he stood behind them looking at them, because he was very interested in this fight and he did not part them. But when these two fellows had fought fiercely for one hour, the debitor who owed the £1 pulled out a jack-knife from his pocket and stabbed himself at the belly, so he fell down and died there. But when the debit-collector saw that the debitor died, he thought within himself that he had never failed to collect any debit from any debitor in this world since he had started the work and he (collector) said that if he could not collect the £1 from him (debitor) in this world, he (collector) would collect it in heaven. So he (collector) also pulled out a jack-knife from his pocket and stabbed himself as well, and he fell down and died there.

As the man who stood by and looking at them was very, very interested in that fight, he said that he wanted to see the end of the fight, so he jumped up and fell down at the same spot and died there as well so as to witness the end of the fight in heaven. So when the above statement was given in the court, I was asked to point out who was guilty, either the debit-collector, debitor, the man who stood by looking at them when fighting, or the lender.

But first of all, I was about to tell the court that the man who stood by them looking at them was guilty, because he should have asked about the matter and parted them, but when I remembered that the debitor and collector were doing their work on which both of them were living, then I could not blame the man who stood looking at them and again I could not blame the collector, because he was doing his work and also the debitor himself because he was struggling for what he was living on. But the whole people in the court insisted me to point out who was guilty among them all. Of course when I had thought it over for two hours, then

I adjourned the judgement for a year, and the court closed
for that day.

So when the judgement was adjourned for a year, then I
came back home and started to treat my wife as before, but
when the judgement of the case which I adjourned remained four months, I was called again to the court to judge
another case which went thus:—

There was a man who had three wives, these three wives
loved him so much that they were following him (husband)
to wherever he wanted to go, and the husband loved them
as well. One day, this man (husband) was going to another
town which was very far away, and his three wives followed
him. But as they were travelling from bush to bush, this
man (husband) stumbled over, he fell down unexpectedly
and died at once. As these three wives loved him, the one
who was the senior wife said that she must die with their
husband so she died with him. Now there remained the
second to the senior and the last one or third of the wives.
Then the second to the senior who had died with their
husband, said that she knew a "Wizard" who was living in
that area, and his work was to wake deads, she said that she
would go and call him to come and wake their husband with
the senior wife then the third wife said that she would be
watching both dead-bodies so that wild animals might not
eat them before the Wizard would come. So she waited
watching the dead-bodies before the arrival of the second
wife with the Wizard. But before an hour, the second wife
returned with the Wizard and he woke up their husband
with the senior wife who died with their husband. After the
husband woke up, he thanked the Wizard greatly and asked
how much he would take for the wonderful work which he

had done, but the Wizard said that he did not want money, but would be very much grateful if he (husband) could give him (Wizard) one of his three wives. When the husband heard that from the Wizard, he chose the senior wife who died with him for the Wizard but she (senior wife) refused totally; after that, he offered the second wife (who went and called the Wizard who woke the husband and senior wife up) to the Wizard, but she refused as well, then he chose the third wife who was watching the dead bodies of their husband and senior wife and she refused too. But when their husband saw that none of his wives wanted to follow the Wizard, then he told the Wizard to take the whole of them, so when the three wives heard so from their husband, they were fighting among themselves; unluckily, a police-man was passing by that time and he arrested them and charged them to the court. So the whole people in the court wanted me to choose one of the wives who was essential for the Wizard. But I could not choose any of these wives to the Wizard yet, because everyone of them showed her part of love to their husband in that the senior wife died with their husband, the second wife went and called the Wizard who woke the husband and senior wife and the third protected the dead bodies from the wild-animals till the second wife brought the Wizard. So I adjourned the judgement of the case for a year as well. But before the date of the two cases expired my wife was very well and we left that town (mixed town) and before I reached my home town, the people of the "mixed town" had sent more than four letters, I met the letters at home, to come and judge the two cases, because both were still pending or waiting for me.

So I shall be very much grateful if anyone who reads this

story-book can judge one or both cases and send the judgement to me as early as possible, because the whole people in the "mixed town" want me very urgently to come and judge the two cases.

After we left the "mixed town," we travelled more than 15 days before we saw a mountain, then we climbed it and met more than a million mountain-creatures as I could describe them.

WE AND THE MOUNTAIN-CREATURES ON THE UNKNOWN-MOUNTAIN

When we reached the top of this mountain, we met uncountable mountain-creatures who resembled human-beings in appearance, but they were not, the top of this "Unknown-mountain" was as flat as a football field and every part of it was lighted with various colours of lights and decorated as if it was a hall, so these mountain-creatures were dancing in form of circles when we met them. But when we reached the middle of them, they stopped dancing and we stood among them and we were looking at the bush very far away from that place. As these "mountain-creatures" loved to dance always, they asked my wife to join them and she did.

TO SEE THE MOUNTAIN-CREATURES WAS NOT DANGEROUS BUT TO DANCE WITH THEM WAS THE MOST DANGEROUS

They were very pleased as my wife was dancing with them, but when my wife felt tired, these creatures were not tired, then my wife stopped, and when they saw her all of them were greatly annoyed and dragged her to continue with them and when she started again, she became tired before them, so she stopped as before, then they came to her and said that she must dance until she should be released. But as she was dancing again and when I saw that she was exceedingly tired and these creatures did not stop at all, then I went to her and said to her "let us go," but as she was following me, these creatures grew annoyed with me. They wanted to take her back to the dance from me by force. So I performed my juju there again, and it changed my wife into the wooden-doll as usual, then I put it into my pocket, and they saw her no more.

But when she had disappeared from their presence they told me to find her out at once and grew annoyed by that time, so I started to run away for my life because I could not face them to fight at all. As I was running away from them, I could not run more than 300 yards before the whole of them caught me and surrounded me there; of course, before they could do anything to me, I myself had changed into a flat pebble and was throwing myself along the way to my home town.

But these "mountain-creatures" were still following me and trying their best to catch me as I was a pebble, although, they were unable to catch it until I (pebble) reached the river which crossed the road to my town and also the river was near my town. But before reaching the river, I was very tired and nearly broke into two, because of striking harder stones as I was throwing myself, but at the same time that I reached the river, they nearly caught me there. But without any ado, I threw myself to the other side of the river and before touching the ground, I had changed myself into man, and also my wife, gun, egg, cutlass and loads as usual and at the same time that we touched the ground, we bade the "mountain-creatures" good-bye and they were looking at us as we were going, because they must not cross the river at all. That was how we left the "mountain-creatures." So from that river to my home town was only a few minutes to reach. Then we entered on my father's land, and no harm or bad creatures came again.

When it was 7 o'clock early in the morning, we reached my town, then we entered my parlour, but at the same time that my town's people saw that I returned, they rushed to my house and greeted us. So both of us reached my town safely and I met my parents safely too, with all my old friends who were coming to my house and drinking palm-wine with me before I left

After that, I sent for 200 kegs of palm-wine and drank it together with my old friends as before I left home. Immediately I reached my home, I entered my room and opened my box, then I hid the egg which my palm-wine tapster gave from the Deads' Town. And so all our trials, difficulties and many years' travel brought only an egg or resulted in an egg.

But on the third day after we arrived home, my wife and I went to her father in his town and met them also in good condition, then we returned after we had spent three days there. That was how the story of the palm-wine drinkard and his dead palm-wine tapster went.

Before reaching my town, there was a great famine (FAMINE), and it killed millions of the old people and uncountable adults and children, even many parents were killing their children for food so as to save themselves after they had eaten both domestic animals and lizards etc. Every plant and tree and river dried away for lack of the rain, and nothing for the people to eat remained.

THE CAUSES OF THE FAMINE

In the olden days, both Land and Heaven were tight friends as they were once human-beings. So one day, Heaven came down from heaven to Land his friend and he told him to let them go to the bush and hunt for the bush animals; Land agreed to what Heaven told him. After that they went into a bush with their bows and arrows, but after they had reached the bush, they were hunting for animals from morning till 12 o'clock A.M., but nothing was killed in that bush, then they left that bush and went to a big field and were hunting there till 5 o'clock in the evening and nothing was killed there as well. After that, they left there again to go to a forest and it was 7 o'clock before they could find a mouse and started to hunt for another, so that they might share them one by one, because the one they had killed already was too small to share, but they did not kill any more. After that they came back to a certain place with the one that they had killed and both of them were thinking how to share it. But as this mouse was too small to divide into two and these two friends were also greedy, Land said that he would take it away and Heaven said that he would take it away.

WHO WILL TAKE THE MOUSE?

But who would take the mouse? So Land refused totally for Heaven to take it and Heaven refused totally for Land to take it away and Land said that he was senior to Heaven and Heaven said that too, but when they argued for many hours, both were vexed and went away, and they left the mouse there. Heaven returned to heaven his home and Land went back to his house on the earth.

But when Heaven reached the heaven, he stopped rain falling to the earth even he did not send dew to the earth at all, and everything dried away on earth, and nothing remained for the people of the world with which to feed themselves, so both living creatures and non-livings began to die away.

AN EGG FED THE WHOLE WORLD

Now as there was a great famine before I arrived in my town, so I went to my room and put water into a bowl and put the egg inside it, then I commanded the egg to produce food and drinks which my wife and my parents and myself would eat, but before a second there I saw that the room had become full of varieties of food and drinks, so we ate and drank to our satisfaction. After that, I sent for all of my old friends and gave them the rest of the food and the drinks, after that, the whole of us began to dance and when they required more, then I commanded the egg again and produced many kegs and drank it, after that, my friends asked me how did I manage to get these things. They said for 6 years, they never tasted water and palm-wine at all, then I told them that I brought the palm-wine etc. from the Deads' Town.

And it was a late hour in the night before they went back to their houses. But to my surprise, I did not get up from my bed early in the morning before they came and woke me up and they increased by 60 per-cent, so when I saw them like that, I entered into my room where I hid the egg and opened the box, I put it in the bowl with water and commanded it as usual, so it produced both food and drinks for all of them (friends) etc., and I left them in my parlour, because they did not go in time. Now, the news of the wonderful egg was spreading from town to town and from village to village. One morning when I woke up from my bed, it was hard to open the door of my house, because all the people from various towns and villages had come and waited there to eat, even they were too numerous to count and before 9 o'clock my town could not contain strangers. So when it was ten o'clock and when the whole of these people sat down quietly, then I commanded the egg as before and at once, it produced food and drinks for each of these people, so that everyone of them who had not eaten for a year, ate and drank to his or her satisfaction, then they took the rest of the food etc. to their towns or houses. But after the whole of them had gone away temporarily, then I commanded the egg to produce a lot of money and it produced it at once, so I hid it somewhere in my room. As everyone of those people knew that whenever they come to my house they would eat and drink as he or she liked, so it would not be two o'clock in the mid-night before people would be arriving from the various towns and villages to my house and they were bringing their children and old people along with them. All the kings and their attendants came too. When I could not sleep because of their noise, then I got up from bed and I wanted to open the door, but they rushed violently into the house and damaged the door. So when I tried my best to push them back and failed, then I told them that everyone would not be served unless at outside, but after they heard so, they went back to the outside and waited at the front of my house. Then I myself got out and commanded the egg to supply them with food and drinks. Now the people were rapidly increasing from various towns or unknown places, but the worst part of it was if they came, they would not return again to their towns, so I got no chance to sleep once or to rest, except to command the egg throughout the day and night, but when I found that keeping the egg inside the room was causing much trouble for me, then I put it together with the bowl outside in the middle of these people.

RECKLESS LIFE AT HOME

As I had become the greatest man in my town and did no other work than to command the egg to produce food and drinks, so one day, when I commanded the egg to supply the best food and drinks in the world to these people, at the same time it did so, but when these people ate the food and drank to their satisfaction, they began to play and were wrestling with each other until the egg was mistakenly smashed, the egg with the bowl broken, the egg itself broken into two. Then I took it and gummed it. But these people still remained there, even they not playing etc. and sorry for the egg which broke, of course, when they were feeling hungry again, they asked for food etc. as usual. So I brought out the egg and commanded it as before, but it could not produce out anything again and I commanded it three times in their presence but nothing was produced. When these people had waited there for four days without eating and drinking anything, then they were returning to their towns etc. one by one, but they were abusing me as they were leaving.

PAY WHAT YOU OWE ME AND VOMIT
WHAT YOU ATE

After these people had gone back to where they came, nobody came to my house as before, and all my friends stopped coming too, even whenever I saw them outside and saluted them, they would not answer me at all. But I did not care for that, because I had a lot of money in my room. But as I did not throw the egg away when broken, so one day, I went to my room and re-gummed it securely, then I commanded it as perhaps it might produce food as usual. And to my surprise, it produced only millions of leather-whips, but immediately I saw what it could produce, I commanded it again to take the whips back and it did so at once. After a few days, I went to the king and told him to tell his bell ringers to ring the bell to every town and village and tell the whole people that they should come to my house and eat etc., as before, because my palm-wine tapster who

300

gave me the first wonderful egg had sent another egg to me from the Deads' Town, and this one was even more powerful than the first one which broke.

But when these people heard so, the whole of them came and when I saw that none of them remained behind, then I put the egg in the middle of them, after that I told one of my friends to command it to produce anything it could for them, then I entered my house and closed all the windows and doors. When he commanded it to produce anything it could, the egg produced only millions of whips and started to flog them all at once, so those who brought their children and old people did not remember to take them away before they escaped. All the king's attendants were severely beaten by these whips and also all the kings. Many of them ran into the bush and many of them died there, especially old people and children and many of my friends died as well, and it was hard for the rest to find his or her way back home, and within an hour none of them remained at the front of my house.

When these whips saw that all the people had gone away, then the whole of them (whips) gathered into one place and formed an egg as before, but to my astonishment it disappeared at the same time. But the great famine was still going on seriously in every part of the town, although when I saw that many old people began to die every day, then I called the rest of the old people who remained and told them how we could stop the famine. We stopped the famine thus:— We made a sacrifice of two fowls, 6 kolas, one bottle of palm oil, and 6 bitter kolas. Then we killed the fowls and put them in a broken pot, after that we put the kolas and poured

the oil in the pot. The sacrifice was to be carried to Heaven
in heaven.

BUT WHO WOULD CARRY THE SACRIFICE TO THE HEAVEN FOR HEAVEN?

First we chose one of the king's attendants, but that one
refused to go, then we chose one of the poorest men in the
town and he refused also, at last we chose one of the king's
slaves who took the sacrifice to heaven for Heaven who was
senior to Land and Heaven received the sacrifice with gladness. The sacrifice meant that Land surrendered, that he was
junior to Heaven. But when the slave carried the sacrifice to
heaven and gave it to Heaven he (slave) could not reach
halfway back to the earth before a heavy rain came and
when the slave was beaten by this heavy rain and when he
reached the town, he wanted to escape from the rain, but
nobody would allow him to enter his or her house at all. All
the people were thinking that he (slave) would carry them
also to Heaven as he had carried the sacrifice to Heaven, and
were afraid.

But when for three months the rain had been falling
regularly, there was no famine again.

MY LIFE AND ACTIVITIES

I am the native of Abeokuta, and I was born in the year 1920. Abeokuta is 64 miles to Lagos. When I was about 7 years old, one of my father's cousins whose name is Dalley, a nurse in the African hospital, took me from my father to his friend Mr. F. O. Monu, an Ibe man, to live with him as a servant and to send me to school instead of paying me money.

I started my first education at the Salvation Army School, Abeokuta, in the year 1934, and Mr. Monu was paying my school fees regularly, which were ⅙ a quarter, and also buying the school materials, etc., for me.

But as I had the quicker brain than the other boys in our class (Class I infant), I was given the special promotion from Class I to Std. I at the end of the year.

After the school hour or every Saturday, I would go to far bush to fetch for firewood, so my master did not spend money on this again.

Having spent two years with my master, he was transferred to Lagos in 1936, and I followed him through his kindness. Having reached Lagos, we were living in an upstair at Bliss St., near Ita Faji.

A few weeks after we arrived in Lagos, I was admitted into a school called Lagos High School. No, I was not the one

303

who was preparing food, etc., for my master, but a cruel-hearted woman, so, before I could go to the school, which is about a mile, this woman would force me to grind pepper, to split wood, to wash plates and to draw sufficient water from the pump to the house before she would allow me to go to the school at about 9:30 A.M., while the school starts at 8:30. And she would not give me breakfast at all before I left home for school.

In the recess time or at 12 o'clock, all the rest of the boys in the classes would go out for their food but I alone would remain in the class to be studying all the subjects taught us before the recess. When we closed finally at four o'clock and I reached home, this woman would only give me a full cup of gari instead of two which could satisfy me and again she would not put meat in the soup for me.

This hard-hearted woman was serving my master to his entire satisfaction, by this trick she had the chance to save some pennies which she ought to use for me. Although I had the chance to complain to my master about this ill-treatment, I was afraid that she would drive me away from my master through bad reports, because she was very trickish and I myself did not want to break my learning.

I attended this school for a year, and my weekly report card columns were always marked 1st position on every week-end, which means I was the first boy out of 50 boys in the class throughout the year. At the end of that year I was in the 1st position out of 150 boys and this was the final examination of the year. For this reason, the Principal of this school promoted me from Std. II to Std. IV and he also allowed me to attend the school free of charge for one year.

The Palm-Wine Drinkard

But having passed from Std. IV to V the following year, I was unable to remain with my master any longer, because the severe punishments given to me at home by this woman were too much for me, so, on December holiday, I told my master that I wanted to go to Abeokuta to visit my father and mother. When I reached home, I refused to go back to Lagos again, but as my master loved me as his brother or son, he came to Abeokuta to know what delayed me.

But still I refused to follow him back to Lagos, because I remembered the cruel-hearted woman, and this is the way I broke my learning. Again, I started to attend the school at Abeokuta once more, the name of this school is Anglican Central School, Ipose Ake, Abeokuta. At this time, I was not under a master, but my father, who was living at a village a distance of 23¾ miles to Abeokuta, was paying my school fees and living. But as I was so young at that time, whenever I went to my father for my chop money and returned to the town (Abeokuta), this chop money would not last me more than 2 weeks before it was finished, because it was not sufficient for my requirements at all, then I would go around the bush that was near the town to fetch for firewood which I was selling to earn my living temporarily. On Saturday, I would go to my father if I needed something from him, but I was trekking this distance of 23¾ miles instead of joining a lorry, because I had no money to pay for transport which was then only 2d. If I left home at 6 o'clock in the morning, I would reach the village at about 8 o'clock in the same morning or when my people were just preparing to go to farm, and this was a great surprise to them, because they did not believe that I trekked the distance but joined a lorry.

305

Having reached the village on that morning and having eaten I would follow my father to the farm to assist him till the evening.

On the following day, which is Sunday, my father would give me my chop money plus 2d for transport, then I would leave the village at about 5 o'clock in the evening to join the lorry at a distance of 5 miles from this village, as from there the transport is available to Abeokuta. But instead of joining the lorry and paying the 2d to the lorry owner I would keep it in my pocket for other purposes, and I would trek the distance to the town.

One day, when I tired of trekking this distance and I had no money with me, I joined a lorry to "stow-away" to my destination, so, this made the lorry owner suspect me that I was a "stow-away," and my forehead was wounded as a result of injuries which gave me a scar on the forehead.

At the end of that year, I passed from Std. V to VI, and after I spent nine months on Std. VI my father, who was paying the school fees, etc., died unexpectedly (1939). Now, there was none of my family who volunteered to assist me to further my studies. Then I left the school and went to the farm or village, so, I started to make my own farm, as I must not touch my father's farm or his properties, as it then belonged only to the family. As I was making this farm, my aim was that if the crops I planted produced fruit I would sell it and have some money to pay for the school fees, etc., because I wanted to complete the Std. VI, but unluckily, there were not enough rains in that year which could enable the crops to yield well. Having spent about a year at the farm unsuccessfully, I went to my brother at Lagos (we were born by the same father and not by the same mother). Then

The Palm-Wine Drinkard

I started to learn smithery. Having qualified for this trade, I struggled and joined the W. African Air Corps (RAF) in the year 1944, as a Coppersmith, as blacksmithing also pertains to this trade. My rank is AAI, and the number is WA/8624.

Having demobilized, I tried my possible best to establish my own job, but after a few months I was unable to carry it on, because I had not sufficient money to establish the work and because I had nobody to assist me. Having failed in this, I started to go here and there for a better job. So, at that time, all the overseas soldiers had come back in large numbers and all were looking for jobs; when a post was vacant, about one hundred persons would rush there. For this reason, it was hard for me before I obtained this unsatisfactory job which I am still carrying on at present.

Amos Tutuola
17.4.52.